Louise becomes Lizette

Louise becomes Lizette

MALIN HL FORSMAN

Louise becomes Lizette
Copyright © 2022 Malin HL Forsman. All rights reserved
www.malinhlforsman.com

Paperback: 978-1-959224-05-1
eBook: 978-1-959224-06-8
Library of Congress Control Number: 2022915457

This is a work of fiction.

Ordering Information:

Prime Seven Media
518 Landmann St.
Tomah City, WI 54660

Printed in the United States of America

Contents

THE FIRST PART

THE SECOND PART

THE THIRD PART

I want to thank the Prime Seven Media in Wisconsin, my aunt in the USA, my beloved dad and mother as well as my friends, my nephew Dante and niece Nike. Finally I want to give a hug to my wonderful Godmother.

THE FIRST PART

CHAPTER 1

The Long Journey

The young Swedish maid Louise would finally emigrate to that enormous land in the west, to that mythical country called North America. In the capital city, Stockholm, the Olympic Games were inaugerated with pomp and pageantry. Louise had heard about it. She often dreamt about a life away from the farm in Värnamo and wished that she belonged to the upper class of Öfvre Östermalm in Stockholm. Louise had surreptitiously read about the fine upper class in the newspaper *Svensk Damtidning* that the mistress of the house had in the main building.

It was a publication that had been published for the first time in 1889 and had rich and newlywed women as its target audience. *Svensk Damtidning* gave tips and advice to new housewives about what being a housewife entailed. Louise was unfortunately a part of the lower class in reality and had to make do with rotten herring, soup and potatoes to stay alive on the farm. However, she had succeeded in saving small sums of money and alms ever since she was a child with the aim of just being able to emigrate to America. Despite her very simple life, nobody could break her strong will or destroy her dreams.

Louise had worked hard on the farms in Småland, as had all of her relatives, ever since early childhood. She had had an aunt who taught her to read and write when she was just eight years old. For Louise, being able to master reading and writing was so valuable not only because it could open up many new possibilities, but also because she loved her aunt. Unfortunately, Louise's aunt died a few years later from pneumonia, a big loss for Louise.

Over the last few years Louise had had to get up at the crack of dawn to milk thirty cows. However, one day a week, she was a companion to the mistress of the house and it was then Louise became inspired to have a different life one day. The mistress of the house was kind to Louise even if she acted nervously from time to time and sometimes screamed. Liqueur was the only thing that calmed these situations and was something the mistress of the house asked for several times a day. The liqueur was stashed in a bureau that the master filled up every month with new bottles. He knew that so long as his wife had drink, he had his freedom to do what he wanted and that meant love affairs with young women. Everybody in the village knew of the master's so-called "hobby" but nobody said a word. Louise thanked and praised the fact that the master had not made advances towards her. For some reason, the fat master liked to seduce married women of the upper class which meant that all maids who worked on his estate, including Louise, could breathe out. The only upper class woman that the master no longer seduced was his own wife. It had all ended a long time ago because he had become terribly tired of her.

Louise thought it was awfully tragic how false life could be and hoped that one day she would find someone who loved her unconditionally and was faithful.

Louise's own family was broken but she had grown up with some contact with her parents. Unfortunately, her beloved biological father had died when she was just ten years old and her mother worked hard on farms far away from her. Louise had heard that her mother and new husband travelled over the whole of Småland and never stayed in one spot for any length of time. Louise, her half-sisters and cousins lived in Värnamo and supported each other in the lack of parents. Their goal was just to survive.

After years of toil, the day finally came that Louise had been waiting for. Her cousins and half-sisters waved at her as she boarded a cabin in Värnamo that would eventually get her to Gothenburg. One of Louise's cousins knew the man who owned the cab service in Värnamo and had succeeded to book Louise on one of the routes. The bumpy and the uneven road made Louise feel sick and being confined so tightly with other passengers irritated her. To make matters worse, she had been placed beside a drunkard, who stank of spirits, for the whole journey to the west coast. Louise's life was and had been hard, but her daily mantra was that everything must be better in America although deep down, she didn't dare to hope for too much.

One day later, Louise had reached Gothenburg to take the boat bound for America via England. Everything she owned had been packed into her only suitcase. After the poor upbringing in Värnamo, Småland, she was finally on the way to her dreamland in the west – The United States Of America – a country that her relatives in the countryside had spoken about throughout her whole upbringing. Now it was finally time for Louise to hopefully find the answer to the meaning of life and get to experience everything good that awaited her in North America. Louise was still young and not in the least bit bitter about anything. Louise had left her childhood, her relatives and the country that she knew behind. In many ways, her life was starting from zero. She was already regarded as a young woman at seventeen years old. She didn't have any idea about what lay in store for her but she knew she would fight with all of her might and belief.

The young and beautiful Louise travelled via England towards the final destination of the USA, a long journey with different conveyances. When the boat had docked in Newcastle, Louise waited several hours before finally transferring to the overbooked train that would take her to Liverpool. The train was cramped with a putrid smell of sweat and unhygienic odors that emanated from third class. Louise, trapped in with other passengers and their unpleasant stenches, almost choked. It made Louise want to vomit but she kept to herself in order to avoid having to deal with the other passengers. It wasn't because she was a snob but because she was a young lady who wanted to be left in peace and avoid danger. After several hours onboard the train, she heard a steam whistle signal the train's welcome arrival in Liverpool.

Louise jostled her way out with the other passengers more intensively than usual, not wanting to be left on the train. Once she was outside in the lovely summer breeze, Louise relaxed for the first time since leaving Värnamo because, in the distance, she could make out the ship Campania that waited to sail her to New York. The maid Louise half ran towards it with her only bag.

She saw a long queue of passengers by the side of the ship. The sun shone and life was full of hope. Louise was full of expectations but even so, a small part of her questioned if this really was her real destiny. She recalled the brochure on the ship Campania that she had read hundreds of times before her journey had finally become reality.

Campania was a steamship that had been built by Fairfield Co Ltd in Glasgow in 1892 for the Cunard Steamship Co. In the worn out brochure that her second cousin had sent to her from America, it stated that: "the steamship Campania was built for 60 first class passengers, 400 second class passengers and 1000 third class passengers." Unfortunately, Louise found herself in the latter category of passengers.

When Louise arrived in the harbor city of Liverpool, the wind blew warm summer breezes as had been predicted this day in July. Louise had been jostling amongst other passengers on the boat as she had done on the train that had taken her to Liverpool. The long journey from Gothenburg had left its mark and Louise was incredibly tired and hungry. She had neither slept on the boat from Sweden or the train that took her through England. That was because, suddenly, everything was completely different from her normal daily routines on the Småland farm in Värnamo.

Despite the fact that she didn't need to wake at four o'clock in the morning for the next three days, she had to look after herself on the trip and keep a watchful eye over her few belongings.

There were petty thieves everywhere and there was no comfort to speak of. She couldn't afford to fall into a deep sleep in fear of losing her possessions, which included roughly thirty dollars that she had placed in an inside pocket of her skirt. The money was maybe needed to get into the USA. Louise had heard that the USA now had stricter rules for immigrants in the 20th century compared to how it used to be. The American customs had started to demand a sum of money for entry into The United States of America, in addition to the obligatory health inspection on Ellis Island.

The following day, Louise stepped aboard the huge steamboat docked at Liverpool's harbor, after a day of queuing, including a humiliating louse inspection of everyone's hair. The poor class were the only ones subjected to a louse inspection. The steamboat that would take Louise to a whole new world kept her spirits up. This trip and the move from her homeland would change Louise's life forever but at this moment, she knew nothing about how her life would turn out.

Louise would share a cabin or rather, a sleep cabin with a dozen other passengers onboard the Campania. She stepped up onto the steep gangway with gusto, making sure that she wouldn't be late boarding and be left in England.

When Louise had jostled her way in to her bunk, she placed her suitcase on the bed and lay down like a heavy stone even though she weighed very little. She was very determined to keep her few possessions, and that nobody would steal them.

Although Louise was both strong and stubborn, she could also be emotional and, to some extent, temperamental. She had never been so tired in her whole life, slowly drifting into a deep sleep. It was a sleep that would last three hours out at sea until she awoke with a jolt. Someone was tugging at her skirt and when Louise had regained her consciousness she discovered a toothless, older and infirm man by her bedside. A man who stank of filth and urine, begged Louise for money. She didn't want to worsen the situation, so she adamently refused to give him any money and just stared at him until he gave up and limped out of the cabin. Louise breathed out and lay down. There was danger everywhere and she knew that she had to keep her wits about her. Louise tried to focus on her happiness at being onboard but if she was honest with herself, there was a pain in her heart from leaving her homeland without knowing what "was to come".

Louise tried to ignore the powerful odors that wafted through the ship. It was as bad as the train. She knew that the stench was contained only within the poor class that she belonged to. Amongst the rich on the upper deck, a different situation probably existed.

After another couple of hours, a friendly woman on the bunk next to Louise said to her in a Northern Swedish dialect that she could watch her bunk if she wanted to wash and get something to eat. Louise had worked together with a person from the north on the farm in Värnamo for a couple of years after school, so she recognized the dialect which made her feel safe. Louise observed the woman carefully and felt, in some way, that she was trustworthy. Impulsively, Louise said yes, took her belongings and walked unsteadily towards the cabin's door. Louise eagerly climbed the steps, almost fainting until the vapors from the food led her in the right direction. She was so hungry that she could eat the meal of a large man if she didn't eat soon. Finally, Louise found herself standing in a kitchen galley where the third class was fed for a small amount of money. Louise queued for a quarter of an hour and ordered two pieces of bread, pork and some warm soup. The aroma from the food and the bread smelt good. She sat alongside boisterous passengers and concentrated on the food.

According to the calendar, she had several long days left at sea. She only had to endure them and make plans about what she would do once arriving in New York. She expected to undergo a medical examination and would probably have to pay twenty dollars for the opportunity of entering The United States Of

America. Louise didn't worry about how she would make a living as it seemed relatively easy for women to get jobs but she took nothing for granted.

Louise slurped on her soup and enjoyed her slightly stale bread as she dreamt of her future life. The rumor about Swedish girls being able to get cleaning jobs in New York and Chicago had spread across the Atlantic. They were the most popular cities to work in during this era.

When Louise had finished her first meal onboard, she felt more like her normal self again. Realizing that she had quite a long journey ahead of her, she looked for the nearest place where she could wash herself. She found a dark room with running water. Refreshing her face felt fantastic but before she returned to her cabin, she fixed herself up and replaited her thick golden brown locks of hair that were hard to control. Just as she was about to turn around and leave for her cabin, a disgusting man barged his way into the washroom and held her hard. Louise felt the large man's repugnant breath and him pressing his penis against her buttocks. She couldn't defend herself as her clothes were ripped by the disgusting bearded man. She tried to scream for help but he clasped her mouth shut. She tried to bite him but nothing helped. Tears flowed down Louise's cheeks as the man penetrated her from behind, causing immense pain. The perfect ideal that she would be a virgin until the day she married had been destroyed. The blood ran abundantly down onto the floor as the man laughed and shouted that he had hit the jackpot. After his outburst, the man zipped up the fly on his filthy trousers and left Louise shaking and violated in the washroom. Louise stumbled to the sink and tried to find the strength to be able to wash herself. She rubbed away all the blood with an old rag, feeling ugly, helpless and disgusting. It felt, in many ways, as if she had been murdered. A part of the beautiful and innocent Louise had been buried for good and she would never be the same again.

Once back at her cabin, she thanked her northern companion for looking after her bunk and after a short while, Louise slept again. The northern woman could see that her fellow passenger looked worse for wear compared to what she had looked like before leaving to eat. She wondered what had happened. All of the new impressions and the trip had made Louise incredibly tired. The rape had damaged her soul and was unforgettable. An anxiety that Louise had never felt before had suddenly streamed into her consciousness. Over the next few days, Louise slept as she had never done before but tried to eat at least one meal a day. She asked herself why but knew that she also wanted to survive and not break down because of the sick perverted madman. Louise was strong even though she was an emotional human being deep down. She would not let anybody destroy her life without her trying to create a more decent existence for herself.

The northern woman eventually introduced herself as Selma Larsdotter. She travelled with her eight-year-old son, Karl, to America to settle down with relatives in Chicago. Their relatives had saved money for her and her son so that they could afford the tickets to America. Selma's husband had died in a landslide accident in a mine in Malmberget when Karl was only two years old and she had had a hard time supporting herself and her son on her own. Selma hoped that a better life awaited them in America. Louise didn't want to tell her about the rape and be reminded of the tortuous experience that could spread tragic ripples across the water. Louise had promised herself never to talk about it to anybody.

Selma and Louise talked about the Titanic's maiden voyage instead on the 15th April 1912. Many people had felt their American dream shaken to the core when the enormous, beautiful ship sank. Sadly, The Titanic had pulled the passengers down into the icy cold water with it when it collided with an iceberg, but they didn't want to dwell on that memory for too long as they were desperate to find and create a better life in the west and had decided to emigrate despite the Titanic's fate. Selma and Louise became good friends on the long journey to America. They shared their dreams and hopes with each other.

Selma told Louise, in a non-boastful way, that she was good at sewing. She would dearly love to be a dressmaker in a rich home in Chicago where her son, Karl, could also live. She could sew new curtains, clothes and everything that was needed whilst Karl could, hopefully, go to a school in Chicago.

Louise didn't know what was really in store for her but she told Selma that New York attracted her and that she would also love to work in a rich man's home. It was the most comfortable and the best place for a girl where she would be well-paid and have a roof over her head.

Despite the age difference between Selma and Louise, it felt as if they formed a sisterly relationship during the unforgettable journey. Selma was twenty-eight years old and Louise seventeen but the eleven years between them felt insignificant. Louise was extremely happy that she had found Selma.

The new found good friends took Selma's little Karl out on deck every day which was a wonderful habit on the summer days. Now and then, a storm would start to whip up over the waves, throwing down lightning bolts and driving rain. It caused many passengers to hang themselves over the railings to vomit violently.

The young women promised each other to keep in touch when they had settled in America. Selma gave Louise the address of her relatives in Chicago so that they could start to write to each other when they had the chance but before they could do that, they needed to pass the health inspection. Their journeys away from the Swedish farming society would really begin if they could both pass the health test with flying colors. America was a country that both Selma and Louise had dreamt about for as long as they could remember.

When Louise finally awoke on the final morning aboard the boat, she heard eager passengers shout that they could see land. Many of them said that New York's silhouette shimmered in the dawn's light. Louise had been fast asleep for hours and would soon take her first steps on American soil.

It became tumultuous in third class when the gangway extended out and everyone forced their way forwards like madmen to step foot on land. Louise had the company of Selma and Karl and they all got off the boat together. Campania hooted and there was a magical feeling knowing that they had now arrived in America unscathed. They were full of hope in finding a better existence.

In 1912, there were 18 117hopeful people that came to Ellis Island in New York. Twelve years earlier, on the 17th December 1900, the French renaissance building built with red tiles and chalkstone was inaugurated on Ellis Island, since the original building had burnt down. It had cost 1, 5 million dollars to complete and five-thousand immigrants could be accommodated there daily.

Louise queued with all the others on Ellis Island the whole night without being allowed into New York. Luckily, Louise had Selma and Karl nearby which gave her security.

Selma and Louise promised each other to keep in contact until they were dead and buried. It wasn't until the following morning that they were finally free after a night on a hard bench. They could hardly believe it was true. Even if the stench from the water in the harbor and the first impression around them was not like a fairy tale, they still felt exceedingly hopeful. Selma took Louise's hand and looked deep into her eyes and said heartfelt: "Louise, I don't know if we will find what we wish for but your friendship is incredibly valuable. Promise me to never give up and write down your thoughts and send them to me. I will always be your friend!" Louise yet again had tears in her eyes, but this time they were tears of joy as she was glad to have a friend in America, their new homeland. Louise hugged Selma for the eleventh time and said in a deep voice:

"Selma, you are the finest friend I have had even if we have known each other a short time, but even so, it's been extremely valuable time! You are the big sister I always wanted. You must know that." Louise continued: "Promise me that you will never lose contact with me because something will break within me if you do. I wish your little Karl and you all the luck and success!" Selma smiled and hugged Louise hard.

About an hour later, they could finally catch the ferry bound for New York and Manhattan, but this boat trip was nothing compared to the long journey from Liverpool to the States.

Once on the mainland, Selma and Louise hugged each other hard again and said goodbye. Little Karl also gave Louise a kiss on the cheek. They all had tears in their eyes; they were both excited to be in America and at the same time, sad about having to part.

Louise looked around curiously and noticed people who carried signs from companies and private families who offered job openings. Louise noted some potentially good employers when someone suddenly tapped her on the back. Louise turned around with worry and raised her eyebrows when she saw a tall, lanky and well-dressed man in a high hat staring back at her. He said something in English that Louise did not understand. The man, upon noticing her confusion, stepped backwards a few meters to a beautiful shiny automobile, something Louise had only seen a picture of on a handful of occasions. He came back with a picture of a maid and a fascinating picture of a fantastic palace-like house. Louise understood that he was offering her work in the impressive house. She nodded a yes and followed the man to the car. The man took her suitcase and placed it on the back seat and opened the door to the front seat of the fine Ford. Louise stepped into the beautiful car and made herself comfortable. The man said something about "Long Island".

They travelled through New York's city center which Louise found fascinating. There was a plethora of cars, horse-drawn carriages and pedestrians that rushed about. The enormous skyscrapers of the time stood as masterpieces and Louise wondered how many people had suffered from vertigo while they built the New York Skyline and how many had lost their lives. New York had such a pulse that Louise gasped. She thought that if she died at that very moment, she had at least been in New York. They continued to drive through beautiful countryside and left the big city behind them. The enormous buildings on Long Island were the most impressive Louise had ever seen.

The man in the hat gave Louise a brochure that described somebody called Vanderbilts and Long Island Motor Parkway and the year 1908. Louise had been completely charmed by travelling by car and could hardly concentrate on anything else. The chauffeur seemed to notice Louise's awestruck expression and smiled to himself.

CHAPTER 2

A New World

Louise had browsed through the brochure she had been given on the road to what she thought was her new workplace. The brochure was full of fantastic grand houses. Strangely, she wasn't especially nervous but maybe that was because she was just seventeen years old. Louise knew that people usually talked about her beauty as an asset, which normally irritated her as she didn't want some filthy man puffing his breath on her neck, but she needed all the help she could get being a long way from home. She suppressed the horrific incident on the boat with a bitter taste in her mouth.

The chauffeur had said a name to her that she assumed was the surname of a family that had job vacancies and with whom she would work for – and it wasn't Vanderbildt but Sinclair.

The car bounced along the pebble dashed roads, finally coming to a stop outside a magnificent iron gate – it was easily two and half meters high. High evergreen trees grew within the giant iron fences that stretched from left to right as far as the eye could see on both sides of the gate. By the gatehouse, a red haired man who probably worked as a guard stepped forward. He opened the gates quickly and Louise and the chauffeur could drive up to the enormous house that in Louise's mind seemed to be a palace.

The whole situation was totally incomprehensible. Louise could never even have imagined that such a lordly manor could exist in reality. The chauffeur stopped and helped Louise out of the car and collected her luggage. First, they strolled over the impressive gravel road and then they climbed all the stone steps which led to an enormous front door made of solid oak.

The chauffeur opened the heavy door and showed Louise in to the grandiose hall. It was an atrium to the large and ornate living room. There were marble pillars everywhere and several walls were dressed in shiny polished mahogany. Louise was almost breathless as she looked at the beautiful home.

At that moment another man, dressed in his livery, approached. The chauffeur bowed lightly towards Louise and said something to the butler that was probably a presentation of her and then left.

Louise really was a stranger in a completely new country. The butler gestured to Louise to sit down and said a word that sounded like "coffee"? It sounded almost the same as the Swedish for coffee so Louise nodded. A real cup of coffee would taste especially good.

Louise sat down and looked through the mullioned windows. The sky was clear blue outside and everything felt as if she had ended up in heaven. If there could have been a sign that she had found the "right" family, she would be thankful for the rest of her life.

The butler came back with coffee and a sandwich after a while that felt more like an eternity. It was a prawn sandwich, a delicacy that had been launched at the end of the 19th century in Denmark. Louise stood up, curtsied, said thanks and then enjoyed the divine prawn sandwich and the sweet coffee complete with a dash of cream.

She started to believe that they had picked up the wrong person; did they not know that she was a maid? Louise had read about prawn sandwiches in *Svensk Damtidning* in Sweden but had never tried one herself, of course. She had read that they were served on the ferries between Denmark and Sweden.

After Louise had eaten every last morsel of the sandwich and drunk the coffee, a lady, dressed in a servant's uniform entered the room. She seemed a little gruff and walked over to Louise to greet her. The lady pointed to herself and introduced herself as Hanna. Hanna then pointed to Louise's suitcase and signaled to Louise that she should follow her. Louise grabbed her suitcase and quickly followed her. They walked briskly through a long beautiful corridor until they came to some marble steps, the most exquisite set of steps Louise had ever seen. They climbed up the sparkling and shiny steps, ascending two floors. Hanna opened a door and showed Louise in.

The small room contained a nice bed, washing facilities and a chamber pot, a desk, a closet as well as an armchair next to the window. Hanna pointed to the bed as Louise brought in her suitcase. Louise understood that she was telling her to rest. Louise laid down and fell asleep as soon as Hanna closed the door behind her and hurried off.

Louise sprang bolt upright after a knock at the door had awoken her from her sleep. She adjusted her clothes, walked to the door and opened it. A friendly looking woman who was elegantly dressed stood in the doorway. The woman introduced herself as "Charlotte Sinclair" and shook Louise's hand. Louise said "Louise" and curtsied. She took Louise by her forearm and walked to a room a few doors down the corridor.

Charlotte opened the door to a room that apparently was a nursery. It had everything a child could ever wish for. In the small adorable "prince bed" lay a light haired little boy in clothes made of velvet and lace. Charlotte told Louise the boy was Andrew Jr, her fantastic son. He was fast asleep. Charlotte put her hand on Louise's shoulder and said "Do you want to be my son's nanny?"

Even though Louise didn't understand any English, she knew what Charlotte meant in some way. She would apparently be given the privileged task of nanny for the friendly lady of the house. Louise was incredibly grateful. It was the best job one could get as a young working woman, especially in this enormous palace-like home which seemed to have personnel for every little thing.

Charlotte took Louise down the beautiful marble steps with iron railings. On the second floor, there was a grand floor with a ballroom, a smoking room for the gentlemen, a magnificent library, ten guest rooms and several reception rooms. Louise's eyes felt as if they were on stalks and about to fall out of her head as Charlotte continued to show her the home. She had never seen as much wealth and tasteful décor on display.

The heat from the summer of mid-July beat against them as they stepped out onto the terraces. It was cooler inside the house except on the higher floors, where the family lived and Louise's apartment was located. The heat tended to linger on the third floor and in the attic.

After they had Viewed the second floor, they went down to the first floor where Louise would meet most of the personnel. There were kitchen staff, groundskeepers, footmen, waitresses, a seamstress and a butler. The chauffeur was not there but he probably had other engagements.

After Louise had met all of the staff, Charlotte instructed her to follow the seamstress. Once in the seamstress' workroom, which was next to the kitchen, the seamstress produced a measuring tape and started taking Louise's measurements. Afterwards, Charlotte came back and collected her new nanny – Louise. Charlotte said something to the butler and took Louise to the front of the house where the chauffeur waited with an even larger car than the one he had picked up Louise in earlier. Charlotte and Louise sat in the back seat and then a young woman wearing a hat got into the car and sat in the front seat next to the chauffeur. She seemed to be some sort of housemaid.

Charlotte mentioned New York and the car drove the same route Louise had travelled before but this time, she believed she knew where she would live and whom she would work for. It was the rich Charlotte Sinclair who would be her new employer in America and now they were on their way to New York together.

Once they reached a place called Manhattan, they travelled to somewhere called "5th Avenue" which had been widened in 1909 to accommodate growing traffic. Anyone who had money went there "and shopped until they dropped" explained Charlotte in such a pedagogical way that Louise understood despite the language barrier.

Charlotte brought Louise to several elegant shops including Lord & Taylor where she wanted Louise to try certain clothes. Charlotte felt they were more appropriate for festive occasions. Charlotte asked "Do you like this one?" repeatedly as they looked through the dresses. Louise presumed that Charlotte wanted her to wear them when the little "prince" would be presented in public with her by his side as nanny. Louise assumed that she would wear the clothes the seamstress made at "home" on Long Island.

After three hours, after they had been in and out of all the shops, they were driven to somewhere called Keen's Steakhouse on 72 West 36 Street. Charlotte ordered soup and salad as a starter and beef as the main course. Louise had never eaten food as sublime apart from the prawn sandwich earlier that day.

Charlotte sat in Keen's and informed Louise about the people there and whispered their names into Louise's ear. Some of the restaurant guests wore theatre make-up; some were incredibly beautiful and looked peculiar. Louise understood that they must be famous people.

This was the best day Louise had experienced since her earliest childhood.

Charlotte seemed friendly, unbelievably generous and considerate.

Finally, it was time to travel back to Long Island and they got up while the maid paid the bill. She had accompanied them and had paid for everything that Charlotte had bought for Louise during their day on 5th Avenue. The finer people, to which Charlotte belonged, apparently never paid for anything themselves except on special occasions.

As they sat in the car on the way out of the metropolis New York, Louise started to think that English was easier to understand every minute. Since Louise was only 17 years old, was smart and observant, she found it easy to learn. She soaked up the American atmosphere, the language, and the customs amongst the rich and famous felt so happy. Everything seemed too good to be true! She had learnt to say "thank you", she curtsied and thanked Charlotte all the time in such a way that Charlotte began to laugh and, in the end, they found themselves laughing together.

The maid who sat in the front seat turned around and wrinkled up her nose. Louise assumed that she was irritated over the fact that they seemed to be having such fun in the back seat, despite their different standings in society. There was an unwritten law which stated that servants should not mix with the upper class but Louise noticed customs were different depending on who one was with.

The car arrived outside the Sinclair's home but before they stepped out, Charlotte gave Louise a small timepiece that could be worn around her neck. It was a silver watch – the finest present Louise had ever received. Charlotte took Louise's hand and said "I do not know where you have been my dear but I am going to treat you dignity and with respect!" Louise replied: "I think you are an angel!" in her fractured English. She had read the phrase on a card while they had been in the city and Louise knew it was precisely what Charlotte was – an angel! Charlotte touched Louise on the cheek and smiled.

The following morning, there was a knock on Louise's door. Louise looked at her new watch. It was six o'clock. Wearing only her flannel nightgown and well rested, she opened the door. It was the seamstress. She stood in the doorway holding Louise's new work clothes. The seamstress was from Holland and called Manon. Manon helped Louise try on the three different work uniforms. Every one fitted perfectly. When Louise had tried on all of the uniforms, Manon said goodbye, left the room and closed the door behind her.

Louise dressed herself in one of the new uniforms after washing. Just before seven, another housekeeper took Louise to the little boy, Andrew Jr. He was only eight months old and one could say that he really was born with a silver spoon in his mouth. The housekeeper who had fetched Louise came from Canada and was called Elsebeth. Elsebeth explained that she had taken care of Andrew Jr ever since he was born but she would shortly go back to Canada and therefore the Sinclair family needed a nanny that could give the little boy all he needed. The boy awoke and babbled to himself as they stood and watched the little bundle of joy. The morning would mark the start of Louise's new exciting life.

Elsebeth gave the boy warm milk and a mashed banana. She showed Louise the different routines the family had. The banana was something that was very exotic for Louise. She had heard and read about bananas in Sweden as early as 1909 but her old master and mistress had not had any. Bananas were hard to keep fresh from their warm climates to Sweden. She remembered and had read that the banana importers were called AB Banan-Kompaniet back in Sweden. The yellow and delicious bananas were a hit amongst the high society according to *Svensk Damtidning*. They were used, amongst other things, as desserts.

Louise and Elsebeth helped to both bathe and clothe the little boy. Later, they went down through the big house where they saw the servants busy with various tasks. Elsebeth said that Charlotte's husband William ("the master of the house") would come home during the following week and that there would be a big party thrown in his honor the weekend after.

Elsebeth showed Louise the way to a separate exit through a room that was like a luxury scullery. Andrew's pram and other things had their own hall and own front door. They placed Andrew carefully down into the pram that had huge elegant wheels. One could really gather that the little boy had everything he could wish for and more besides. The little boy's big blue eyes looked intensively at Louise from where he lay. For Louise, it was love at first sight.

Sinclair's "Mansion" (a word Louise had learnt to call the big house) had a magnificent park and garden that had been finely clipped and landscaped in every minute detail.

Elsebeth showed Louise around the garden's "labyrinths" and pointed out the greenhouse, pavilion and the pool house. Andrew Jr seemed snug in the pram and seemed to be well. It was a pure luxury that the Sinclairs had both an outside pool and a separate pool house. There was even a dining room where they served light meals and cocktails by the pool when the Sinclairs had guests, explained Elsebeth.

They went into the greenhouse where the groundskeepers lovingly took full care of the most exquisite cut flowers Louise had ever seen. There were two men who worked with tending roses, lilies, irises and orchids amongst other things. Their scents were wonderful and the heat in the greenhouse took Louise's breath away.

Louise and Elsebeth strolled their way in the direction of the sea and left the hot greenhouse behind them. The weather was warm and sunny as they passed by large trees on the plot. Louise eventually learnt their names - Cherry Blossom and Oak.

When Andrew Jr started to cry, Elsebeth gave him a small pacifier to suck on. It was an invention that the religious frowned upon but which the Sinclairs allowed. "Anything goes so long as their baby is happy" said Elsebeth. A month previous, Charlotte and William had pointed out the huge controversies and debates in the press about the use of pacifiers. Elsebeth thought that the debate would continue to be a source of conversation for years to come.

They continued to walk on the grounds with the pram in the direction of the sea. On the way to the beach, there was a long well-kept lawn. As they kept walking, the white sandy beach took over and towards the end of the beach, there was another incredible house. Elsebeth said briefly: "There's "The Beach House" where suppers are served and organized special events are held in the spring, summer and autumn". She continued: "Sometimes guests are allowed to stay there if they want to be by themselves".

The women went into the beach house which consisted of a large living room, two bedrooms, a small kitchen as well as a bathroom with shower and tub. Louise was dumbfounded to everything that she could see in front of her; even the beach house was more exclusive than any house she had seen during her childhood in Småland.

When they had finally pushed the pram to the beach, Louise was almost blinded by the bright white sand and the mighty ocean. Louise thought that it was a place where she could bring little Andrew Jr for many hours. They sat themselves down on some beach furniture without cushions, leaving Andrew Jr in the pram in the shade. Elsebeth tried to explain the daily routines to Louise and she mostly understood them. Elsebeth had a blueprint of the whole estate with her including the plots and all that could be found on the grounds. She pointed out the spots where Louise could take little Andrew Jr on excursions, all within the Sinclair's walls and gates. During the first few days, everything was so incredible, in so many new ways, that Louise was confused every night when she went to bed. Louise knew that, first and foremost, she would be busy learning English and finding her way around.

One day, after Louise and Andrew Jr came back to the main building, which really was an exclusive mansion, there was a message waiting for her from Chicago. She was beside herself with joy – "it must be from Selma" thought Louise. Louise had kept her word and written a letter during the first days spent living with the Sinclairs. The chauffeur had taken the letter into the city. As it turned out, the message really was from Selma who had written about her everyday life and host family in Chicago. She had already been given the task of sewing curtains and that her little son went to kindergarten, paid for by her host family. It was part of her salary for which Selma was grateful. Selma wished her son all the best and if he could learn English right from the start he would be able to go to the schools that were to be reckoned with and become something great one day.

Selma felt at home and saw her Swedish relatives every week. She ended the letter by saying that she hoped to meet Louise as soon she could and that they should do something together. The letter brought so many emotions that were inside Louise to the surface. She kissed the letter and said out loud: "Thanks Selma for your letter!" Louise cried a bit and thought about the rape onboard the boat. She had a nagging suspicion that she was pregnant. She had not had her period since then. She had prepared some sanitary napkins through many late nights of crocheting. Louise had always worn them since she started menstruating at the age of twelve. They handled her monthly visitor and she was used to this awful and bloody "porridge" and women were on the whole considered normal if they had it. It was also considered as valuable as it meant that they had the possibilityto bring a child into the world, but a certain ambiguity existed. A woman was called a whore if she gave birth to a baby outside marriage and it was never the man's fault. Everything was the woman's fault if the child was branded a bastard and she was frozen out while the man was regarded as a virile charmer.

CHAPTER 3

The Welcome Dinner

The Bratt Brothers family who owned Regular Oil would be a part of welcoming William Sinclair home from his long journey in Europe. The brothers had recently demolished their family's phenomenal fortress-like home from 1897 and had started building a new house on the same plot. The project had started in 1909 and was supposed to be finished 1915. The house would have all of the latest mod-cons including exclusive pools and fountains, almost like a castle. It would be there that they would hold so- called Gatsby-parties where the champagne flowed and the partying never ended.

"The Great Gatsby" was a novel that was written during the roaring twenties by the prominent writer F. Scott Fitzgerald and the book was released in 1925, when the luxury life of the rich in America was at its peak in New York and Long Island but, right now, it was only 1912.

Louise was daydreaming in the little prince Andrew Jr's nursery where the décor was blue. The beautiful velvet wallpaper was adorned with golden trumpets and the furniture was made out of stained oak. The floor and shelves teemed with the most modern toys.

Louise had dressed Andrew Jr in his pajamas. He smelt so good after his bath. Louise received the help of a maid every day to warm the boy's bath water. Before Louise left the boy for the night, she turned off his small gilded music box that played a beautiful melody. It seemed to enchant the little boy and send him comfortably to sleep.

Louise had been invited to the welcome dinner in the evening and she was now on her way to her room to freshen up. She would, for the first time, wear one of the beautiful dresses for special occasions that Mrs. Sinclair had bought for her in New York.

One of the maids, who assisted Louise, had been given the task of guarding Andrew Jr's bedroom for this magical evening, just in case the boy woke and needed something. Louise had a very special position amongst the house's servants and she was completely taken with her new role. She could hardly believe that she had such luck and thanked her lucky stars every evening prayer.

To live in this beautiful manor-like palace gave her a huge sense of security even though she knew that she belonged to the class of servants and didn't own anything. Louise was young and full of dreams and hope but she didn't feel any bitterness in belonging to the lower class of society, only bitterness towards having lost her virginity to a revolting stranger. For Louise, everything was still attainable but without her being aware of how and why. To be in America was like a fantastic fairy tale, like a dream. That "lower class feeling" and the sense of not being "good enough" had been completely blown away by this promised land, even though Louise knew, that when it really came down to it, she was still an employee, "but you could not blame a girl for dreaming no matter the position she was given".

After she had freshened up, Louise put on the white silk stockings that she had received as well as the beautiful clean cut deep green dress Charlotte Sinclair had chosen for her. It suited Louise extremely well and complimented her golden brown hair. Louise soaked her unruly locks with a towel and tied them up in a bun.

Louise didn't own any jewelry but she hung the watch that she had been given around her neck. There was a knock at the door and Louise rushed to open it. It was none other than Charlotte Sinclair herself who asked if she could come in. Louise asked her to sit in the only armchair in the room while she sat on the edge of the bed and looked in amazement with sparkling eyes at the elegant and sophisticated Charlotte.

Mrs. Sinclair was worldly and carried herself like a real lady. She had an aura of power and money but her exuberant personality made her not only interesting and exclusive. Charlotte had empathy, humor and under the luxurious surface, she was also an extremely nice and considerate person. Louise thanked her lucky stars every night in her prayers for the luck in having ended up with the Sinclair family. Charlotte cleared her throat and said to her young nanny: "It's an important Friday evening, an evening when my husband will come back to be the head of the house after a long trip abroad. I want everything to be perfect, no negligence and I don't want to see any disgruntled faces. You, Louise, are the most essential person in our household because you are responsible for Andrew Jr. Our son is indescribably important to us as you must be well aware of. Andrew Jr. Sinclair is the heir to an enormous fortune and you, Louise, have shown yourself to be very able in taking care of him. I saw that right from the first moment!" Louise smiled and replied in her new language: "Thank you, Madame!" Charlotte then pulled out a small box and gave it humbly to Louise: "Here, this is for you my favorite nanny!" Overwhelmed, Louise accepted the silver colored little box that Charlotte begged her to open. Two pairs of earrings and a beautiful bracelet lay in the red velvet soft lining of the box. They were beautiful and fitting for a young lady without being too showy. Charlotte continued to say: "Louise, you represent our family now and you are the one amongst our staff of servants who is closest to our son. When we have special parties, I want you to wear this jewelry. Please, feel free to vary between the two pairs of earrings for different dinners!" Louise was speechless but extremely thankful and happy – it felt as if everything was a dream. Despite her happiness, Louise remained so down to earth and was aware that if she made one small grave mistake, she would be thrown out of this privileged existence. Charlotte Sinclair inspected Louise in her new outfit while Louise put on one pair of the earrings and the beautiful bracelet. Louise looked absolutely radiant and carried the new clothes with an elegance that could easily have been mistaken for that of an upper class girl on the way to her first party.

Then Charlotte Sinclair took Louise under her arm and they both went down the grand staircase in their high heels. There were approximately a hundred guests in the house. The whole of the second floor was filled with guests who talked and laughed. A new champagne called Piper-Heidsieck from France was served alongside *hors d'oeuvres* from Sinclair's own kitchen.

Florens-Louis "Piper" Heidsieck founded his vineyard in France in 1785 (he dedicated one of his wines to Queen Marie Antoinette who he had met personally). Piper was an unbelievably good businessman and entrepreneur in his time; he travelled round the world to advertise his champagne. Eventually, the reputation about his fabulous champagne reached William Sinclair through one of his travels in Europe. Therefore, William Sinclair had installed a large number of bottles of Piper Champagne in the wine cellar on Long Island.

William had not only taken home champagne from Piper's vineyard, he had also travelled around Paris and visited the most distinguished clothing boutiques. William adored his beautiful wife and had bought several beautiful and unique furs made of mink and sable for her. To add to this, he had also bought jewelry at Boucheron for his wife, Charlotte, whom he regarded as his better half. William had always praised his wife as a valuable person and she really was his best friend.

Charlotte came from a family of high lineage and so did William, but there had been losses in both their backgrounds; both families had lost everything they owned at some time during the course of history. Luckily, their ancestors had always been enterprising and had always succeeded in recuperating their fortunes. Nowadays, William and Charlotte managed a joint heritage even if it meant working hard for it.

This was the summer of 1912, two years before the First World War would break out in Europe; a war where all the great super powers would come to be involved. William, who was also a prominent man within politics, had had some unpleasant premonitions on his European trip but since he could not predict the future, the trip had, above all, been a pleasure. He had missed his beloved wife and his fantastic son Andrew Jr throughout his journey.

William and Charlotte had a party planner who knew "everybody who was worthy of knowing" and knew the right people to invite to different types of parties and events. His name was James, a 38-year-old who lived in New York. James was a flexible type who could charm anybody even though he was neither particularly memorable nor handsome. His most important quality was that he had an unbelievable memory and remembered every person he had met as well as their names and titles. In addition to this, James was a good judge of character and all of his qualities were made for the profession that he exceeded in. He was engaged, born to do it. He was sought-after to arrange all socialite parties and knew how important his value was.

Charlotte and William had known James for many years. He had the ability to bring the most unique blends of people which usually led to fantastic results both for the hosts and the invited guests. James was a lifesaver for the upper class when it came to both "match-making" and business relationships in New York and in the noble houses around the bustling metropolis. James was always well-dressed and lived on 5th Avenue on Manhattan in an elegant apartment he had inherited from his parents who had unfortunately passed away tragically early. He had grown up with glamorous people since his first stumbling steps. They included everybody from actors to writers to musical geniuses to high ranking politicians. James' parents were known for their generous and spectacular parties. He had been fed the finest world with all its pomp and ceremony from childhood. James had grown up as the only child in a huge apartment on Manhattan. He had received a lot of loving attention from his parents during his upbringing. They had had him very late in life so he had been enormously awaited for and was naturally spoilt right from the outset. When James was to choose the path in his life, he could himself choose what he wanted to be. James loved and adored his parents who never judged him for his different sexual orientation. They gave him unconditional love which was something that very few children in the world get to experience. Charlotte suspected or knew that James preferred men over women as partners but James was a very private person and nobody troubled him with any questions. He was the best at his job and it was all that mattered.

The party had started and Charlotte went round with her nanny Louise who she introduced as the important link to the master's son. She became "Louise from Sweden – only seventeen years old". Louise had, in a short time, become very well looked after by her host family and it was something she enjoyed immensely.

There were many wealthy friends of the hosts on the guest list that evening. Among them were colleagues from the oil industry as well as a copper and industrial magnate who was a senator called Spark. Senator Spark had become a widower early but had met a young, new wife with whom he had two daughters. Two years earlier in 1910, they had moved into a house on 5th Avenue with one-hundred and twenty-one rooms! The senator had filled this gigantic dwelling with French art on every wall. Senator Sparks, who owned railways, copper mines, newspapers, sugar and tea plantations and properties, amongst other things, was described at the time by The New York Times as either the richest or second richest American. The only person who was understood to outshine senator Sparks was John D. Rockefeller. When Sparks was accused of bribing his way to a seat in the Senate, he replied calmly: "I have never met a person who wasn't for sale."

When all of the prominent guests had arrived, they enjoyed the Piper- champagne that flowed freely. They were seated at the tables according to the dynamic arrangements made by the party organizer, James. Louise had never seen anything quite like it or dared to think that these elegant rich people existed for real. The upper class in Stockholm whom she had read about in *Svensk Damtidining* was not even close to this abundance of wealth. It was all inconceivable for Louise but as a nanny in this society, it showed her this new life on all fronts.

William Sinclair cleared his throat to start his welcome speech. The buzz in the enormous dining room fell silent and everyone who sat around the beautifully set tables turned their attentions to the stylish host. William started his speech with everybody's gaze focused on him: "Everybody in this room means so much to me and my family. I want to wish you a hearty welcome and I am honored that you want to be here to celebrate my return from Europe this evening." Then he told several anecdotes from his European trip and towards the end of the speech, he asked his beloved wife Charlotte to rise and he thanked her for bearing him a son – Andrew Jr. William said: "My father was called Andrew and now, with my own son, my own flesh and blood in the house, has also the given name of Andrew Jr, of course, in honor of my father." William continued: "Without my father's enormous strength and stubbornness, the family empire would never have survived all the tests that we have gone through over the years." William finished: "So I want to make a big toast to all of you who are here tonight and make sure you have fun and enjoy what our personnel have worked so hard for! Yes, feel like kings when you eat and drink and a toast for my father, my beloved wife and the newborn apple of our eyes".

The huge cheers and applause from the happy guests rattled around the golden room where the food would be enjoyed for several hours ahead. The staff dressed in black and white uniforms ran around and attended to the prosperous and handsome guests.

The champagne, the toast and the imported Russian caviar was enjoyed over the first hour.

Louise had been placed at the main table but further down by the table's edge which didn't faze the young girl in the slightest. Louise sat opposite a young man called Philip Brenner. His hair had been combed with water; he was well-dressed and boastfully spoke about his work on Wall Street. His sparkling brown eyes looked curiously at Louise in a way a young man had not looked at her before.

Louise's English was far from fluent but she understood, weirdly enough, a substantial amount. The waiters poured champagne constantly and Louise started to feel drunk, happy and in a haze. The seafood and condiments were served at the right time.

Philip whispered in Louise's ear: "Lobster is my favorite delicacy. What do you think, Miss?" Louise became slightly embarrassed by Philip's self-assured flirting. Louise replied and pretended to be worldly: "I agree with you. I love lobster!" The lobster, mussels and prawns were amongst the finest tasting food Louise had ever eaten. Foie gras was served as a side dish and it was something different. After a good while, the main course was served that comprised of juicy meat together with heavenly potato cake, red currant jelly and a thick brown cream sauce. Louise was in heaven. What luck she had had coming to America. If she had not done that, she probably would have lived on fermented herring and rotten potatoes until she died. Of course, Louise realized that there were very few host families in the world who were as generous as the Sinclairs. She knew that she was very *very* lucky.

It was finally time for the dance to complete the magical evening. Most of the men retired to the smoking room beforehand which was only for men to enjoy a Havana cigar and a glass, or several glasses, of port. The men told each other about the "latest news" in the smoking room. It was worse than real gossip that old wives would tell. When it came to these prominent men of status and success, it was not considered to be gossip however – more like "oral traditions" at a high level.

When the music started, Louise was invited to her first American dance ever by her neighbor at the table, Philip Brenner. She felt her hands were embarrassingly sweaty and that she had started to blush. The orchestra played happy tunes whilst a known singer from Manhattan performed the latest numbers one could see and hear on Broadway. Louise did her upmost to follow her dance partner's definite steps. Philip held Louise's chin carefully after a short while on the dance floor and asked her to look into his eyes instead of at his shoes.

Louise felt like a princess and wished that the evening would never end but nothing lasts forever. Charlotte Sinclair approached the young couple and whispered: "Can you follow me out onto the veranda?" Louise and Philip finished their dance and followed Mrs. Sinclair through the crowd of guests. Out on the veranda the music stopped playing at a distance. It was a place where they could all breathe.

The evening was warm and the sound of crickets could be heard clicking in the garden. Charlotte asked Philip and Louise to sit down and ordered the waitress to fetch some cool lemonade for all of them. Louise was petrified that she had gone over the boundaries and now would be fired on the grounds of her dance with the finer people but it wasn't the case at all. Charlotte said: "Philip, I would appreciate it if you could help my new found Swedish nanny Louise with a little extra tuition". Charlotte continued diplomatically: "As Louise takes care of our son, she needs to be a good role model, teacher and someone our boy feels safe with". Charlotte turned to Philip and said: "Philip, you go to Brown University and we know your family well. I have spoken to your parents but I'll leave it to you to decide whether you want the small assignment. What would you say about teaching Louise English, American history and general societal issues two evenings a week?" Charlotte added that she liked Louise right from the start and believed that she was of the right mold for the world on

Long Island. Charlotte wanted her nanny to be treated well, as if she was a member of the family.

Everything she could do and did would affect the little "prince" Andrew Jr. Philip coughed and stared at Louise and exclaimed: "I gladly accept, Mrs. Sinclair!"

It was almost midnight and Charlotte asked Louise to say goodbye to Philip for the night and retire. They had all come to an agreement and Philip really wanted to teach Louise. They decided that Louise should meet him the following Tuesday night at the Sinclair's library.

Louise felt much appreciated and spontaneously gave Charlotte a hug and then apologized if she had stepped over the class boundaries. Louise shook Philip's hand and he whispered sensually: "Good night, my sweet!" Louise curtsied and hurried back into the large house. She pushed her way first through the happy guests that mingled in the great hall. The music played loudly and cheerfully with smoke fogging over the beautifully dressed noble guests. Louise ran towards the huge staircase and this time, she was grateful that her hands were not sweaty. It was the only thing she could think about. Philip smiled when the beautiful Swedish girl had left them on the terrace. Charlotte looked at him and whispered: "You must not hurt her, Philip!" Philip blushed and said politely: "I have absolutely no intention of doing that, Madame!"

Within a few minutes, Louise was residing in her chambers and had finished getting ready to slip into her comfortable bed. Louise rocked herself to sleep with a smile on her lips from the memories of the evening.

CHAPTER 4

Life with the Sinclair family

Louise was a quick learner and was soon able to speak English fluently. She spoke a lot with Philip Brenner and she loved history. It was an exciting time for Louise and the months rolled by.

Little Andrew Jr loved his "nanny" Louise and had grown every day. Louise had strong feelings for the boy and Charlotte Sinclair, his beloved mother, invited other children of the same age home for activities over the weekends. Charlotte and Louise planned the weekends together with different themes which included: treasure hunts, circus performances, playing by the pool and more besides.

Ever since William's welcome home party where Louise had been "fixed up" with Philip Brenner, she believed life was a party. Louise had both the intelligence and the ability to take advantage of her new found knowledge which made everything easier and more fun. Philip Brenner was a very handsome young man who had an enormous legacy to uphold. A few months later, he realized that he was seriously in love with Louise. He didn't dare to approach her; especially since he knew his parents expected him to marry Miss Sophie McLean, a family friend and millionaire's daughter.

Louise looked forward to every "school night" with Philip in the library. It made her see a positive future. It seemed as if everything was possible in America and she loved working as a nanny for the Sinclair family. Philip stimulated Louise intellectually with every lesson and she could feel her heart pound faster when she was in his presence. Louise felt the emotions that sparked between them but tried to ignore it in various ways. Her ticket to the fantastic life was to devote her life to the family and be faithful to them and do a good job. She was terrified that she might lose her wonderful position and no love in the world could be allowed to destroy it. But she was in love with Philip.

Louise had early on learnt not to involve herself with the "refined people" in a romantic way. It was too dangerous and could only lead to misery and alienation and nothing could be worse for her than that. Louise and Philip hid their feelings from each other but Philip felt as if he would explode after several months of teaching Louise. At the start, he thought Louise was just a cute little nanny, far from his own social position and also a girl he shouldn't have been interested in. But when he later understood that both his parents and Charlotte Sinclair had deliberately placed him near Louise on that first evening to get to know her, he realized that she was special. He didn't have an inkling when they danced for the first time at William Sinclair's homecoming party from Europe but she had something he liked and he was more than willing to be her teacher. Aside from the Sinclair family's generous fee, his feelings had grown exponentially during the months he had spent with the young and beautiful Swede. Louise was just as beautiful on the inside as on the outside and at the same time she was healthy, alert and had a wonderful sense of humor.

After two evenings, on one particular week as Philip taught Louise, he could no longer stop thinking about her. Louise was the one that filled Philip's whole existence, without her being fully aware of it. Philip could hardly concentrate on his own studies at Brown University. The only thoughts he had were those of Louise. He daydreamed constantly about her and planned their lessons more carefully than he needed to. Unfortunately for Louise, it was the reverse. She was having nightmares. She felt that her body was different and sensed that the horrific rape onboard the ship to America could have led to her now assumed pregnancy. Louise's agony and anxiety grew exponentially within her. She knew that she would have to tell her much loved Charlotte as it was the only thing she could do. They would soon see the large bump that she tried to hide every day. A few days later, when they were sitting in Andrew Jr's bedroom, the opportunity arose for a candid conversation between them where Louise revealed the worst thing that had happened in her life. "Charlotte, I think I am unfortunately expecting!" Charlotte froze. Louise felt tightness in her chest and said shaking: "Charlotte, I was raped onboard the boat on the way to America. It was the most devastating and humiliating experience I have been through despite being born as a poor girl and always having it tough." Charlotte held Louise and answered: "My poor angel, I wish I could get the good-for-nothing who did this!" Louise cried uncontrollably for the first time in her life while Charlotte comforted her and gave her all the support Louise had never dared to expect.

The following day, Charlotte arranged for a trip to see a doctor on Manhattan, who aborted the growing fetus. The doctor warned Louise that she might not be able to become pregnant ever again. Louise cried but knew how cruel the world could be. She nodded while biting her lip.

In the car home, Charlotte said: "Louise, I want you to understand how much we love you!" Charlotte dabbed Louise's bloodshot eyes dry and held her tightly. It pained her to see how Louise had suffered from the abortion.

As December drew closer, everything was about Christmas and all of the special preparations in the house on Long Island. Philip had long thought about Louise and how they needed to have a serious, undisturbed, private conversation. Philip felt that Louise had sometimes looked at him surreptitiously. Both their hearts beat faster in each other's presence. They were two young gifted and enamored people but had different roles in life. Their love could destroy each of their lives, that is, if somebody knew of their feelings for each other.

Even if American society was less snobby than Europe, Philip Brenner belonged to its elite despite his young age. He was an heir to a fortune and was expected to marry the "right" girl, manage the family dynasty and pass it on.

Philip's commitment to the young "Louise from Sweden" had changed her broken English to a fluent language with an upper class dialect and American elegance. Nobody could tell that she was foreign and had only been in the USA for six months. As a student, Louise had absorbed all the new knowledge like a sponge thanks mainly to having interest and a good head for studying. However, Louise knew that she also had learnt to appreciate beautiful clothes, perfumes and jewelry by watching her "mistress" Charlotte Sinclair. She would never be able to study hard science or be able to lecture on history but she really loved the luxury life she had learnt to live on Long Island with the fantastic Sinclair family. They had placed her in a superb and fantastic world, a paradise far away from the poor life in Sweden. It was a solace for her soul in many ways. Louise never ever wanted to travel back to her homeland even if she missed some of her relatives sometimes, but for Louise, there was no return. America was somewhere she didn't want to leave. Louise had come "home" in the end. Even though she was so young, it felt as if her life had not really begun until the summer when she came to Long Island and started to work for the Sinclair family. It felt as if her first seventeen years had only prepared her for the life she now lived. America was worth its weight in gold and was a place that Louise got to know as a paradise on earth.

At the end of the first week in December, the whole Sinclair mansion was decorated like a wonderful fairytale castle. There were lavish decorations of angels, stars and Christian motifs everywhere. The Sinclairs were Catholics and respected their faith and church but they weren't overly religious and seldom went to church. Louise realized that Christmas felt more spiritual and glamorous in the USA compared to the simplicity of Sweden.

Although Louise had had an abortion, Charlotte's support calmed the pain and shame. Louise repressed the persistent pain that remained and she would for many years to come. She pretended that it had been a nightmare so that she could be the happy girl that she was on the inside. The sad and tragic incident had, in many ways, changed her but Louise refused to lose herself because of the rape. Life went on and it could have been worse. On the whole, she had been extremely lucky.

Sometimes, the Sinclairs had a choir that sang for their guests at simpler festive gatherings before Christmas which fascinated Louise. When she got to be a part of the festivities, she would drink tea whilst Andrew Jr played on the floor in the same room and enjoyed the songs. Louise was constantly at Andrew's side and she really loved the little boy who would soon celebrate his first birthday. Charlotte Sinclair thought it was important for her son to listen to the singing and the music right from the very start.

It was the week before Christmas. Philip Brenner was finally on Christmas holiday and had asked his parents if he could take his student, Louise, or, in other words, Sinclair's nanny, to see a play on Broadway. At first, Philip's parents didn't like the idea but when Philip explained that Louise's experiences and knowledge influenced little Andrew Jr Sinclair's whole life and that Mr. and Mrs. Sinclair would appreciate it, they changed their minds. Charlotte Sinclair told Louise about Philip's invitation during dinner. Louise blushed and became so happy that she wanted to scream "YES" which would have been frowned upon. Instead, Louise thanked Charlotte for the request and said she would probably go – only if Charlotte and William agreed to it.

Louise dried Andrew Jr's mouth and took the boy up to his bathroom to give him his evening bath. She thanked her hosts first, curtsied and later, left them with their coffee. Louise almost flew up the stairs to get ready for her first "date". Andrew Jr babbled happily as if he understood that his beloved nanny had something wonderful to convey. When Louise laid Andrew Jr down to sleep, she read him a bedtime story and got him to sleep soundly, she crept out of the fine nursery and half ran enthusiastically to her simple maid's room. She took out her diary and started to write, adding an entry to the book she had been writing for five months. Of course, she wrote in Swedish so that nobody else could read it. It was like having a secret language in her own "little box in the bureau" that only Louise could interpret. Louise wrote in her diary about all of her impressions from her new found world and about its quality of life as well as the horrendous personal feelings of the heinous rape. Maybe, one day, her writings would become a novel but it wasn't anything Louise planned now. She knew that it was unrealistic to even be able to have such dreams as a nanny.

Thanks to Louise's youthfulness and positivity, she wasn't bitter or cynical as many other poor people. The Sinclairs had praised her to the skies and had almost adopted her to their own world where everything was possible. Louise was born under a lucky star. She read The Lord's Prayer every evening after she had got ready for bed and fell asleep quickly as she had done every night in America with the Sinclair family.

Louise woke early, around five o'clock the following morning. She decided to eat breakfast with other members of staff in the personnel's kitchen. For the most part, Louise ate all meals with Andrew Jr but on this Tuesday morning, she was too early for the little prince. Andrew Jr ate breakfast a little later in the morning, giving Louise time to get herself ready, get dressed and braid her hair. After this, she ran down to the personnel's kitchen.

All of the fantastic Christmas decorations breathed magic in the Sinclairs' large house and since the previous evening, Louise thought they glistened even more in the spirit of love on this early Tuesday morning, at the thought of being alone with Philip for the first time. It smelt of pine and Christmas baking throughout the mansion. Louise was happy.

The Broadway play they would go and see was in four days, on a Saturday evening in December, which felt completely unreal.

First, according to Charlotte Sinclair, they would enjoy a dinner party on Manhattan. Louise beamed with joy and looked forward to it as she walked through the giant house on her way to eat breakfast with the rest of the staff.

Butlers, maids, the housekeeper and the driver were in the staff's canteen in order of rank. Louise, who very rarely ate there, had her seat at one end of the kitchen table where the gardener ate. Some of the staff envied Louise's place in the house but most of them didn't care at all. There was a fairly harmonious atmosphere amongst the staff and it depended, naturally on the fantastic Sinclair couple. They knew how they could really get the best response and appreciation from the staff and everyone enjoyed working there.

When Louise had finished with all of the day's chores with Andrew Jr, Charlotte came to them to spend time with her son and to talk to Louise before the dinner. Charlotte told Louise that she wanted to give a different Christmas present to her nanny before her weekend date with Philip and gave Louise an envelope with a beautiful red seal.

Charlotte said to Louise: "You can open this envelope on Christmas Eve 1917 so that we know that you'll remain here as Andrew's nanny for five years with all that the job entails. He needs security and during that time, we will do everything to provide you with solid foundation."

The words went straight to Louise's heart. She hugged her boss and "second mother" Charlotte with a strong sense of gratitude. This time, it all felt natural and Louise was like their "extra" daughter. Louise chirped back: "Charlotte Sinclair, I love you dearly! More than words can say".

The Second Part

CHAPTER 5

The Christmas Present 1917

The First World War in Europe had been raging since 1914 and America had also become involved. It was a horrendous time for all the American mothers who got a telegram or a visit telling them that their husbands or sons had died in battle. The only positive outcome from America's involvement was that it created jobs within the American war industry. But it was a terrible price to pay with horrific losses that would forever leave its mark on many people.

Louise realized how lucky she was because she had a good life on Long Island far away from the war in Europe. Since William Sinclair was politically active, everyone talked constantly about the war.

Louise had now worked for the Sinclair family for more than five years. She had reached twenty-two years of age and really was a beauty. She was, however, more sophisticated and well-read now compared to the young and inexperienced girl that had arrived on Ellis Island. The wound from the abortion had healed and she felt whole.

Louise had been in love with Philip Brenner since William Sinclair's homecoming party from Europe in the summer of 1912. Philip Brenner had taught her English and America contemporary history twice a week during a year. After he had finished his two years at Brown College, he was sent to Harvard Law School. Louise missed him more than words could say. She knew that he was of a different class than her as she belonged to the working servant class. The problem was that deep down she didn't feel it to be so. The Sinclair family had done everything so that she would feel like one of them and had actually spoilt her as if she was their own daughter, but at times at a distance. Louise and Philip had kissed several times, making Louise feel as if she was in seventh heaven. The first kiss was in New York when they had watched a Broadway play together. Later, during 1913, they had carefully kissed at times in secret when nobody could see them but it had been extremely hard to be completely alone. Philip's parents insisted that he should meet the young heiress Sophie McLean. Sophie studied at the Women's College Radcliffe that was situated near Harvard University. Louise almost died from the shock of hearing about it.

Louise didn't meet Philip Brenner much after the spring of 1913. She buried herself in her work. She also offered to help with other errands as well as tending to Andrew Jr when time allowed and was needed, but Charlotte didn't want to burden her precious Louise. Andrew Jr and Louise spent a lot of time together and it was a consolation for a broken heart that longed for Philip Brenner.

Charlotte told Louise that she had booked a beauty treatment session for herself and Louise at 5th Avenue's Spa and Beauty Institute shortly before the Christmas of 1917. She had also spoken to the maid who would take care of Andrew Jr instead of Louise on the day. Everything was planned and ready. Charlotte told Louise that the beauty salon was owned by one of the richest beauty queens Helena Rubenstein. Charlotte revealed enthusiastically that HR was one of the most exclusive beauty brands on the market at this time and would probably remain to be so if she could predict the future. Rubenstein had class just like her followers which included Elisabeth Arden and Estée Lauder.

The December morning came when Louise would make her premiere visit to the famous beauty salon with her "second mother", the rich and generous Charlotte Sinclair. Louise really looked forward to her and Charlotte's day there. At nine o'clock, both women sat in the large car, where the chauffeur had opened the back seat for both women. Louise was now undeniably a woman and not a girl any longer.

Charlotte had requested Louise not to eat breakfast at home that morning for they would enjoy a fine breakfast in New York. Once in the heart of the city, they soon arrived at a café on 5th Avenue and munched on divine smelling croissants that were as fresh as they were warm. The strawberry marmalade tasted luxuriously sweet and the coffee was at just the right temperature.

Charlotte looked at Louise deep into her eyes and said in a heavy voice: "Louise, it's soon time for you to stand on your own two feet, leave us and find your own way. Andrew Jr is soon turning sex years old and it's time to send him to a boarding school and you, Louise, are more than ready to spread your wings!"

Louise nearly choked on her food and wondered if they would throw her out now. It was winter and the freeze had taken hold of the New Yorkers. Where would she go? Louise started to panic.

Charlotte continued: "Have you still got the letter I gave you five years ago? The letter you shall soon open?" Louise nodded with tears in her eyes. Charlotte was the mother she had always wished for and the Sinclairs had done so much for her during the years. Louise had been overwhelmingly happy to have been a part of their fantastic lives. She became paralyzed in fear of losing everything despite being her normal calm and collected self. Charlotte continued: "The letter will explain your new situation. You don't need to be afraid and we will, of course, continue to keep you near us and I will always be your guardian angel, my dear! Everything will sort itself out".

They stepped out into the cold and climbed into the car waiting outside. The chauffeur took them to Helena Rubenstein's premises where they spent half a day enjoying the beauty treatments. At two o'clock, they were ready to leave the salon. Louise had never felt so beautiful and clean. The rose oil stung her face slightly but generally, she felt like a new-born with baby skin. But, at the same time, wild thoughts flew like birds inside her troubled head.

When they arrived back at the house on Long Island, they all ate lunch with William and Andrew Jr. Christmas Eve was approaching and the Christmas magic, once again filled the atmosphere of the Sinclairs' "mansion".

Louise watched all of the wonderful people closely as if it was the first time, and the thought that her time with them would soon be over, pained her. She didn't know what awaited her. What would become her fate now?

The Sinclair family and the staff celebrated a fantastic Christmas Day morning in the exclusive palace on Long Island.

Little Andrew Jr who had now started to become the big boy was drowned in presents. The beautifully decorated tree filled the room with a fantastic scent and the candlelight created a warm and wonderful ambience. Louise was slightly downcast over leaving the home that had meant the most to her in the whole world. She soaked in the atmosphere and cried internally over the fact that she would leave the Sinclair family. Charlotte Sinclair could tell that Louise was unhappy, approached her and gave her a kiss on the cheek followed by a pat and said: "The best is yet to come!"

She asked Louise to fetch the envelope with the red seal that she had given to her five years earlier. Louise walked away with heavy, forlorn steps up the majestic staircase. For the first time in all of the five years, which at her young age was a very long time, she didn't want the stairs to end.

Louise went slowly to her sweet little room that had been her home. She opened her closet and dragged a drawer towards her at the bottom of the closet. The mystical envelope had been placed in the drawer, unopened for five long wonderful years. Louise blew away the dust and flipped it around; the powerful seal glistened towards her. She had wondered what the envelope contained sometimes but, at the same time, she had controlled her curiosity.

Somehow, she sensed the letter was part of her future but it had been protected until now. It was now December of 1917 and there was no turning back.

Louise hastened her steps down the staircase and into the grand living room to join the family again but this time with the mystical envelope. The warm atmosphere met Louise in the shape of little light haired Andrew Jr who bounced towards her, crying out for "his" Louise to show her what he had got for Christmas.

Charlotte and William asked Louise to sit down on the sofa. Charlotte said:

"Louise, you have been precisely the fantastic nanny we had hoped for when you first came here five years ago. We gave you a second test to see if you were as good as we thought you were from our first impressions. You were given this envelope five years ago as a guarantee for your future security. We have understood that you have not opened this envelope and have been faithful to us in every way. Right here and now, the time has come for your life to move forwards. Andrew Jr needs to start at the boarding school where William also went and to learn to socialize with other children of the same age full time. Dear Louise, you need to find your own way now." Charlotte continued: "You are twenty-two years old, Louise, and we want to help you and thank you for all that you have done and meant to our "little prince" and our family. Now, it is time for us to really thank you! In other words, you passed all of our tests gallantly and here is your reward. It's time to open the envelope!"

Louise felt dazed and wondered what in the whole world was hidden in this special envelope. William gave her a letter opener and she opened the magical envelope. In the letter, written in Charlotte Sinclair's beautiful and stylish handwriting on expensive writing paper, it said:

"Louise, if you are the golden egg that we believed you to be from the start when you landed here from Sweden in 1912, you are now the rightful owner of an apartment on 5th Avenue in New York. You will have a maid to assist you and a servant when need arises. Besides this, you will receive a monthly allowance of seven-hundred dollars which you can do with what you will. The apartment's costs are paid for by us on a yearly basis as is your staff. You will also receive a bonus of ten-thousand dollars every year in December that is to be saved and treated as a buffer.

In return, we wish that you continue to be a part of Andrew's life and in all of his major endeavors which will maybe include four to five meetings a year. We want him to know that you will remain a figure in his life. You have the possibility to study art, economy or politics and will also have to take courses in order to act as a hostess in wider society. We also hope that you eventually get married to the right man.

Finally, Louise, we want you to travel with Charlotte to Palm Beach in Florida and to Grosse Pointe in Michigan at the earliest opportunity. We have friends who live in all of these places and they are all fantastic places. You are the daughter we never had and a good friend to Charlotte. Remember that you are the girl and now the woman we always wanted to have!"

The fantastic content of the letter was overwhelming and had been signed with: "With love and devoted wishes from William, Charlotte and Andrew Jr Sinclair who wish you all the best in your life".

Louise was speechless and almost shook from shock after reading the letter. When would she wake up and realize that it was all a dream? Charlotte smiled and said to Louise: "You made it and you have been more valuable than you could possibly know." William cleared his throat and said: "I have never met a girl better than you, Louise, in our home besides my wife". William blinked at his beloved wife. Charlotte and Louise laughed. William continued: "My wife and the others love you Louise! You have never gossiped behind our backs! Our son has got all the security, stimulus and guidance he needed his first years thanks to you. You have never complained and you have been unique in viewing your occupation as a gift. We will be eternally grateful to you, Louise!" William smiled and finished his goodbye speech with: "You will be economically independent for the rest of your life as a thank you from us." Louise cried tears of joy and didn't know how she would ever thank them. The content of the sealed envelope had muted her.

This was a ticket to the "good life" despite not having a job to go to. Louise would get to live her own life with company and friends. The thought both terrified and fascinated her. How would she ever be able to thank her host family? Ideally, the best thanks would be to see Andrew Jr become successful, the adorable little boy that Louise had helped shape during the first important years of his life.

Louise walked over to Charlotte and gave her a hug she would never forget. She liked that Louise had given so much of herself and both she and William realized that it was time for Louise to have her own life. If Louise had not fulfilled her duties regarding Andrew Jr in the Sinclairs' home, she never would have got the chance to open the fantastic envelope and reap its generous rewards.

William asked the staff to come in with a bottle of Piper champagne and a jar of Russian caviar. They drank the golden drops with deep heartfelt feelings and enjoyed the exquisite Russian caviar. It wasn't the first time Louise had got to be a part of the "fine people" during her twenty-two year old life but this time, it felt like new – she was her own master. After the toasts and well wishing, Charlotte asked Louise to get dressed for a trip in to Manhattan later on in the day.

This time, Louise ran up to her small quarters where she changed her clothes to represent somebody more conservative and elegant and at the same time, packed her small handbag she had got as a birthday present from Charlotte earlier that year. When Louise came down to the hall, Charlotte was already there. They walked out of the front door and into the cold winter afternoon. Charlotte Sinclair's private chauffeur had just pulled up in a recently purchased Rolls-Royce that William had given his wife as a wedding anniversary present a few days previous. The black Rolls-Royce was an exclusive means of transport with an inbuilt fridge for food and drink. Louise sat, for the first time, in the luxury car as a real lady and could hardly believe what had happened. The only thought in her mind was that she was indescribably thankful to Charlotte Sinclair and her family. They had changed Louise's life into a real fairy tale. At the same time, Louise didn't take anything for granted even if she was drifting along on a cloud. She refused to fully believe that everything would be astoundingly wonderful for the rest of her life.

Charlotte opened the small fridge in the Rolls-Royce where she found an appetizing cheese sandwich and freshly brewed black coffee that they could enjoy. Charlotte said: "We can wait a little with more champagne. We want to be fairly sober when we enter your new home Louise! That is to say that we can drink it there!" Louise laughed happily at Charlotte's comments and showed her how she had to pinch herself in the arm to realize that it wasn't a dream.

Louise was brimming over with emotions that she had never before dared to feel. It was like an enormous endorphin of joy for the girl who had grown up as a maid. Now the world seemed to lie suddenly at her feet and she could hardly believe it was true. That she, Louise, would get to live the luxury life. It was completely unbelievable! She prayed silently with a prayer of gratitude to herself.

When the chauffeur had parked on 5thAvenue, the ladies walked out into the cold winter weather, dressed for the chilly winds. The falling snowflakes created a fantastic romantic Christmas spirit as they were dressed in fur coats. Louise was in a hurry to see her new apartment. An apartment that wasn't just any old apartment but one of the finest you could get – a fantastic home of her own that meant the beginning of a new life, thought Louise excitedly.

When they had walked up to the eleventh floor, the landing was as exclusive as the marbled interior of a bank. Wreaths with red bands hung on the massive doors that lead to Louise's new neighbors. Charlotte took Louise's hand and gave her beautiful a bundle of keys on a golden key ring. Louise stood, frozen to the spot, and she could barely get a word out. Charlotte laughed and led Louise to the front door. Louise hand was shaking lightly as she waited for Charlotte's support. Charlotte exclaimed: "Louise, open the door to your new home!"

Louise poked the key into the lock and pressed down the door handle. What awaited her was like an indescribable dream. The fantastic rooms had been decorated in the elegant but trendy style that the upper class appreciated at the time of the First World War. In one room – the music room – stood a grand piano and hanging mirrors with exquisite gold frames everywhere. The sofas had been ordered from Boston and were completely new and looked so inviting that you wanted to sink slowly into them. The view over Manhattan was breathtaking through the numerous amounts of windows. A grand staircase in the enormous lounge led to the second floor. The apartment had two floors! An exclusive "master bedroom" was on the second floor where Louise would sleep for many years to come. There was an amazing four poster bed with wooden posts made out of mahogany in amongst all the luxury you could imagine. There was a bathroom with all the modern conveniences that the era had to offer. There was running hot and cold water, a separate shower with a fascinating array of accessories with several showerheads for fountain like sensations. The new bathroom trends with working plumbing had already come to the USA in 1908. It was a luxury to have a water closet that you could flush. The bathroom was so spacious that it even had a built in scale. Louise had understandably seen a fashionable bathroom in the Sinclairs' house, but this bathroom seemed to be a copy of the one she had seen in a film starring Gloria Swanson.

In 1899, Gloria Jospephine May Swanson, the star of the silent movies, was born into the world. By 1919, she would get her big break, becoming a goddess to both men and women through the silver screen. Gloria Swanson's life, clothes and home created enormous attention and was copied by everyone who had money.

When Charlotte had showed Louise around the exclusive home, Louise almost felt intoxicated by everything and could hardly say a word. It was a long way from Småland in Sweden where she had always been subjected to poverty and the cold. Charlotte suggested that they should eat lunch at the Astoria and later drive back to Long Island. When they left the apartment, Louise's first impressions of her new home span around in her head. The huge library had been built to show silent movies. The dining room was perfect for large banquets. The fine guest rooms and, especially her enormous bedroom, were pieces of heaven. Louise felt numb and tried to make sense of her new reality.

Louise clearly had to give thanks to the little, adorable Andrew Jr who had given her the opportunity to be able to live the dream life. She had felt a big sense of responsibility towards Andrew Jr and had done everything for him as his nanny. It was clear that the Sinclair family loved Louise and as a thank you, they had now given her a reality that she could never ever have imagined to exist.

Louise was on the path to becoming a refined lady with a twelve room apartment on 5th Avenue and she was only twenty-two years old. It was what you could really call transcending the boundaries of class, from the dark woods of Småland and from the hard toil to luxury and vanity of New York where she could experience all of life's riches.

After the winter had passed and been replaced with spring, Louise had started studying and went on a course to become a prominent hostess on 5th Avenue. But she knew nothing about what would happen in the future. She was really still just a child. The First World War that USA had been involved in, both politically and militarily, had finally ceased towards the end of 1918.

CHAPTER 6

Selma

Selma and Louise had corresponded all the years they had spent in their new homeland. Selma's son was now big enough to be without his mother for two weeks. He would live with his relatives while Selma came and saw Louise in New York where they had said farewell six years earlier. They had shared each other's lives on the boat that had taken them across to the new country in the west. Since then, the First World War had raged in Europe but they had been secure in the USA and they had been exciting years for both of them.

Louise thought that her service as a nanny had been pleasant but after the taste of freedom and the economic independence since 1918, she wondered how she had been able to feel so good previously.

Selma and Louise met up at Grand Central Station in New York in the summer of 1918. Louise had lived there for several months by herself in her grand apartment. It was the first time in her life that she been completely by herself, with her thoughts and wants, which was a pure luxury in itself. The fact that she had received all the luxuries a woman could ever ask for was the icing on the cake.

Louise recognized Selma at once when the train from Chicago rolled in and the passengers streamed away in different directions. Louise rushed to Selma who waved at her for attention. They were both surprised at how wonderful it felt to meet again. They were like two sisters who had finally got to meet each other again after an eternity of being apart. Selma was thirty-six years old but still beautiful. She made all of her own clothes herself and Louise was fascinated by how capable she looked. Louise said to Selma directly: "Selma, you look fantastic! You should be a designer and live with me!" Selma laughed tears of happiness and they hugged each other. They would spend two weeks together. After that, Louise had an obligation to the Sinclairs before the autumn term started for Andrew Jr.

Louise hailed a taxi and both women put themselves and their luggage in the car. They giggled like two young girls who would finally go on an adventure together. When they pulled up outside 5th Avenue and paid for the taxi, they hurried out of the vehicle. They were on route to Louise's own apartment and Selma was really curious to see the jewel Louise had told her about.

When they arrived, Louise unlocked the heavy oak door that had a copper letterbox, doorbell and keyhole. She then turned to Selma and said in a Småland accent: "Welcome to my home!"

Even though Louise had told Selma in detail about the apartment in her letters, it didn't stop Selma's jaw from dropping. The apartment was not only a dwelling; it looked as if it was a part of a palace! Selma said in a choked voice to Louise: "Dear Louise! You have done so well! You're doing so much better than anybody else I know. Not even my employer has a place as lavish and big as this! I wish your family in Sweden could see you now!" Louise became sorrowful. "Selma, I found out that both my parents are dead. I have no idea where my brother is. So I am all alone in the world." Selma hugged Louise: "Dearest friend, I am so sorry, I had no idea about that." She continued: "It was fate that God sent you to the Sinclair family!" They cried, laughed and held each other. Louise composed herself whilst she mopped up her tears and called out for her maid Sarah. Sarah had good credentials and her parents had emigrated from Ireland to Ellis Island at the end of the 19th century.

"Sarah darling, my friend Selma is here and I want to celebrate with some champagne. Fetch a bottle of Piper out of the wine cellar and some entrées. While you do that, I want to show Selma to her room."

Selma and Louise proceeded enthusiastically to the guest apartment. They went through the elegant rooms with the view over Central Park. Finally, they came to Louise's finest guest room. Inside, there was a separate bathroom and a large closet with several mirrors. There was also a silk bathrobe for Selma to use. Selma fell in love with her room at first sight. Louise hugged her friend and asked her to unpack, take a quick shower and join her in the large living room.

"First, we can take it easy and toast each other with Piper champagne in our bathrobes. Then we will decide what we want to do this evening. After that, maybe we can go and paint the town red and eat out. Or we can stay here and just chat about the last six years! See how we feel! There's plenty of the same gourmet food here as out there. I have prepared for your stay, my dear friend."

Selma blew a kiss at Louise who rushed back to her bedroom. After twenty minutes, they were back in the living room or the lounge, or in other words, the largest reception room. They sat in their silk gowns and enjoyed each other's company. Sarah hurried in with the well-chilled champagne and several gourmet entrées. The black caviar was Russian and very popular within the upper class society.

Sarah had previously ordered all the food from the exclusive food boutique Rocco Lupo & Sons on 310 West 39th Street until it went bankrupt 1908. She had later heard that the owner had illegally entered New York in 1898 on the run from Italy where he had been sentenced for the murder of a rival shop owner. In New York, he continued to work within the food branch, which he did with honor but nobody knew that he threatened his competitors. Lupo had worked with his father in Palermo in the same business since 1887. He had opened a number of businesses since they moved to New York in 1902. The first shop became the talk of town where Lupo had worked with his brother. The New York Times described the shop as "the most pretentious shop in the quarter with goods that are fascinating and amazing to the customers."

The exclusive horse drawn carriages that travelled to Lupo's shops with all the goods was the most pompous form of delivery anybody had witnessed in the neighborhood.

When the shop closed, Sarah had to rely on her network of butchers, fish shops and the many delicatessens that had all of the supplies Louise needed. Sarah was in her forties and very spritely, quick and reliable. She reported all expenditures perfectly and only wasted money when it meant buying the best quality because she knew that is what the upper class wanted. But when it came to necessities, she was very economical.

Sarah served Louise and her friend supper and there was certainly celebration in the air. The young women toasted and told each other about their experiences when they first moved to America in 1912.

Selma admitted after a second bottle of champagne that her employer, Mr. Brown, had visited her in the evenings to, as he thought, make love to her. She had been appalled when it suddenly happened after seven months of working for him in Chicago. It was humiliating and tortuous. The man's putrid breath and sick fantasies disgusted Selma. Louise sympathized and dried a tear. Selma continued to tell her story. The situation worsened throughout the years but Selma daren't to say no because she had her son Karl to think about. She didn't have a choice and had to give in. She had sex with her employer for two years before he died of a heart attack, luckily for Selma. His wife, Heather Brown, had become a widow and it wasn't until that moment that Selma's life was worth living. The widow, Heather, didn't grieve

her late husband but, instead, enjoyed the wealth he had left her
and started to live again.

Selma and her son were given a better room in the large
apartment. They were treated well by Heather. She loved Karl as if
he was her own son and sent him to the best schools in Chicago.
Selma was also much better paid and became more of a companion
to Heather than an employee.

Louise listened to Selma's story for several hours. To lighten
up the atmosphere, Louise told Selma about how her employer,
Charlotte Sinclair, had rejoiced in her transition from nanny to
lady. "Selma, I often hear from Charlotte that I fit like a glove in
upper class society. Charlotte also thinks that I bring more heart
and soul into rich men's circles," laughed Louise happily. "There,
people with good hearts like I have got are needed says Charlotte."
Louise continued: "It doesn't irritate her in the slightest that I have
been spoilt because Charlotte loves her expensive transformation
of me. It was "her secret project" she said to me with a twinkle in
her eye".

After Louise had finished speaking, both Louise and
Selma laughed until tears spurted from their eyes. They felt such
gratitude and warmth towards each other as two young women
on adventures could only feel. They were both extremely grateful
and would never forget where they had come from. They had
succeeded in the land of opportunity, which America really was.

Sarah came in and suggested a dinner made up of lobster and
other delicatessens. Louise and Selma decided that they would
stay home the first night because they felt that they needed a little
time to get to know each other again. When they had eaten dinner,
they drank coffee and later enjoyed more champagne long into the
evening. They carried on talking until it was two a.m. They said
good night and dragged their shaky tired legs to their bedrooms,
happy to be each other's friends.

The following morning, Sarah served strong coffee with
scrambled eggs, bacon, croissants and strawberry jam in the library.
Louise and Selma had agreed to eat breakfast in the library and

forge plans for the upcoming weeks together. They had both got themselves ready and were dressed, perfectly made-up and smelt good from the latest perfume - when they entered the fantastic library. The library contained leather bound books: poetry and prose from the whole world that William Sinclair had assembled for Louise's sake as a moving-in present.

There was also hand darned leather furniture in the library but also wooden furniture by Chippendale amongst other pieces such as a masculine English desk with a serious business-like appearance.

Both of the young women were happy and appreciated that they had each other. They preferred eating their breakfast sitting on the beautifully crafted wooden chairs by Chippendale with velvet inlay that stood beside its respective table with high legs in one part of the library.

The Chippendale style was established by Thomas Chippendale who was a furniture designer in London born at the start of the 18th century. In 1754, Thomas Chippendale published a handbook for furniture designers called "The Gentleman and Cabinet Maker's director". The style broke through initially in Western Europe and in America but in modern times it is mostly found within the manufacture of new cutlery. Chippendale's furniture has a Rococo character but at the same time has a comfortable form featuring both straight lines and curves. In other words, a mixed style of Rococo, Louis XVI and China.

Sarah poured the good strong coffee out of a silver pot and asked Louise if they would eat lunch together at home later so that she could plan the day's food. Louise friendly replied that Sarah could take the rest of the day off and said to Selma that they would eat lunch at the Astoria and eat dinner at a club. It was therefore convenient for Sarah to not be back until the following morning. She thanked Louise, curtsied and returned to her room.

Louise suggested to Selma that they would have a "spa day" together. Elisabeth Arden had a beauty salon on 5th Avenue since 1909 and it was there that her "Red Door" salon had all the exclusive beauty treatments that you could think of having. Elisabeth Arden was seen as a pioneer within cosmetics. Arden made women in high society carry make-up as an everyday accessory which had not been considered appropriate before unless you worked in a circus, theatre, or prostitution. Elisabeth Arden's beauty and make-up was exclusive and sought-after. Louise was a VIP customer at Arden's salon and could get an appointment time for Selma and herself at short notice. Louise suggested that they must shop every day at the finest shops as long as Selma was in New York.

At the end of breakfast, they had enjoyed several cups of coffee, croissants and scrambled eggs when Selma was surprised by Louise's announcement that she wanted to throw a party in her honor. Charlotte Sinclair had provided lists of potential guests that Louise always found useful. One list for small parties and one for large parties. Louise had got permission from Charlotte that she could call herself "Louise Af Sinclair" as it could open many doors. Selma reacted to the announcement with a blissful smile. She was willing to meet the cream of New York's people. She had been alone for too long and with Louise by her side, she felt strong and filled with the lust for adventure. Selma was open to all suggestions.

They booked a time for eleven o'clock at Arden's beauty salon the same day. They started to pack their cosmetics, fine lingerie and a change of clothes.

Louise had a chauffeur at her disposal during the whole of Selma's visit. The Rolls-Royce eventually stopped outside the famous red door of Elisabeth Arden featuring her ingenious brand that would symbolize her perfume "Red Door" over sixty years later. The young women stepped into the salon without wearing any make-up. Despite that the women inside turned around and eyed them from top to toe. A short well-manicured blonde girl greeted them. Both Louise and Selma, although devoid of make-up, looked good and seemed to create curiosity amongst the other customers who wondered who they could be. They were ushered into a changing room where they got left their belongings and changed. Afterwards, they sat in the lounge attired in fluffy bathrobes they had been given in the reception. They received some sort of health drink to sip. Louise and Selma sat for fifteen minutes and talked about the things they never understood about Sweden and laughed until their therapists came. They would both undergo a mud treatment – a "scrub" to get rid of dead skin cells and deeply clean both the face and body. After this, they were treated with a kind of face mask with calming cucumber slices for the eyes.

In the treatment room, they continued to talk about the shortcomings of Swedish society while their therapists treated them from top to toe. Selma exclaimed: "Our old Sweden is such a peasant country, wouldn't you say Louise?" "Yes, compared to New York and Chicago. Back home, everybody's eyes would pop out if they saw us now!" answered Louise, bubbling over with energy. Selma started laughing while at the same time getting the hiccups. They both laughed until tears ran from their eyes. Louise stopped after a while and interrupted Selma's hiccups. "Hopefully the whole of Sweden, not just Upper Östermalm in Stockholm, will get to enjoy their time in the future. It's simply tragic that people work so hard. Sometimes I have a guilty conscience that I have all of this splendor. It's like I sometimes wonder if I will wake up from a rosy deep sleep, Selma." Selma nodded with a more serious countenance and patted Louise on the hand.

After fifty minutes, it was time to shower and wash away all of the mud. Then it was time for them to lay down on their stomachs on a bench where they received a lovely and thorough massage by their masseuses. They both enjoyed it immensely and had never felt so looked after. It was an enormous luxury for two women that had started right at the bottom of society. They had both, against all of the odds, landed up at the top. Well, Louise had already hit the top with Selma on her way. Louise had sensitive feet and absolutely loved the foot massage. They both fell asleep during the hour-long massage. When they awoke and the treatments were over, the women dressed themselves in the bathrobes provided and wobbled like newborn calves into the changing room. They were now ready to face New York. The clock read two o'clock in the afternoon. They had spent three fantastic hours at Elisabeth Arden and when they stepped out into the summer breeze, they looked fantastic.

Louise's chauffeur took them to a club that Louise had heard people talk about at Ardens and it was said to be *the* place to go to. They decided to skip the Astoria and leave that for another day. They climbed out of their Rolls- Royce, well-dressed and looking pretty with subtle makeup that made heads turn.

They sat down in the smoke screen that at the time was a common feature at the exclusive diner for the socialites. Louise and Selma ordered a large lobster with vegetables and various condiments as well as a bottle of champagne. This time, Piper was replaced with Louis Roederer Champagne Brut Vintage from 1912, which would become the "film star's champagne number one" in time. It was really a lunch for "the jet set" and Louise, who had grown up as the ugly duckling but had become a beautiful full-feathered swan, had quickly allowed herself to become a young, spoilt upper class woman. Despite this, she still had her heart in the right place and she had even started to learn that you could take part in different charities, which was something special and valuable. Louise had, in other words, finally become the happy fortunate woman who people admired but certain obligations came with the new position. It was something she appreciated but she also realized that whatever she did or tried to improve, there were always people who backstabbed her. Louise had actually felt the jealousy and irritation from "the old upper class". From the moment she had moved into her fine apartment, the neighbor's had gossiped that she was from the lower class and had only succeeded because of her beauty.

The ridiculous thing was that there really wasn't an old upper class in America, a country that was still young for the influx of emigrating Europeans. In upper class society, like all other classes, there are always people who love to talk badly about everyone and everything. It was humanity's negative instinct, thought Louise with contempt. Those who don't have a life of their own are the ones who love to speak ill of others. It was something Louise didn't understand. Why didn't they just struggle to achieve their own goals? It was a motto she had learnt from her biological father at the age of ten. Her beloved father had given her all the self-confidence she needed in life to be able to get by and overcome life's challenges, regardless of class. Louise smiled to herself and later said to Selma: "If my father had been noble, he would have been at least a baron". Selma smiled and nodded: "It is from him that you probably inherited your warmth and elegance!" Louise looked at Selma with a serious gaze: "Mother and father moved around Småland during my upbringing so I lived with my aunt permanently in Värnamo. When my father passed away, my mother met a new farmhand she worked with on the farms around Småland but my much loved, biological father gave me all the attention that I needed to get through life and nobody can take that away from me." After talking about the sad memories, Selma smiled and replied: "If my mother had come from the right circles, she definitely would have been a countess". Selma and Louise both laughed because they realized that it was "life's lottery" that decided where you landed up on the steps of society which was both frightening and fascinating. Louise said abruptly: "Some of the lower classes would have been more suitable amongst the noble than some who are born into it, I can safely say." They both became pensive and melancholic after they thought about how hard their parents and ancestors had fought to just have food for the day and a roof over their heads.

Slightly jaded, they remained seated, enjoying the lobsters and a whole bottle of champagne. Louise frowned and said to Selma: "You almost feel guilty when we can have an unbelievable and incredible gold rimmed existence, don't you think Selma?" Selma replied: "We still shouldn't forget that we, ourselves, worked really hard during our whole upbringing!" Louise rose quickly and walked around in her high heel shoes "á la latest model" and sat back down again opposite Selma at their window table. The waiter came in with yet more champagne and served it to the beautiful ladies. Louise said solemnly within earshot of just Selma: "Selma, there is something I have never told you but when we were onboard the trip to America, apart from us finding each other." Louise grimaced, choked, cleared her throat and continued: "Selma. I was raped onboard the boat the day you looked after my bunk!" Selma's face dropped and she put down her full glass and whispered: "Why have you never told me about this or written to me about it?" The memory of the disgusting and terrible rape didn't make Louise shake any more but the tears still fell from her cheeks. "Dearest Selma, I didn't want to worry you and jeopardize our relationship. I hope you understand!"

They shifted uneasily at the table and returned to their champagne and suddenly, they were back in their luxurious reality as if someone had waved a magic wand. They realized that they were enjoying a superb lunch. They raised their glasses and toasted each other, thankful for everything that was good in their lives. Louise said: "We should be thankful that we ended up here and we should never forget it!" Selma nodded and enjoyed the chilled champagne and cheese with figs that the waiter had served. After a while, Selma looked Louise deep into her eyes and told her about the humiliation and sorrow that the years of sexual abuse by her employer had caused her. It felt easier to tell Louise now that they had grown close again; she could not hold back her feelings. Selma had hidden her horrible experiences from her son during all the years in Chicago, but in Louise's company she finally felt secure enough to tell Louise about her horrific experiences for the second time.

Louise patted Selma on the cheek and comforted her dear friend. Then she said that they both had got a new start in life and that the disgusting men, like Selma's abuser, would not be able to affect their lives again. Those people had no influence on them and were worthless. The important thing was to ignore them. Selma dried her tears with a serviette and wondered how Louise, who was many years younger than her, could be so wise? Louise finished her champagne and calmly said: "I guess, that I am an old soul but now, we should make the most of the rest of our lives and 'carpe diem' - seize the day – as I have learnt that to mean!"

During the time spent at the restaurant, two young men had been looking at them. After a while, they plucked up the courage to ask them if they could join them at their table. Louise bit herself lightly on the lip and told them that they were having a private conversation. Selma looked at Louise with a puzzled expression as she had longed for the day where a man wanted to court her, especially now that her son had left and she was alone. Louise added: "But gentleman, it would be fine if you want to talk to us later." The men looked at each other and invited them to dinner at the Hotel Savoy the same evening. They agreed to meet them at the Savoy at eight o'clock. The men asked where they could pick Selma and Louise up but Louise said they would get there themselves, surprising the men. The men happily bid the women adieu.

When the young men had left, Selma and Louise felt slightly embarrassed and broke out with hearty laughs. One man had introduced himself as George Summer and the other as Oliver Nelson. Selma had already fallen for the well-dressed and stylish George Summer. Louise had tried to forget her love for Philip, her ex-teacher from her time spent with the Sinclairs who was now engaged to Sophie McLean.

This was the first time she could experience a "real" date the American way as a wealthy independent young woman and Louise remarked on the fact that she had not had a man in her adult life. She found Oliver appealing but too young – but what did it matter? It was just fun to go out and eat as two couples.

Selma and Louise hurried back to Louise's apartment with the help of the chauffeur. The two young and happy women prepared themselves for their dinner dates. They curled their hair, sipped coffee and nibbled on small entrées. They laughed and sang with the music that streamed out from the funnel of the gramophone.

Suddenly, the phone rang and interrupted the evocative atmosphere. It was Selma's employer, Heather Brown, who told her that Selma's son, Karl, had scraped his knee playing a game yesterday. It wasn't anything serious but she wanted to tell her regardless and wondered when Selma would be coming home. Selma, who was on holiday for the first time in her life, was already missed by her son and Mrs. Brown, and knew that it was a request for her to get back to Chicago. Selma said that she would be back within a week and ended the conversation with Mrs. Brown. Louise encouraged Selma to try to relax until her return trip. They both felt better and helped each other to get ready for the evening's dinner with the two young strangers. Eventually, it was time for the ride to the Savoy with Louise's chauffeur.

When they arrived and entered the Savoy they heard the beat, the buzz and the laughter. They could also see a screen of smoke, smell perfume and the sound of clinking glass. An orchestra played new modern music, which continued to entertain people throughout the 1920s. They were shown to a window table where the young men were waiting. George stood up quickly, beamed a smile and led Selma to a place next to him. Oliver stood up too, looked deeply into Louise's eyes, took her hand and kissed it before offering her a chair. When all of them were seated comfortably at the elegant table, beautifully set with silver candlesticks and art deco details, George raised his hand discretely and attracted a waiter who came immediately with the champagne they had ordered.

Selma was completely enchanted by George. Selma was fifteen years older than Louise and George, she guessed, was in the middle of them in age but this didn't seem to concern George. He loved mature women. They, in some way, represented the answer to life's mystery for him. He had always enjoyed the company of mature women.

Oliver asked Louise where she had gone to school. Louise grimaced with a little irritated reply "Sinclair's College". "Ah ha!" said Oliver and followed up by asking her what she had majored in. Louise said sourly: "Everything from history to political issues!" Oliver didn't ask any further questions but Louise politely asked him where he had studied.

Oliver answered: "I served some time at West Point and later studied a couple of years at Yale. My family is from Boston." He added: "I have a big sister and two older brothers. I am the youngest of them and am, probably, the most spoiled". Oliver raised a charming smile towards Louise. Louise looked in wonder at Oliver and was captivated by his sensual eyes. Oliver continued without looking away from Louise: "My mother was responsible for my childhood home and the staff whilst my father has always been a businessman, engaged in the financial world on Wall Street here in New York". Oliver flirted with Louise and admitted that he knew his parents both had lovers when they were apart. Oliver began to laugh: "No, my father has had mistresses and my mother lovers."

The champagne and hors d'oeuvres were served. All four newfound friends drank happily, and enjoyed the delicious food. The Russian caviar was perfect, hard and round, and dissolved on the tongue when you pressed it against the palate. They seemed to like each other and the young ladies knew that their first impressions had been right. After dinner, Louise suggested everybody should go back to her apartment.

They stepped into the Rolls-Royce that had waited, ready the whole evening with her faithful chauffeur at the wheel, who drove them to Louise's apartment. When they had arrived, Louise called for Sarah who immediately came from her room, ready in her white ruffled apron that she wore over her black dress.

Louise asked Sarah to serve them a little evening drink each and some small delicatessens. The music that streamed out from the expensive gramophone started to entertain them all. The music came from the 78 records, the new arrivals for the season.

Oliver invited Louise up onto the floor and they danced tightly together whilst Selma and George sat on the sofa and talked intensively. After some time, Selma and George started to kiss each other passionately. Louise thought to herself that it was exactly what Selma needed. After some drinks and delicatessens, they had all started to become tired. Selma took George's hand and they disappeared into Selma's guest room.

Louise started to kiss Oliver and asked him if he was unmarried. "For the moment," was the answer. It didn't sound especially encouraging – why yet again be caught out with someone who was maybe already taken?

Their dance moved in slow motion and they started to tear at each other's clothes while kissing. The maid, Sarah, showed up and saw what was happening and left for the servant's quarters by the kitchen. Oliver sensually removed Louise's silk garments. He took off her shoes and took off her silk stockings with his teeth. Louise was very aroused but wasn't sure if she could taste the forbidden fruit. Suddenly, Oliver said in a sexy voice: "May I suck on your toes?" Louise felt as if she was about to orgasm from Oliver's delicate foot job. Oliver got up from Louise, who was lying on the table, lifted her up and, mumbling, asked where the bedroom was. Louise exclaimed with a happy laugh: "I can show you if you let me down!"

Once there, the pair stumbled into the bedroom where Oliver made Louise come three times with a fountain of orgasms. He sucked her clitoris as if it was an exclusive exotic flower. Louise shook with pleasure. They made love with each other until the early hours.

Both couples slept until twelve o'clock the following day. The maid, Sarah, had stayed away until Louise rang the bell and ordered breakfast.

The evening's party had been in Selma's honor even if there had only been four participants. It didn't matter to Selma as she said that she didn't want a large party and thought that everything had gone better than planned. They had all enjoyed extreme pleasure and enjoyment from each other's bodies.

Selma and George spent the rest of the remaining days of Selma's holiday together. Oliver had to travel back home to

Boston. Louise travelled to Long Island instead and met her old host family, the Sinclairs. Andrew Jr had a lot to tell and showed everybody all of his new things. Louise thought that the little prince had grown up to be a very stylish young boy. Charlotte wondered how Louise was doing. Louise told Charlotte about Selma and George, how her friend had found somebody that she really needed and how it had pleased her. Louise didn't mention her own escapade that made her blush at the mere thought of it. Louise stayed with the Sinclairs a few days whilst Selma and George made use of Louise's apartment on Manhattan. The maid, Sarah, took good care of them.

Louise returned to her apartment in the city a few days later. Everything was in order and Selma was packing everything for her journey home. She was on cloud nine and was filled with everything George had told her. They were deeply in love and would exchange letters when Selma returned to Chicago. She was so happy and asked Louise time and time again if George really could be the one for her. Louise said that only time would tell but she hoped that he really was her sake.

They stood at Grand Central Station the following day. Selma took Louise's hand in hers and thanked her for the completely wonderful time. They promised to contact each other again soon. Louise waved as the train left for Chicago with a whole different Selma onboard compared to the one who had come to New York. Louise waved until the train left her sight and felt both happy and excited. Love was a fantastic feeling, thought Louise, and everybody should experience it.

CHAPTER 7

The Start of
The Roaring Twenties

"The good life" had, despite everything, not gone to Louise's head. She had had a year of studying politics, English at a high level and history as well as having undergone fun and sophisticated "conduct and etiquette" courses. She had met a friend there the same age called Alice who was from a wealthy family from the west. Her rich mother thought it was too rural at home in Ohio and sent her daughter east where "everything" happened. Even during this era, New York was already "the city that never sleeps".

Alice's mother wanted her daughter to learn how to behave as a successful hostess for the cream of New York's high society. In addition, Alice was studying literature studies so that she could converse in an intelligent and well-read way. Even so, Alice had a cool attitude and whispered to Louise "that rules are made to be broken". Alice said that at the periphery of conduct and etiquette, the upper class led a life that was free and licentious. That was true for shopping, food, drink, good cigarettes and whom one currently had as a lover.

Louise blushed at all of Alice's sexual stories, which she had claimed was going on within the upper class. Louise had started to notice that there was actually a little truth in it. It was true and she, herself was a part of it, but she hadn't witnessed anything during her fantastic life with the Sinclair family on Long Island.

But what did she know?

Alice upheld that everyone was very smart but careful when they were playing their "games" – unless the whole gang was crazy – because then everyone was with everyone and partied and laughed without excuses. During the year 1920, Alice and Louise were inseparable. They went out and saw reviews, dances and studied together. A successful review that they saw, where the song "Swanee" was the most loved hit, was an amazing experience. A new musical genius, George Gershwin, who appeared on Broadway heaven with this review, had written the melody "Swanee" which was performed by Al Jolson. George Gershwin, who came from Brooklyn, had Russian ancestry and was born in 1898. When his family bought a piano, his future was sealed. George created many of America's most loved melodies during his short life and already had his first song published in 1916. George and his brother Ira would rule the American song world during the twenties, which included the major hit "Lady be good".

Alice took Louise on shopping trips and taught her to enjoy the luxuries and vanity. Alice's family had a lot of contacts and they were invited to a plethora of parties. Life was like a fairy tale for Louise.

It was trendy in the twenties to have peacock feathers as attachments in headbands made of pearl, gold and velvet. The fashion was luxurious but also restrained and androgynous as a reaction to the First World War when women had carried the weight of men's work during the war years.

It was no longer accepted to be as distinctly curvy as in the previous centuries. Women within the upper class society would have a slender, almost skinny figure, which had the effect that the clothes hung off them in a provocative way. Showing more skin and make-up was a must. Most wealthy women had an ivory cigarette holder and the queens of high society wore a variety of jewelry. You would wear many pearls and long necklaces but also eye-catching bracelets and gems like rubies, sapphires and, naturally, diamonds. The dresses were short and straight – glamour was the word of the day!

Suddenly, Louise had become one of the most sought-after hostesses on 5th Avenue. She was young, beautiful and had money, thanks to the Sinclairs, to live the good life. The large hairstyles gave way to the simpler page hairstyle with a shingled back. Louise, who found herself in the middle of the optimistic twenties, with the buzz of vanity in upper class circles, was no exception.

Alice took Louise to a hair salon and the moment she had dreaded happened; Louise's locks fell down to the floor and Alice gasped in amazement, as did the hairdresser. Louise closed her eyes until everything was finished. When the hairdresser had finished she said: "You can have a look now and see the new you in the mirror!" Louise opened her eyes slowly and carefully. She was dumbfounded. It was the Louise from old Sweden who sat in the exclusive salon in New York but the reflection in the mirror was of someone she had never seen before! Thanks to Louise's naturally curly hair, her new short hairstyle was full of volume and lifted her whole personality. She was really satisfied and felt like a real adult. The popular and renowned hairdresser invited both women for a coffee after the haircuts. The hairdresser gave them a tip about a new designer whose work was available in the department store Macy's.

Louise and Alice looked at each other, liking what they saw, and when Louise paid for her new look, she gave the hairdresser the expected tip. They rushed to Macy's where they would enjoy lunch and discuss the most ridiculous concepts with great enthusiasm.

At Macy's they tried on hats and laughed many happy laughs. Alice exclaimed: "Louise, you snob! I bet you'll be a countess some beautiful day!" Louise laughed and grimaced in front of the mirrors. Both Alice and Louise were wise and intelligent but Alice was more mischievous and got Louise to do things she had never previously done. Alice said in the middle of the hat department: "Louise, I will let you into the 1920s most coveted games!" As Alice provocatively grabbed her bust, she said: "Louise, there is a man who is older and boring in Ohio who wants to marry me but I have absolutely said no. An abrupt no!" Alice was, perhaps, not especially thoughtful but slightly arrogant and knew what she wanted; she didn't want to do the things that people expected her to do. Nobody got to decide for her. Yes, she was a little wild. Alice brought a new side of Louise out which had never been able to indulge in luxury during her upbringing at home in the dark forests of Småland, in Sweden. Louise had only worked to survive whilst Alice had always had everything she wanted without working.

They complemented each other in a brilliant way and Louise helped Alice become a little more thoughtful and learnt how about other people's lot in life. They were a good duo and had a lot of fun when they studied together. They had the best results in their class and the teachers were both impressed and amazed. The only bad marks they received were from being too outspoken according to the "etiquette" teacher, which made them laugh even more.

One afternoon, the girls took off from school early, directly after their lesson, playing truant so that they could eat strawberries and ice cream at the Astoria. The Astoria was still feeling secure in its spot but the site would later become the Empire State Building in the 1930s and the Astoria would move to a new building.

At the Astoria, Alice coined "Lizette" as Louise's new name. Alice exclaimed in a cocky manner: "You are supposed to hold court for the whole of society and that calls for a swanky name that's not as corny as Louise".

Louise answered: "You are crazy Alice but I believe I dig Lizette as the new glamorous me!" They both laughed while the creamy ice cream melted on their tongues. Louise thought about it and pulled a face towards Alice, thought for a moment and then said to her: "OK, that's that then, I am Lizette!" She reflected over her new name together with tasting the sweet strawberries.

"Louise becomes Lizette!" Louise felt slightly affected but it was, in some way, just like being a child again, a sort of childhood that she had missed out on. It was something she needed to be completely whole as an adult. Louise made up for her first years when there hadn't been any ice cream and strawberries to eat and it was neither allowed nor possible to be mischievous and rich. Everything has its time, thought Louise.

When Alice and Louise left the elegant hotel, Alice told Louise enthusiastically: "There is a coveted bachelor who lives on Long Island and he asked me if I would want to join him for a weekend out there with good company". Alice added: "Lizette, you're coming with me, aren't you?"

Lizette answered: "Louise doesn't want to come with you BUT Lizette will say yes to a pleasant luxury weekend and everything that goes with it!" Alice laughed whole-heartedly and said: "OK Lizette! Let's go and pack our weekend bags!" Both the young women went home to their respective apartments and packed.

Over the following hours, they sat in Lizette's chauffeur driven car en route to Long Island but to a different area to where the Sinclair's mansion was situated.

Anthony Barrow opened the door when Lizette and Alice arrived on this special evening. The house was big and dark. The Gothic style didn't immediately enamor Lizette to it. It was imposing but drearily black. Anthony Barrow welcomed them both with a kiss on their cheeks. When Alice and Louise walked into the living room there were some well-dressed couples who examined them as the special additions to the weekend. Snacks were served and the champagne flowed. A maid took care of all of their luggage. A skilled pianist appeared and the music flowed through the house whilst one of the guests started to strip. The clothes flew into the air and after a large quantity of prohibited spirits had been drunk there was a whole room of naked people. Lizette didn't understand how it came to be that she too was suddenly naked and laying on a divan after a few hours of drinking champagne. A man was licking her down below whilst other pairs around her groaned loudly. Everyone in the room was into their own respective lovemaking.

The man between Lizette's legs wondered: "Can I spice it up by smearing Russian caviar on your attractive triangle?" Lizette could not help but smile and nodded with pleasure, feeling both ashamed but at the same time, enjoyed the bizarre situation. Lizette was now an upper class creature of her time and she really didn't know if it was right or wrong. The man licking her down below suddenly made her convulse of pleasure and she grabbed the pearls around her neck when orgasm after orgasm was reached on the divan.

CHAPTER 8

The Matchmaker

When Louise had reached the age of twenty-seven in the summer of 1922, she got a phone call from society queen Claudia Harper. Louise had heard a lot about her but had never met her. Charlotte Sinclair had, with Louise's knowledge, started to worry about Louise who seemed never to meet a man to share her life with. Louise had partied and reigned in her fantastic apartment for a long time and Charlotte started to wonder what Louise's sexual orientation was.

Charlotte realized that Louise was completely normal but she understood that Louise probably needed a little help to get on track. Charlotte didn't know about Lizette's temporary conquests.

In any case, Claudia Harper presented herself to Louise: "I am familiar with both the Sinclairs and the party planner James as you probably already know!" Yes, Louise had met the mythical James through the Sinclairs on Long Island. Claudia continued: "I have a proposal to invite you to a charity event where a part of the British high society and nobility will be involved".

Claudia added with a calm and assertive deep voice: "There will be a polo match and women should wear hats as they do at Ascot in England!" (even if it was horse racing at Ascot and not polo). At the Hamptons in New York, it was polo and other types of entertainment that mattered.

It usually involved refreshments in the form of drinks and other goodies like buttery pies, chicken drumsticks, potato gratins and, of course, salmon of all types. The rich guests usually almost bathed in the champagne relayed Claudia and gave a dry laugh. Louise listened and realized that it was just another game for the upper class. Since she was new to this world, it was fantastic but also slightly taboo. But Louise was no ascetic however; she thought that everyone should have the chance to climb the ladder of society to reach their goal.

At any rate, Louise lived a comfortable life and would never want to get on her knees to polish the floor or wait on others again. Louise had, in other words, become a part of "the good life".

Claudia Harper told her enthusiastically about the Polo Club Meadow Brook that was founded in 1879. The club became a corporation in 1881 and the first polo field for general use was built in 1884. It was still hot news to do a sort of pilgrimage to the polo competitions at the start of the twenties and it would be more and more popular over time, said Claudia to Louise. She added that she usually had a feeling for these things. Claudia was proved right when in 1925-26, several years later, polo was one of the most popular sports amongst the rich.

Louise friendly commented that it sounded very exciting and asked politely how big a donation was expected to be and which charity was intended?

Claudia cleared her throat and mentioned in a light voice that it was usually around five-hundred dollars per person and that the money would go to a home for orphaned children. Louise's heart beat twice. She felt very strongly towards the orphaned children. The most needy children were the ones who Louise wanted to help and she quickly said to Claudia to count her in. "Can I bring a guest?" asked Louise a few moments later.

Claudia surprised her by saying that it would not be possible as the guest list had been planned down to every minute detail and that Louise could look forward to meeting many other interesting people. She understood that there weren't many people who received an invitation to Claudia's special parties. Louise thanked her, said yes and hung up.

The following Saturday, Louise arrived at the polo competition at Meadow Bridge on Long Island in the Sinclair family's car. They had sent their chauffeur to fetch her despite not being able to be there themselves. Louise was dressed up in a new, large and elegant hat that she had bought at Macy's. One of the characteristics of polo was that all present were finely dressed and that you showed your status with the clothes. The hostess, Claudia Harper, had carefully planned the seating arrangements and when Louise arrived with her chauffeur, she met Louise personally by the car which Louise thought was peculiar but nice. What Louise didn't know was that Charlotte Sinclair and Claudia Harper had planned Louise's participation and that an appropriate gentleman had been chosen to sit at her table so that she could find "the right one". The man in question was a nobleman from England called Lawrence Stewart. He was a count, owner of an estate and had a stable full of fantastic horses that he adored.

Lawrence was thirty-two years old and a very sought-after bachelor who didn't seem to engage seriously with women. He had dated one after another but had never had a serious long lasting relationship.

He had come to New York on the ship Mauretania that from now on left from Southampton instead of Liverpool, a few days earlier. He was staying at a small, charming hotel, The Inn, on Long Island by the water because he loved to do things in a different way.

The Inn was a wooden structure and was in a white east coast style with hammocks on the porch. The hotel only had twelve rooms, three of them suites and Lawrence's suite had a marvelous view. On the bottom floor, there was a lounge with a small library and open fires where the hotel guests would gather, relax and have a drink.

Claudia Harper wormed her way through all of the guests at Meadow Brooks. Louise really got a royal reception and was presented to everyone Claudia deemed appropriate.

Louise, who thought it was a little too fantastic to be true, was hardly surprised at all as her life had become one big party. Unaware of Charlotte Sinclair's involvement in the party, Louise smiled on and greeted all of the other guests. The champagne flowed and the sun shone – what more could you wish for thought Louise.

When it was finally time for lunch, the happy buzz of people was interrupted by a trumpet fanfare. Claudia Harper greeted the well off and polo interested crowd with a welcome and finished by wishing everyone a good day. She encouraged them to enjoy the lunch, and the interesting company while the polo competition rolled on. Many had their own binoculars to show that they were real polo connoisseurs and ardent fans of competition. Some studied not only the sport but also the crowd of people who had showed up. Just as Louise sat down at a table, an attractive man in a well-cut tweed suit turned towards her and said in a low voice: "My name is Lawrence Stewart and I assume that you are my dinner partner." Louise shivered with pleasure. What a man! In addition, he spoke British English, which made him even more exciting. They were both from Europe but Louise didn't want to tell him that. Her simple upbringing had been changed into something completely different and it would remain that way.

When Lawrence sat down beside Louise, she became spellbound. The feelings between them were so obvious to other guests that they turned to look at them. Louise and Lawrence discussed everything in life while their eyes sparkled at each other. They started to lose themselves in each other's eyes and could have been sitting anywhere. They didn't pay any attention to the polo, the cries or the cheers from the crowd. Something had happened and Louise never wanted it to end.

Lawrence finally asked Louise in a deep, sensual voice: "What's your name?"

Louise laughed and had to think carefully before using her newfound nickname: "My name is Lizette". She pulled out her cigarette holder with the intention of making herself look more sophisticated.

Lawrence took the cigarette holder from her and stopped her from looking for a cigarette and said: "I will give you everything in the world, if you quit smoking!" Louise smiled back at her newfound friend and said: "It would have been my first cigarette anyway so you don't need to worry!" Louise burst out in an infectious laugh.

Lawrence looked completely perplexed and admitted that he had never been so fooled by a woman before and was now indebted to her. Louise said to him: "The only thing I want to do is go for a walk with you after dessert!"

They enjoyed the lunch but only had eyes for each other. Lawrence told her about England and fox hunting which his father and grandfather had let him take part in since his childhood. He mentioned that his love was not the hunt itself but the horses. He admitted that even if he was "only" a simple count, he felt like a prince when he galloped over the estate at dawn. It gave him an inner peace and he felt a deep sense of admiration for the horses. Lawrence argued that without horses, humans would not have come as far as they had.

"Without horses, people would have, for example, not been able to transport trees from a forest to build houses" said Lawrence enthusiastically to Lizette and felt it was just one of the many qualities a tame horse possessed.

Now, for instance, they were present at such an exciting polo tournament thanks to the horse, according to Lawrence. Lizette agreed and looked at the handsome man who had popped up in her life as a fascinating and interesting stranger. He seemed to have everything Louise looked for in a man; he was the man of her teenage dreams.

After lunch, they got up from their table simultaneously and Louise, or Lizette, the name she had decided upon, put on her thin summer gloves. Lawrence carefully took her by the hand and ushered her out from the crowd and from the restaurant. They then walked hand in hand to the stables where Lawrence wanted to introduce her to someone he hoped she would like.

They made a very beautiful pair and Louise's heart pounded. When they reached the magnificent stables, Lawrence led her to a stall with an attractive iron gate.

"Lizette, here is Faye! She is a jewel amongst my horses and she is, naturally, an English thoroughbred. They are the world's quickest horses. The English thoroughbreds are the best for racing, dressage and eventing. Faye has won many competitions and has been mainly trained for polo. Do you know anything about polo?"

When Lizette answered no, Lawrence patted Faye and continued: "Polo came from Europe via the British officers who discovered the sport in Pakistan. It had originally come from Persia. The word polo can be traced back to the Tibetan language. Before they called the sport "polo" it was called "Tschugan" but later changed to "Tzykanion" during the 5th century. "Pulu" means ball and they were made from a soft wood originally."

Lizette stood outside the stall and was dazzled by both the horse's beauty and its owner. She looked Lawrence deep in his eyes and said jokingly: "Amen!" as if she was listening to a sermon. She smiled, laughed and said: "No. I'm only joking. It's really very interesting! Is there anything else I need to know about polo?" wondered Lizette and stared at Lawrence. She laughed sensually when Lawrence came out of the stall and kissed her hand.

He informed her that a polo field is just as big as twelve football fields but the most interesting addition to the horses is the audience. "Above all, the original hats that you ladies wear and naturally, the bubbly champagne!" Lizette was a little confused but pointed out that they maybe needed a little top up and that she wanted to watch the exciting polo competition for a while. Lawrence thought it was a good idea. His horse, Faye, would compete the following day so they had plenty of time to socialize.

Before they were to leave the stables, Lawrence took Lizette in his arms and gave her a long, hot kiss. Lizette understood that she had never known what a real kiss was before this magical moment. Lawrence held Lizette gently in his arms, tightly towards his chest. The smell of the stable was suddenly completely wonderful. They hardly noticed the stable staff that had come into the stables clear their throats when they passed the "lovebirds". Lawrence whispered in Lizette's ear: "You are everything I have been looking for!"

Lizette felt drunk from both the champagne and Lawrence's loving flirtation. They finally staggered out of the barn with their legs feeling as if they had been on a long ride. The sun shone in a clear blue sky and life felt wonderful.

The hostess, Claire, stood a short distance away and observed the successful pairing, Lizette and Lawrence. The Sinclair family would be very satisfied, thought Claire.

Claire Harper had, as always, kept her promise. She was expensive to hire but in this case, the investment would bear a fruit in the form of a count from England with big assets and exclusive contacts. Whether the relationship would last was not Clair's main concern. She had done her bit. Louise or Lizette, which she was apparently called in certain circles, was in a good place regardless if she became a partner of the British count or not.

A lucky and dazed Lizette went to her car with her count Lawrence in tow. He prayed and begged her to follow him to his romantic hotel on Long Island and suggested that they eat dinner there so they could enjoy the seabreeze. Lizette answered: "Another time, my dear count. I have things that I must take care of at home".

Cunningly, she continued: "If you still feel so intensively for me next weekend, you can always call me!" Lawrence came closer to Lizette with long steps and said humbly: "I will do everything to meet you again!" Lizette gave him a kiss on the cheek and sat down in the car.

"Towards Manhattan, my friend", said Lizette to her chauffeur and enjoyed her perfect exit. It was said that men had the desire to hunt so this fantastic man should hunt me, thought Louise as she sat in the back seat.

Louise felt herself becoming intoxicated by life. She was now officially Lizette and an English count had shown interest in her as if she, herself, was of nobility. It was like living in a film where the actors played their parts and everything was in color. The lead role had been given to Lizette and it felt completely wonderful. When they had travelled more than half the way, the chauffeur asked Lizette if all was well on the back seat. Lizette thanked him and said that everything was fine.

But the buzz started to wear off, the buzz she got from love as well as the golden drops of champagne. Lizette started to feel anxious without knowing why. She sighed and thought about how unfair life was.

Some were born with everything and some had nothing. Her own "class journey" was very unusual but she was forever thankful. Lizette let go of the idea of classes. She now thought instead of how she could play her cards right to become Lawrence's woman.

It was hard for her not be caught up in the carousel of love and sometimes she only wanted to run into the woods, sit on a stump like she had done as a kid in the forests of Småland when things became difficult. It was a solace to be protected by trees, to smell the scent of pine needles and ferns and deeply inhale them in. Imagine how much the simple things in life could be worth!

When they had arrived back to Manhattan, Lizette asked the chauffeur to greet and thank the family and say that she would soon be in contact with Charlotte Sinclair. The chauffeur followed Lizette to the entrance where the doorman let Lizette in to the fashionable property on 5thAvenue, which was now miraculously Lizette's home.

Lizette awoke the following day in the afternoon, which was an unaccustomed luxury she would never learn to take for granted. Her whole upbringing had started with an alarm clock, which chimed at four o'clock in the morning. She was tremendously thankful that she could now get to sleep when and how long she wanted. Her old life felt like a stranger compared to the way she lived her life now. Sometimes Louise (or Lizette which was now more of a fitting name for the person she had transformed into) was still scared that she had become something of a diva. She sat, dressed in her silk morning robe and with her feet in comfortable swan-down slippers. After she had finished in the bathroom, she went to the living room where Sarah wished her good morning even if it was almost noon.

Lizette asked if anybody had called but got a disappointing negative answer. Sarah disappeared out into the kitchen to fetch Lizette's breakfast tray. While Lizette waited for her morning coffee, she looked quickly through the headlines in the New York Times. While she enjoyed the coffee, she booked a spa afternoon at Elisabeth Arden's salon. When it was booked, Lizette chewed slowly and with pleasure on the delicate croissant, which Sarah had baked, with a little strawberry marmalade. The croissant that Sarah had baked was perfect and she had of course made the marmalade herself too.

Lizette had, in her childhood, grown up with always being hungry and when she did get to eat, it was only to put something in her stomach. Lizette was now, in other words, in heaven when it came to food and drink. She had to make sure that she didn't become fat!

A waist belt that vibrated could be found in all the beauty salons during this era. The magical belt would keep the rolls of fat at bay and the waist small.

Lizette had become encouraged by her previous employer, Charlotte Sinclair, who was generous, beautiful and slender, to try to enjoy the upper class life to the full. Now that the fashion amongst the rich and affluent women suddenly had become a very small silhouette, Lizette found herself compelled to follow the slender fashion, otherwise she would not be able to live up to her new position.

Lizette thanked Sarah for the breakfast and went to her room where she packed a change of clothes in a brown leather case as well as make-up and perfume. When she had packed everything, Lizette took the lift down from her apartment and went out to get a cab on 5th Avenue for the short distance to Elizabeth Arden's beauty palace.

Once there, Lizette went to the changing room and changed into her swimming costume, stuffed her curly page styled locks in a swimming cap and put on a bathrobe. Afterwards, she went to the pool with a towel in her hand.

Once she had entered the small warm pool, Lizette swam for half an hour while at the same time thinking about Lawrence. She thought about him so intensely that her head almost hurt and her heart thumped. Lizette was well aware how it could hurt being so in love after she had been let down by Philip. She was, in other words, very scared that it would happen again.

When she lived and worked for the Sinclair family, she had felt that she was on her own when Philip flirted with her. Now she had her own position, money, even her own life and some confidence.

Lizette knew how cruel love's twists could be regardless of class. She sensed that she was maybe a little too sensitive for her own good, but this time, she would be strong – Lizette knew her own worth, which she had never before.

The swimsuit had a narrow belt at the waist. Lizette was conscious of the fact that she had always had a small pot belly and that her stomach had never been completely flat. After swimming she did some gymnastic exercises in the training room where there was a "magic belt". Lizette was smart and realized that belt couldn't reverse her genetics but could improve her shape.

Apart from the little pot belly, she had long, slender legs as well as a nice and firm butt. Unfortunately, she wasn't as flatchested as the time's fashion dictated.

Lizette had always had a relatively big bust and the men always gave her "breast looks" which Lizette detested. She also realized that no matter what the fashion dictated it was her bust that was always right in the men's point of view! This didn't apply to men who preferred other men, of course.

When Lizette had exercised with rings, hoops and jumps, she finished with "the magic belt". She was sweating but despite this, spent the last hours in the hot sauna.

Lizette didn't want any beauty treatment this afternoon. After an ice cold shower, she applied her own eye make-up, brushed her hair and put on a sober marine blue robe. Lizette had spent nearly three hours behind the famous red door, a door that was the brand logo for Elisabeth Arden's salon.

It was already afternoon when she returned home to her fantastic apartment. Today, the hall and the whole lounge were unusually beautiful because of a dozen red roses that were for Lizette.

Sarah came and met Lizette with her eyes wide open and an envelope in her hand which she gave to Lizette and said: "Here is the letter that came with the roses!" The envelope read: "To Lizette". Lizette eagerly opened the envelope and read: "Dearest Lizette! You are the one I have been waiting for too long. I must travel back to England tonight but I want to see you as quick as possible. Lizette, you are all I think about! Can you come to England with me in a month? I have some business to finish. I'll send you a ticket for the Mauretania which leaves from New York to Southampton on the first of September."

Lizette almost felt faint from happiness and staggered backwards with the letter in her hand looking for something to grab a hold of, falling backwards onto the sofa behind her. There, surrounded by the jungle of long-stemmed beautiful roses in the most beautiful vase her maid could find, Lizette burst out laughing. The maid, Sarah, clapped her hands and gave out a light shriek which was unusual for the otherwise quiet Sarah but this fantastic woman really did do everything for Lizette. Sarah was full of kindness for her employer just as Louise had been with the Sinclairs.

Sarah asked in a shaky voice: "Is Miss Lizette going to travel?" Lizette was deep in thought but gave the answer: "If I don't go, my friend, I will regret it for the rest of my life, so I think you have a lot of packing to help me with, dear Sarah!"

CHAPTER 9

The Trip to England

In March 1922, the renovation of the old, fine luxury cruiser Mauretania had been finished after she had been battered as a warship during the First World War. Her maiden voyage had left the docks in 1907 and she had been the fastest ship to cross the Atlantic, a record that held for twenty-four years.

In the autumn of the same year, Lizette would enjoy her trip to England onboard this boat in first class. The Mauretania had seven decks where first class was a palace just like the Titanic whose maiden voyage had ended in disaster. The Mauretania, however, was considered "the grand old lady" and had been reliable and stable through several decades.

Just like the Titanic, the Mauretania had been built with cabins decorated in different historical styles. In first class, there was luxury in the form of music rooms, smoking rooms, lounges, a café with veranda and much more.

As first class passengers, it was easy to get a feeling of living in a hotel, not onboard a ship.

Charlotte Sinclair gave Lizette a lift down to the harbor in New York when the Mauretania would depart. The autumn morning felt fresh and there was a fantastic clearness in the air with a hint of something wonderful and great. "Lizette", said

Charlotte with feeling and consideration. "I hope that you will have a wonderful journey and a wonderful time in England."

Taking Lizette in her arms, she continued: "I have heard about Lawrence and who he is but we should all be on the safe side. He is apparently a count and owns a fantastic castle and a manor outside London." She looked deep into Lizette's eyes and added that Lawrence was one of the most sought-after bachelors in Europe. She finished by asking Lizette to be careful so that she didn't end up being hurt and to be strong regardless of what happened.

Lizette hugged Charlotte again and said that she shouldn't worry. She herself believed that if she had managed to make it across the Atlantic in third class and had survived in old Sweden during her upbringing, she would easily make it through the upper classes' schemes. Lizette said to Charlotte:

"And you have given me so much and taught me to be independent so I will be thankful to you until I am cold in my grave!" Lizette's fresh and spontaneous thoughts made Charlotte laugh. She said goodbye from her husband William and Andrew Jr just as Lizette boarded.

Sinclair's chauffeur helped Lizette with her bags and trunks. He informed Lizette that once in Southampton, first class passengers disembark first and get their own porter to help them leave the boat as easily as possible. Lizette knew that Lawrence would meet her at the quayside there.

Lizette was finely dressed in a fur and hat. She carried her handbag made out of beautiful leather where she kept her most important belongings for the journey. A piccolo showed her the way to her luxurious first class cabin. There, Lizette would live in a type of suite that was in keeping with the turn of the century's fashion. The cabin had velvet curtains and warm colors, which was fitting for the drab autumn days. She had her own bedroom and living room as well as a fantastic bathroom that had a tub with lion's paws.

Lizette thought to herself that it was a real difference compared to third class. Actually, it was really absurd how man had divided up people into different classes but at the same time, Lizette was not a socialist. There was a certain charm in having climbed up the ladder of society and to be almost at the top. To have the possibility to do this was something everyone could live for. It would be very boring if everything was as "flat as a pancake" and there wasn't anything to strive for.

Lizette was intelligent enough to understand that it would not work if all of the world's population were on the same level, even if it was terrible to think about hunger, war and disease. Life's different levels were so enjoyable that everyone should have the possibility to reach these levels regardless of what class of society you came from. To dare to take a chance and get to the top was the allure, to be able to fulfill your dreams and make it through the world. It could happen in America but not in the same way in Europe. Lizette was very aware of this and blessed America for its possibilities.

The Piccolo placed Lizette's luggage in the cabin and gave her the keys while she looked for some coins to give him a tip. Afterwards, the man saluted and welcomed her onboard the Mauretania.

Lizette through off her mink fur and sat on the comfortable, wine red sofa and breathed out. She was finally onboard and on the way to meet her big love. After a moment, there was a knock on the cabin door and she answered: "Yes, come in!"

A waiter came in and asked politely if he could fetch her something to eat and drink while the second and third class passengers boarded and the ship was being loaded. Lizette said, in a slight upper class accent, that she would rather like a bottle of Dom Pérignon champagne and something light to eat. She had learned, over the past year as one of high society's most coveted hostesses that it was the most sought-after champagne that had come out the previous year.

Dom Pérignon was made up of 55% Chardonnay and 45% Pinot Noir which were the grapes Lizette loved. During the latest year, she had got a taste for the most appreciated wines and champagnes that were on the market. Dom Pérignon was a "vintage-wine" which meant that it was made during the best harvests and that all the grapes used in the wine were picked the same year, a difference that separated it from other champagnes.

Lizette asked the waiter to bring in a bowl of black caviar too and if it was genuine Russian black caviar from Russian sturgeons, Beluga or star sturgeon. "Naturally, my lady" said the waiter and smiled. Lizette answered quickly: "Wonderful! I'll have a little toast and butter too, thanks!"

The waiter and servant saluted and backed out of Lizette's exclusive cabin. There was a knock at the door shortly afterwards and a young girl came in with twenty-two white roses in a vase and the card read: "for Lizette Af Sinclair". Lizette thanked the girl and gave her a tip.

Deep within herself, Louise could feel a nagging sensation that everything was too good to be true and would, probably, end but these doubts soon subsided. Despite her upper class charm, she would never take anything for granted but, of course, she had changed with all her added assets and material nobility. There was no way she would go back to dark forests of Småland as a maid. That she was completely sure about in all entirety. She would rather sell perfumes and cosmetics at Helena Rubenstein's or at Elisabeth Arden's shop at Macy's in New York with a low wage and live in a closet than poor Småland, anything to be closer to the flashy and upscale 5th Avenue.

There was yet another knock at the cabin door. The waiter came in with an elegant cart filled with delicatessens. Lizette gave the waiter a tip and locked the cabin door after he had opened the champagne and filled up a glass for her. Lizette had barely been on the ship a few hours and she already felt as if she was royalty. It was a real quality of life that could be bought for money! Yes, Lizette loved the luxury and it was nothing to be ashamed of. Despite having learned in Sweden to not try and be somebody she wasn't, she had acquired the language fit for a movie star.

It was probably her wonderful but eccentric father who had given her the belief that she could do anything, which he had deeply installed into Louise without being aware of it. Her father, Björn, had always thought that you should enjoy everything from the little things as well as the big things. So even though she had grown up without parents for a large part of her life, her mother and father had always been there for the first few years.

When Lizette had enjoyed some delicious Beluga caviar and the toast, dripping with butter, she called for the female cabin maid. A girl called Doréen came immediately to Lizette's cabin. She ran a hot bath and unpacked Lizette's bags. Lizette had been told that she should be properly dressed for all occasions and even if she intended to spend most of the journey in her cabin, she wanted to look around the beautiful ship and eat lunch or dinner in the dining hall now and again. For that reason she had a few changes of clothes with her.

Lawrence had given her strict instructions to only bring one trunk as he wanted to take her to London to buy all that she would need in the damp English autumn air, as a present from him. It made Lizette laugh to herself while Doréen ran the bath.

Doréen curtsied when everything was finished and dismissed herself with a generous tip from Lizette. She saw herself in the young girl and said several friendly but meaningless words like "Thanks! How good you are!" Lizette knew tips meant the most.

Lizette locked the cabin door once more. This time she hung a "do not disturb" sign outside on her cabin door. She undressed and walked slowly into the bathroom with the Dom Pérignon bottle in an ice bucket, which she placed, by the side of the bathtub. She climbed into the warm bubble bath and sank comfortably in. She stuffed her wild locks of hair into a bath cap that she found amongst the toilet accessories in the bathroom. Lizette breathed a large puff of air and poured a second glass of champagne as she sat in the fragrant steam created by the bath. She breathed deeply and felt as pleased as she could be.

Lizette could hardly believe that she would soon meet Lawrence. It felt unreal. She had been without a partner for almost the whole of her life. Some of her friends, the same age, had either two or three children although some had decided to only have one or none at all.

It was more difficult in these times as there weren't any contraceptives and the man tended to use the withdrawal method to stop the lovemaking in time. Lizette had heard of this method despite her young age and despite not having much experience in the lovemaking jungle. If the truth could be told, she wished that she was still a virgin.

It was considered shameful to give birth to a child out of wedlock. The child in question would always be called a bastard and Lizette would not let this happen to herself. She didn't wish to make life difficult for a child or herself. Life was challenging enough already.

Lizette suddenly tore off her bath cap and sunk down in the bathtub surrounded by the rose scented bath foam. She knew that there was a risk that she would never become pregnant and this weighed down on her. The bath water was invigoratingly warm and Lizette suddenly got the urge to wash her bushy pubic hair and get rid of the unhappy thoughts. It was nice to relax completely and be on the way towards something lovely and exciting.

The boat's horn honked and it was time to leave. Somebody knocked on the cabin door and shouted that it was time for departure towards Southampton, England. Lizette filled a third glass of champagne and shook her head. Nobody was supposed to knock according to the sign. Not that it did any harm but what if Lawrence and Lizette were making love in the room. Lizette's face became blood red at the mere thought.

It would take approximately nine days to reach Lawrence in England. Before she had gone onboard, Lizette had read about the "Atlantic Blue" band, which was a trophy, awarded to the fastest ship that crossed the Atlantic. The competition, and its prize, was introduced in the 1860s by the transatlantic shipping companies. RMS Mauretania could apparently reach twenty-seven knots. It had been said that the Titanic, on its maiden voyage, sailed at maximum speed in an attempt to win the record, which ended in tragedy.

You might as well be a little bit drunk or tipsy on the whole journey just in case it all went wrong thought Lizette and sucked up the last drops of the fantastic champagne. Then she stepped gracefully out of the bath but at the same time, jumped slightly. She was both the "wild Lizette" and "wise Louise" in one.

The fluffy towels were lovely and while she dried herself, she, with high expectations, thought of Lawrence waiting for her on the other side of the Atlantic. It made her happy. Suddenly, she felt terribly tired because of all the new experiences on the first day of travelling. She put on her bathrobe and slid between the sheets in the bed and fell asleep at once.

Several hours later, Lizette awoke and sat up in her comfortable bed. She looked around the fine cabin. The white magnificent roses were in the other room and she could see them from the bed. The walls were clad in stained oak, which Lizette liked very much. The wooden floor was just as beautiful and covered in the finest rugs imaginable in burgundy and dark blue. She looked at the clock, which showed 17.35. Carefully, Lizette got up and pulled the dark blue curtains aside from the window and she could see that it had started to get dark and that the boat was well out at sea. The ocean was calm and still.

There were wooden chairs with comfortable cushions out on deck where a well-dressed couple half slept while they held each other's hands. "How wonderful!" thought Lizette. Soon perhaps, for the first time in her life, Lizette would be part of a loving couple made up of herself and the count Lawrence Stewart in England!

Lizette sat in the darkness of her luxury cabin and stared blindly in front of her for a long moment. Her thoughts swirled between Småland, Long Island and New York in confusion. Suddenly, she remembered that it was time to get herself ready to go out amongst the other passengers. She walked lightly into the bathroom and put on her make-up. She turned on all the lights and a fantastic atmosphere spread across the luxurious cabin that would be Lizette's home for the nine days, travelling towards the unknown.

She still wore her silk bathrobe and wondered what she would wear for dinner while she opened the well-filled closet. It was necessary to make an elegant but sophisticated entrance; who knew who she would meet onboard in first class?

It was not as if she wanted to flirt with anyone other than Lawrence at the moment, but the world was small, as Lizette had quietly noted in her circle of acquaintances in recent years. It was best not to make a fool of herself, at least, not too much thought Lizette and smiled to herself.

After Lizette had put on her stockings and ribbons, she chose a dress designed by Coco Chanel; a dress that she needed shoes with comfortable heels for, a casual style that was also fashionable. She also had the latest perfume with her, namely Coco Chanel's No.5, which had just been released and was a perfume Lizette appreciated. It had a special scent (both a little chic and sensual). Lizette's big idol was really Coco Chanel who had undergone an enormous class journey like herself.

Lizette liked Chanel's well known quote that was presented when the perfume was launched "This perfume is not only beautiful and aromatic. It contains my blood, sweet and a million crushed dreams."

Lizette liked Coco Chanel's style of clothes – bien sûr! Coco's masculine and liberating patterns with a feminine touch gave Lizette the feeling of identity that she liked.

Lizette had devoured everything that had been written about Coco Chanel who was the pioneering French fashion designer that created male inspired fashion for women in an exclusive and elegant way. Chanel influenced "Haute Couture" from the first day and was already a legend during her lifetime. Her philosophy changed the way many women saw themselves and Lizette was one of them! For Lizette loved being a woman while she also wanted to be a determined young lady with spunk, which Coco Chanel's clothes conveyed in exactly the right way.

Coco Chanel's creations revolutionized the fashion in the 1910s as she liberated women from the corsets, which had been a necessary evil towards the end of the 19th century. She could really tailor make clothes for the independent and successful women of the 1900s because she created the fashion that women like her wanted. The precise combination of femininity and masculinity with the right sophisticated attitude.

It was time for dinner and Lizette wore a satin dress to suit the occasion, which was not a Chanel model. This evening she wanted to be a little "soft" and invisible, one of the crowd that no one would notice. But she dressed nicely and her mischievous bangs were the icing on the cake together with the right jewelry and shoes. When Lizette was finished she grabbed her crocodile skin handbag and opened the cabin door. Before she left her cabin, she took the "do not disturb" sign off the door and threw it into the cabin. She then walked down the corridor and one flight of stairs up to the party floor. Lizette felt at ease and looked forward to some friendly "mingling" and eventually a good dinner. Lizette would sit and dream if no conversations with fellow passengers happened.

Right now, she didn't really have any great need for socializing but wanted to be surrounded by people. Lizette walked up the beautiful, broad stairs to the lounge. When she had reached the top and walked with long strides like a model, men in the lounge turned and looked at Lizette. Lizette saw some window seats and walked towards them quickly. As she went to sit down in a leather armchair, a man approached her quickly and helped to pull the seat forward. Lizette thanked him abruptly, showing him that she wasn't interested. She then took out a cigarette and a cigarette holder. She didn't smoke very often but thought that the only way to get rid of the unwanted person was to blow smoke in his face. The red-faced middle-aged man coughed and departed as quickly as he had come.

Lizette breathed out a heavy sigh.

A waitress approached Lizette dressed in a black uniform with a white apron. She asked politely if Lizette wanted something to drink. Lizette ordered a whisky as she had the money to be able to order it. She had promised herself to be a little tipsy during the trip, so that if the ship sank as the Titanic had a few years earlier, she wouldn't notice. As a young seventeen- year-old girl, when she had emigrated, she had no choice but to be sober. Her maiden voyage, a long time ago, across the Atlantic had been spent sleeping away tiredness.

It was another life thought Lizette with slight bitterness, but she had, in any case, kept her heart in the right place. She was a wee bit more spoiled compared to her younger days, she admitted to herself as she sat in the deep English armchair. Well, she was twenty-seven years old and more mature and more sophisticated.

The whisky came and Lizette sipped and enjoyed the powerful, rounded taste. It was not an American whisky but a Scotch. Lizette could smell the aroma of seaweed and ocean. After intensively being a hostess in New York's high society in recent years, she had learnt everything from table settings and party planning with the right groups of guests in mind, to knowledge of wine and spirits.

While Lizette sat alone and drank the whisky, she picked up a newspaper that had an article about the alcohol prohibition in the USA: "While it is forbidden to distribute or make beer, wine or any other alcoholic drink, it is not forbidden to use alcohol for private use. The prohibition allows Americans to have alcohol in their home and use the drinks for family and guests, so long as it stays within these circles and is not distributed, sold or given to anyone outside the home".

Lizette laughed to herself. The only thing that prohibition affected so far was to increase the interest in alcohol intoxication, parties and glamour. The twenties was the decade of parties, thought Lizette, which was so incredibly paradoxical!

The more they ban, the more attractive it gets thought Lizette objectively. It had been written in the American constitution in 1919, as an amendment, that they would ban a certain amount of the alcohol flow into the USA, but at the same time as consumption fell, doctors treating patients with liquor as "medicinal care" increased. The black market had also become more violent. All of this made Lizette smile. She continued to read the newspaper seriously, unaffected by the looks that sought her attention. She enjoyed the whisky.

Lizette had a lot in her head and sometimes could not understand how certain women could only think of physical stimulus. Lizette (and even the girl Louise who was still deep within herself) had always liked to revel in knowledge. Lizette's intellectual needs were strong and demanding. If she didn't get the stimulus, she withered as a person. However, she loved luxury and vanity and trivial matters too. Everything had its place in life's jungle and a bit of everything is needed, thought Lizette.

Lizette sat happy and content but she realized that she had started to become a bit hungry. It was almost seven o'clock and it was time to eat dinner in the first class dining room. RMS Mauretania offered a three-course menu and those who wished for a cognac or liqueur could do so in the music or smoking rooms after the dinner.

Lizette shifted uneasily in the leather armchair and noticed that the first class passengers were making their way to the dining room. Suddenly, a woman in her thirties stood in front of Lizette and said: "Do you remember me? I am Vera from New Haven. I was at a party you threw last spring on 5th Avenue." She showed Lizette her gorgeous diamond ring that she wore on her left hand and said that she and her new husband were on their way to Europe on their honeymoon. Vera asked Lizette if she wanted to eat dinner at their table. Lizette thanked her with a yes and was introduced to Vera's husband Luciano. He originally came from Italy and worked within the food industry in Boston. Lizette greeted him with a gentle gesture and they all walked into the dining room together. Luciano chose a seat in the middle of the table and Vera and Lizette sat to the sides. As Lizette sat down, she already felt half bored. How would she pass the time with these two? Fortunately, another man sat to her left. Before he sat down, he asked: "May I have the pleasure of sitting beside someone as attractive as you?" Lizette felt slightly embarrassed. The man in question was very stylish and probably twenty years older than her. The unknown man introduced himself: "I am Justin O'Fly and come from Ireland but I have been living in California for many years". He spoke with a passion about the legendary gold rush to the Klondike, where he had become so rich that he was rolling in it. He continued to say that he had come over to America as a poor farmhand aged fifteen.

Their waiter served champagne and toast with prawns as a starter. It was a dish Lizette never tired of. When everybody at the table got their starters, the noise started to get louder as the wine and drinks flowed. People toasted happily and everyone was in a good mood it seemed. There were, at least, several hundred people at the dinner session. The meals were served in two sittings in first class. They were told, while they ate, that the RMS Mauretania had reached twenty-five knots. Everybody started to applaud and the orchestra started to play. Justin whispered in Lizette's ear: "Do you know how many passengers are on board in total?" Lizette played stupid and exclaimed: "I have no idea!" Justin revealed that there were two-thousand and thirty-five people onboard, with only a few hundred in first class. Justin followed up with another question: "My dear, do you know how much a ticket over the Atlantic cost in the different classes?" Based on this question, Lizette started to think that Justin was a typical example of someone who had just become rich but he had some sort of personality. "Well?" repeated Justin. Lizette took a hefty swig of white wine and answered again: "I have no idea!" That usually pleased men, thought Lizette cynically, that the woman didn't know much and that the men got to tell them. Justin took Lizette's hand and said: "I guess that you miss, never need to think about such things in your position, but here are the following prices: In first class, the tickets cost approximately two-hundred pounds. In second class, they cost seventy-five pounds and in third class, barely ten pounds."

"Ah ha", answered the bored Lizette, but added: "That's so interesting!" If she had been honest, she would have admitted to being completely uninterested.

The dinner progressed and Luciano and Vera sat to the right of Lizette and were completely engrossed in each other, which Lizette appreciated. She turned to Justin halfway through the main course, which was a well-cooked meat dish and asked what he remembered of his childhood's Ireland. Justin looked emotional for a couple of long seconds and answered that what he most remembered were the intense storms in the autumn and the waves that smashed against the cliffs that drew his attention and imagination towards the horizon.

Justin told her enthusiastically: "I have three sisters and I am the youngest of all siblings. My sisters and my mother have always spoiled me and said, ever since I was little, that I could be what I wanted in life". He would be grateful to these fantastic women for the rest of his life. Justin was now on his way "home", thirty-five years later, to his mother's funeral. He added that he was thankful that he had sent her money during the years he become rich so that she could live well. Justin's father had died a long time ago and had barely understood the extent of Justin's fortunes during his lifetime.

Justin, who was a gentleman, continued to tell, after several glasses of wine, that he had gifts of the highest American quality to give to his sisters but when he met Lizette, he wanted to give them all to her just based on her beauty and personality alone. Lizette began to giggle and said: "Justin, take it easy! First, you need to sleep off the alcohol but I thank you for your kindness". Justin just smiled and continued to flirt with Lizette.

After the dessert had been finished and the men went in large groups towards the smoking room, Justin asked if he could leave her. "Of course!" answered Lizette.

When Justin O'Fly had disappeared out of sight, Lizette stood up to leave. There wasn't anybody to her right anymore as Vera and Luciano had vanished. Lizette felt quite tipsy and wobbly legged as she climbed the magnificent stairs that led to her nice cabin.

Once in the cabin, she locked the door and lit all the lights she could access. The sight of a huge number of vases with twenty plus roses in each, made Lizette gasp. There was a card in one of the bouquets that read: "I can't control myself. I can't wait until you are here by my side! Love/Lawrence". Lizette kissed the card and felt overwhelmed by love; it was surprising and quite wonderful. Lizette had never, except for the occasional times of being bewitched by Philip in the Sinclair's library, felt like this about anybody. Even if it was a long distance relationship, it was still glitteringly romantic and satisfying. A meeting at a polo competition and Lizette had been hit by Cupid's arrow for the Englishman.

Lizette went into the cabin's bathroom and could hardly wait until the boat arrived in Southampton. How would she last another eight days?

After getting ready for bed, Lizette lay down on a freshly made bed and enjoyed the fresh scent from the newly ironed sheets. She sank into a deep sleep and dreamt about her poor years in Småland's dark forests when she was a child. She wasn't sad as a child and had inner strength back then mainly thanks to her dear father but it was a paltry existence both in terms of food and money.

There was a knock at the door! It was morning at sea and the whole cabin basked in the light. There was another knock and Lizette swore to herself in bed. She had a splitting headache. Outside the cabin's door she heard: "Miss Af Sinclair, your breakfast is served in the breakfast room!"

Lizette regretted that she had forgotten to order breakfast to the cabin instead. Now she had to force herself up and go up to the breakfast room, which wasn't something, she looked forward to, especially when she considered all the strangers and that she had a headache from hell. She wondered how the time had gone so fast.

Lizette was not a morning person. She could certainly see the beauty of dawn but so long as she could be herself and wake up slowly and comfortably, she was happy. As a maid and nanny, it had never bothered her because she had responsibilities and did not have the luxury to know what her real needs were.

Now there was nothing to do but to crawl out of her comfortable bed and take a shower in the bathroom. Lizette knew herself best and knew that if she didn't eat breakfast, both her head and temper would explode. Once ready, Lizette went to the breakfast room, one floor up. She had had such a rich social life recently that she just wanted to go and hide but she as met the gaze of other passengers, it still felt good to be surrounded by well-dressed and proper people on this sunny morning.

Lizette sat down at a window table by herself. The waiter came quickly, offered coffee and suggested that she look at the menu. After a short moment of studying the menu, she asked for toast, scrambled eggs, bacon and a big glass of juice as well as the New York Times.

As Lizette sat there and enjoyed the breakfast and the newspaper, somebody tapped her suddenly on the shoulder. A red haired diva like lady stood behind her and exclaimed: "Are you not the Louise that the Sinclairs gave the whole world to? Are you not the nanny from Europe? Are you on the way home now that the money has dried up?"

Lizette almost choked on the toast. "And who are you?" she asked. "My name is Madame Hazard and I am from Georgia." Lizette invited the mean, wrinkled ginger head to her table. The lady in question said no and said that she would rather sit down with her slaves at home in the south, turned around and left.

Lizette was shocked but the only thing that she could think about was that President Lincoln had prohibited slavery in the USA in the 1860s! Lizette had never felt so exposed or ridiculed in her life. She should have followed her instinct and hidden herself away earlier. Who was this wrinkled witch who looked as if she had lived during the early 1800s? She probably would spread awful rumors about Lizette throughout the whole of first class. Lizette was furious and tearful. It was day two and a whole seven days remained of her journey before she could curl up into the arms of Lawrence in England.

Lizette sat upright and held her coffee cup with both her hands so that it wouldn't rattle against the saucer. She tried to concentrate and thought strategically; she had climbed up the ladder of society in the USA as many had done.

Actually, she should have just ignored the old woman Hazard. Lizette had not done anything wrong and she understood that the bitch was just jealous. Maybe her husband had appreciated Lizette one time and that had started the ball rolling, making the ginger Madame Hazard see red! Lizette had thrown high-class society parties on 5th Avenue in New York and a bad reputation was nothing that she cared about. Now she couldn't stop what Madame Hazard would spread lies about.

Suddenly, she didn't feel as hungry as she had done before. She patted her mouth dry and left the table. She felt people whisper around her in the dining room. Mrs. Hazard had probably already spread some nasty rumors about her but instead of rushing directly to her suite as her instincts told her, she went out on deck. The fresh autumn sea breeze felt good.

Lizette sat down in a deckchair with soft, beautiful pillows. A waiter rushed up and asked if Lizette wished for something to drink. "Yes, please! Can I have a Bloody Mary, thanks!" said Lizette and sat comfortably on the chair with her face pointed towards the autumn sun.

"Bloody Mary" was a new and trendy drink that had been popular for a year. A man called Fernand Petiot claimed that he had invented the drink after Queen Mary of France who murdered a mass of people in an enormous bloodbath – the Bartholomew night. Petiot thought the name was fitting after the drink was made up of tomatoes coloring it red.

And now, Lizette wished that the red haired witch Hazard could also be slung into a bloodbath and, therefore, never bother her again.

Fernand Petiot said that he composed "Bloody Mary" while he worked at a bar called New York in Paris that Americans frequented; a regular guest was Ernest Hemingway. Lizette could recall that she had read about it in the New York Times. In 1922, the famous writer had married Elizabeth Hadley Richardson and moved to Paris where he worked as a foreign correspondent. Lizette thought that Hemingway looked so masculine in pictures, yes, a real man's man. Well, Lizette liked this drink that was good for a hangover and subdued hunger.

Just as she had finished thinking about the drink, somebody stood in the sunlight, blocking it. It was her table guest from the night before, Justin O'Fly who coughed and asked if he could sit down. Lizette hesitated at first but agreed. The waiter returned with Lizette's Bloody Mary. Justin ordered a cognac even though it was early morning. Lizette said jokingly as an excuse that she ordered the Bloody Mary as an energy restorer but thought at the same time that it was way too early for a cognac. Justin answered quickly: "Cognac is made out of grapes so it can't be that dangerous?!"

This led to them having a conversation about prohibition in the USA and all the secret exciting places in New York where all the spirits flowed regardless. Lizette said that the time of prohibition only increased the interest in alcohol. Lizette said that it would be impossible to ban it forever and Justin O'Fly agreed. It was really easy to talk to Justin but Lizette was thankful that she wasn't attracted to him. It would have made things more complicated in the position she now found herself in.

Justin O'Fly sat in the chair beside Lizette and asked: "My dear, do you want a quilt?" The chilly autumn ocean breeze made itself known. Lizette said yes and Justin O'Fly got up immediately and went towards a pile of blankets that were stacked on a wicker table. When he came back to Lizette, the waiter had returned with Justin's cognac. Lizette sipped slowly on her Bloody Mary and looked out at the horizon and smelt the scent in the air as did Justin. Lizette felt really at ease in Justin O'Fly's company. It wasn't every day that you could be quiet without creating a strange atmosphere.

When they had sat for a few hours discussing world politics in between pauses of silences, Lizette started to really freeze. She turned to O'Fly and said in confidence: "Thank you for being such a good friend onboard this journey!" She then excused herself by saying that she needed to warm up in the cabin and write some letters.

Justin O'Fly asked Lizette: "Can we eat dinner together a little later?" Lizette thanked him for his kind invitation but declined. She continued: "I feel a little feverish and don't feel completely well, Justin, so I think that I will stay in my cabin a while."

Justin O'Fly took Lizette's hand, kissed it like a true gentleman and said that he would be there for her regardless of when she needed him – she just needed to shout. "Oh!" thought Lizette to herself – dangerous! Dangerous! Why can men and women never be just friends?

Lizette walked briskly and strode towards her cabin. Justin O'Fly stared and took in every step she took; he had fallen for this fantastic woman in every shape and form. Was Justin O'Fly finally in love?

Lizette couldn't cope with more nasty taunts from the horrible Mrs. Hazard from Georgia so she avoided the crowd in the restaurant. She couldn't handle all the chitchat amongst all the prominent passengers when the conversations were all at such a low level – Lizette wanted peace and quiet and went to her cabin. It wasn't a bad decision because the cabin was fairy tale like.

This would be where Lizette would spend the last days until the boat had docked in Southampton or at least this is what she had decided. It would be "room-service" from now on until she met Lawrence.

But Lizette had not taken into consideration Justin O'Fly's obsession with her. When she was in the bathroom to remove her make-up, she heard three intensive knocks at her cabin door. Lizette put on her silk bathrobe and walked slowly to the cabin door. She heard a familiar voice outside say in a firm voice: "I have news, Lizette, from Long Island!" Lizette flinched. Was Justin serious? Lizette didn't want to hear terrible news. Lizette opened the door to a refreshed man who was prepared to seduce the woman who had charmed him. He surprised Lizette as he first closed and locked the cabin door behind him. He then lifted her up and carried her to the bed where he coaxed off her bathrobe and nightgown with an intensive male grip. Yes, Justin had beautiful hands that were gentle but determined. He kissed her on the stomach and clambered upwards with his tongue, devouring her ample bust. Lizette knew it was wrong. She wanted Lawrence but was drunk and now felt the desire that she couldn't deny. Suddenly, Lizette loved sex without comparison; she was wet, slender and radiated sex, glamour and money. He took her from behind, from the front, licked her clitoris so that it was blessed with pleasure. Lizette moaned with desire and satisfaction.

Justin O'Fly could get a woman to spin and Lizette span with every cell of her body. She took his stiff cock in her mouth and sucked gently but forcefully as they both gasped for breath and were sweating with ecstasy.

They literally lived in Lizette's bed and ordered "room-service" when they weren't making love. Sometimes the boat rocked in time with their orgasms and they both laughed and admitted that it made the job more difficult.

Justin bound Lizette's hands with the silk ribbon from the exclusive bathrobe for some sessions. Lizette could not break loose while Justin licked her in every corner of her femininity. Lizette's clitoris was so stunned by the pleasure and orgasms. Lizette had never experienced anything like it before. Justin made love to Lizette passionately over the following days on the way to England until Lizette cried with anguish and asked him to leave the cabin.

CHAPTER 10

Lawrence

Lizette had chosen to pack her large trunk herself after making the decision to be by herself for the last day onboard. She had deeply regretted her escapades with Justin but at the same time, she knew that her Lawrence was a "ladies' man" and had had his own conquests. Lizette tried, instead, to focus on her packing. She had conservatively packed, in comparison to what she was used to having in her own closet, and hoped it was a clever move. Lawrence had promised that he would buy her new fitting clothes when she was in England. Lizette was sad and now wondered if she deserved it. It would probably be a good idea to give the impression that she would not stay forever, thought Lizette.

It was these small things that could scare away some people. Within the upper class, it was the norm that you would marry the right person who was of the same class, but also to have a lover or mistress if it was needed in a loveless relationship. Everything was an act. Lizette had never imagined the machinations that happened behind closed doors. It was, however, now clear in her mind that Lawrence was the man for her and she would do everything in her power to be treated in the right way. Lizette was head over heels in love and only had a few "skeletons in the closet" like Justin O'Fly.

Lizette wondered how she could be in love with Lawrence but at the same time have sex with someone who was only being nice.

She had started to wonder who Lawrence really was over the nine days on the Atlantic. Had she had fallen for a charmer who would tire of his ladies as quick as he changed shirts? But she had done the same thing herself! Hm!

Lizette knew that there was a difficult situation that waited around the corner but she was grateful that through the years, she had become more down to earth and thought more clearly. Lizette laughed to herself, feeling a bit embarrassed.

Lizette's biggest joy was the Sinclair family where she had got her first and only employment in America, which had given her economic freedom. It was thanks to them that she didn't need to be dependent on a man or endure a loveless relationship. She could still hardly understand that she had had such tremendous luck.

Sadly, Lizette was still very tired of being alone in her fashionable apartment on Manhattan even if she was very popular and surrounded by people most of the time. Lizette longed for a close relationship with a man who could be her companion, lover and best friend.

Then, suddenly she heard a signal through the Tannoy that the boat had docked which meant they had arrived in Southampton. RMS Mauretania had shown her strength on her way across the Atlantic but this time, newly renovated and in a grander style.

Lizette woke up out of philosophizing and checked her Chanel dress with matching coat in the mirror. Since her teens, she had heard that it was cold and damp in England and that a coat was needed. The icing on the cake was her gorgeous hat from Macy's. Finally, after checking her make-up one last time, Lizette put on her leather gloves and took a deep breath.

She was now ready to meet Lawrence face-to-face, make or break she thought calmly. There was a knock on the cabin door and a bellboy came to carry Lizette's trunk while she carried her fine leather handbag. She followed the all too skinny bellboy. The boy was stronger than she imagined. Lizette smiled to herself while she thought that the bellboy would have a brilliant future with his humility towards rich women. Maybe one day, a rich widow would take him under her wings and he would get, just like she had, to live in opulence. Life was strange and anything could actually happen!

Lizette believed in fate but because the world was so unfair, maybe you would be born again in different guises to be able to try the life of both the poor and rich through reincarnation? It was something she imagined and who could argue with her? Nobody actually had the answer.

The passengers from first class disembarked first when the RMS Mauretania docked with care. When Lizette came to the gangplank, she was greeted by cheers and hurrahs, which felt unreal.

The passenger's loved ones welcomed their relatives to Southampton and England but Lizette was on her own, nervous and a little tense before her meeting with "the flirt" she had met at a polo competition on Long Island in the summer.

Lizette didn't have any regrets yet. When she was almost on land and had just stepped off the gangplank, she heard a whistle and turned towards the sharp sound coming from the sea of people. And there he stood! Her own Earl Lawrence Stewart! He was just as charismatic, as masculine and as good looking as she had remembered. It wasn't difficult to fall into a trance again when she looked at this wonderful man, thought Lizette to herself.

She still didn't know whether or not he was really "hers" but she intensely hoped that she was not considered to be his new mistress.

"Lizette! This way!"

Lawrence came up to Lizette and took her hand while she held onto her hat with the other. A fresh wind blew while the sun shone on this beautiful autumn day. Lizette's bright red lipstick on her relatively small lips dazzled the surroundings. Yes, the new trend was to have really red lips. If Lizette had been truthful, wearing the red lipstick was a little bit too much but what wouldn't you do for beauty's sake, she thought as she happily took Lawrence's hand.

After passing through the toll, they came to Lawrence Stewart's car, the famous Rolls-Royce Silver Ghost featuring a chassis that had been built during the early 1900s. Lawrence smiled when he saw Lizette's fascinated expression from the sight of his beautiful cream-colored cabriolet. He took the trunk from the bellboy and laid it in the back of the car together with Lizette's smaller leather handbag. The bellboy stood waiting as Lizette opened her small handbag and gave him several coins. Lawrence apologized and said "My dear, I usually don't take care of such things as giving tips to the personnel." Lizette coughed lightly and looked sternly at him. Lawrence kissed her on the cheek and apologized again with an effective cheeky beautiful smile that made Lizette melt and forgive him.

When they had driven out into the countryside, away from Southampton, Lawrence asked how the journey had been. "I will tell you everything later", said Lizette subtly, "but first, tell me about this wonderful car."

Lawrence laughed and said: "The motor has six cylinders. It can reach 65 or 70 miles an hour and one can drive 10 to 12 miles per gallon. The Silver Ghost model has won many reliability tests during its production time including the Alpine Trial in 1913" he explained. Lizette felt her love increase again during the short time together with Lawrence Stewart. He had charisma and radiating masculinity that made her breathe faster and blush from her strong feelings.

Lawrence continued: "When I heard that "Lawrence of Arabia" talked well of the Rolls-Royce Silver Ghost and that the car gained a reputation of being one of the best in the world, I became enchanted" said Lawrence with an air of male sensuality.

He continued: "One admires this Lawrence, a British officer, author and archeologist". Lawrence smiled and said that he knew all the gossip that had been told about Lawrence of Arabia alias

Thomas Edward Lawrence who had anonymously applied to the Royal Air Force under the name John Hume Ross recently.

Lizette felt that she sat beside the "right man". It was real somehow. Just to hear him and be near him made it possible to feel waves of pleasure inside. Had she found the right place in the end?

They continued to drive for over an hour after they had left Southampton. Lawrence suggested that they stop and eat, and Lizette, who was always a little hungry, agreed. Lawrence drove up an entrance to a restaurant after a half an hour of searching for an inn with a golden rooster as a motif.

When they had parked, Lawrence turned to Lizette and looked deep into her eyes and kissed her hand. Softly, he said: "I am so happy to be finally reunited with you, my darling". Lizette shivered with pleasure; she had never experienced such an electric contact with anyone else.

Lizette looked happily at Lawrence and said: "You seem to be almost too good to be true!" Lawrence smiled back and said it was totally mutual. He promised to try and never let her down.

"Try?" exclaimed Lizette in a light shaky voice. Lawrence helped the worried Lizette out of the "Silver Ghost" and said: "I promise, Lizette, to never let you down!" Lizette coughed and kissed Lawrence on the cheek before they both went into the inn "The Golden Rooster".

The local people who sat in the restaurant looked curiously at the stylish pair who had just entered. Lizette ignored the strange reception. Lawrence made her feel secure regardless of the places they would visit. Lawrence pulled out a chair by a window table and a waitress came and asked them what they wanted to eat. Lawrence asked Lizette if a meat dish would be good. She nodded because she loved all kinds of food, from fish and seafood to a real steak. Lawrence ordered a pint of a locally brewed beer with the meals.

Lizette laughed hysterically at the British English that she was not accustomed to hearing having spent many years in the USA. It made a lovely and different change. Lawrence took her hands and whispered sweet compliments to Lizette until they were served with their beer.

Lawrence stretched and said with seriousness: "Lizette, regardless of how you experience being in England this month we have together, you must tell me if you miss anything or how I can get you feel more at home".

Lizette nodded happily and sipped the beer; she enjoyed being "the Lady" and having a man who cared for her. After a moment of small talk and looking at each other with love in their eyes, the food was served and they enjoyed the delicious steak and drank more beer. After this, it was time to return to the winding English country roads.

Lawrence was wearing a leather cap, which was fashioned like a pilot's model, and he even had goggles to block out the wind in the open convertible. Lizette still had her hat on, held in place by a beautiful woolen shawl. It started to get dark and in the enchanting autumn evening they drew closer to Lawrence's family estate, which was a fair distance outside London. It was beautifully situated in a fantastic forest. It looked like a castle out of the fairy tales Lizette had read to little Andrew Jr that were about the kingdom of England.

They drove through a long avenue with stately trees that lined both sides. Lizette felt as if she landed up in a fairy tale. In addition, she had this wonderful man who owned all of it next to her. If someone had said that it was only a strange dream Lizette would have believed it, even if the Sinclair family had accustomed her to the fine world at the highest level during a number of years. Lizette would never forget where she came from and it was both good and bad.

Lawrence looked in Lizette's direction and took her hand. They parked in the large courtyard outside the manor after having passed through imposing stone pillar gates. Lizette had been a little bit cold in the car during the tour in the chilly autumn evening. She breathed out now that they had finally reached their destination. A servant rushed towards the car and greeted Lawrence a welcome home. He took Lizette's trunk out of the car's boot and carried it in. Lawrence asked a servant, called Patrick, to carry up the trunk to the guest suite on the third floor. Patrick nodded first towards Lawrence and smiled shyly at Lizette.

Lawrence stood in front of Lizette and took her hands and embraced her

lovingly, which made Lizette weak at the knees. He then whispered sensually into her ear: "Welcome to my home, my darling!" Lizette couldn't help kissing Lawrence back as an answer. There they both stood, in the fantastic autumn evening in England, and kissed each other intensively.

Patrick suddenly came back and coughed to get their attention. He wanted only to tell his lordship that a supper was waiting in the dining room that had been cooked especially by Mrs. Smith, the cook, as a welcome dinner. Lizette started to laugh and asked Lawrence: "Are you going to fatten me up to turn me into a Rubens' model?" Lawrence answered emphatically: "Maybe, my dearest, because then I would have you all to myself!"

Lizette answered with a small laugh: "I suppose that this is what the new fashion requires – that us women should be thin as twigs and dance otherwise we will be thrown to the wolves – or what do you say?"

They walked from the car through the castle grounds to the stately entrance with two high pillars in front of the steps that framed the enormous oak doors. Patrick had, at the same time, walked briskly in front of them with Lizette's luggage, which made her smile humbly.

Imagine how lucky she had been to be excused from being a nanny forever even if she felt a certain amount of pride from all the hard work she undertook as a child. It felt as if it was another life. Now Lizette felt as fine and on the same level as the people she had socialized with within the upper class. She realized that everything was just a "game", but with huge implications depending on whether you were poor or rich.

Lizette breathed in the clear, fresh autumn air and felt at ease after the long journey. She was there with Lawrence, a man who she had only believed existed in fairy tales. As Lizette had had to wait so long for love, she could have said "good things come to those who wait". However, there was some skepticism within her – everything could also be too good to be true. Lawrence put his arm around Lizette when they stepped into the stunning castle like manor, which was considered to be an actual castleas royals had lived in it once for some time.

The original castle was built in the 1700s during the reign of King George who belonged to the House of Hannover from Germany. The palace was completed at the start of the 1700s and was a morning gift to a noble relative of Georges' who was a prospective consort to him. Nothing became of it but the manor got to keep its castle status. Lawrence's family, the Stewarts, had an exciting family history and had royal, noble and ordinary people's blood in its veins. Lawrence whispered to Lizette: "I feel so honored that you wanted to come to my home in England!" Lawrence continued to whisper in Lizette's ear: "You have courage, beauty and a very exciting personality Lizette!" He kissed her and added: "I feel so happy together with you, my dearest!"

They walked into the grand hall where the servant, Patrick who was still carrying Lizette's luggage, rushed up the stairs towards her room.

Lawrence asked Lizette to wait in the dining room with him so that they could rest a while. A maid showed them in to the fantastic dining room, a hall with spectacular views over the estate and, at the far end, an incredibly beautiful bay window that was almost an orangery, where they would enjoy their supper.

They walked three steps down into the glazed bay area that had an open fireplace, sturdy furniture and a harmonic atmosphere. The candles were lit and a crackling fire wooed them on this fabulous autumn evening.

The question was whether it crackled just as much between Lizette and Lawrence like the fireplace? They sat down in the deep ox-blood colored leather sofa and Lawrence rang a bell. The maid came in with a wagon loaded with the most delicious seafood.

Lawrence gave a light cough and reminded Lizette that it was lobster season. He stood up and opened the champagne, a Dom Pérignon. Lizette asked if she could take off her shoes and put her feet up on the sofa and leaned against the soft cushions. Lawrence answered quickly: "Your wish is my command, my darling!" Lizette sat comfortably for the first time since she had set foot on English soil. Lawrence gave her a glass of champagne, filled up a glass for himself and sat in the armchair beside the fire.

While the maid made the table with lobsters and side dishes, Lawrence said in a deep and sensual voice: "I hereby welcome Lizette Af Sinclair with a toast of admiration, love and a thank you for having come all this way home... I mean to my place, this autumn of 1922!" After the toast, Lizette felt warm, surging waves of love inside her. It felt so wonderful; maybe it was home after all!

Lawrence lit a thin cigar and surprised Lizette: "So St. Louis Brown "Baby Doll" Jacobson helped to beat the Tigers in September?" Lizette sat upright in the comfortable leather couch and answered irritated: "Do you really want to question me about sport?" and briskly added, "If that is the case then you have met the wrong woman as I hate sport!" Lawrence laughed and was so charming that Lizette felt her heart pound. Lawrence slightly shifted from the subject of sport and asked: "But what about Polo? It was at the polo competition on Long Island that we met."

Lizette blushed slightly and felt caught because she was at the polo competition for a completely different reason than an interest in sport. She said firmly: "I was there because I love horses and because I had been invited to the lunch". Lizette looked at Lawrence in a slightly defiant way. He raised a beaming smile and blew a kiss at her through the smoke from his Cuban cigar.

Lawrence asked Lizette, who really knew Broadway like the back of her hand, if she had seen all the new musicals like "Make It Snappy" or "Spice of 1922" which had had their premiers recently or "The Passing Show" which premiered the day before her journey. They had been performed in the Winter Garden in New York, which was a theatre on 1634 Broadway; it had 1482 seats and was opened in 1911.

Lizette rarely lost face but now felt frustrated that Lawrence knew so much about her city and was so well-read within the areas where she should have had the upper hand. Suddenly, she felt like an inexperienced teenager without any training or knowledge. It seemed as if Lawrence knew his "faux- pas'". Lawrence put out his cigar and went over to Lizette who was lying on the sofa with one hand on her forehead. He took her little hand in his large and powerful hands and said tenderly: "Lizette, excuse me for joking with you but you bring forth so many feelings within me – even my childish side!" He kissed her long and intensively. Lawrence tasted of tobacco but it didn't matter. He still tasted divine and she wished he would never stop kissing her.

Lawrence poured some more of the champagne that was in the wine cooler. He lifted Lizette out from the sofa and sat her by the little table that had been laid out with a tablecloth and the awaiting lobsters.

Lawrence rang a bell and while they waited for the maid, they toasted once more and enjoyed the rich droplets of champagne. The maid came in with toasted bread and Russian caviar as a side dish for the light seafood supper. Lizette enjoyed sitting opposite the irresistible man while munching on English toast and eating delicate lobster. It was almost dark outside and although Lizette had had a long journey, she didn't want the evening to ever end.

The maid came and cleaned the table. Lizette wished her a good night. The older lady curtsied and thanked Miss Af Sinclair and wished Lord Lawrence the same. Left alone, they looked at the smoldering fire when Lawrence exclaimed spontaneously: "Now my lady, I want to carry you to my suite; first for you to freshen up after supper and also because I think you want to!" Lizette was dumbfounded, but Lawrence actually did carry her from the orangery, through the dining room, up the very majestic staircase to the second floor.

Lizette started to laugh and asked if she was too heavy for poor Lawrence. Lawrence answered with sincerity: "You are light as a feather, for being a gold bar!" Lizette laughed and jolted her elbow lightly into Lawrence's stomach. Lawrence whispered in her ear: "Never hit those who carry you, my lady!"

They came into the unbelievable suite that Lizette would have as her own home during the next few weeks. Lawrence put her down on the gigantic bed, which had a bedspread with woven gold threads. Lizette wondered if he could hear her heart pound. Lawrence said excitedly that he had waited for this moment ever since they had met in America during the summer and now it would soon be winter. Lizette was as happy as he was and didn't care about playing hard to get. She wasn't a virgin but they had both waited for each other for a long time and Lizette was more than ready to make love to this man who she pined for with her whole soul.

Lawrence excitedly undressed Lizette, from her silk stockings to her modern bra she had bought before she came to England. When Lizette lay naked on the bed, Lawrence quickly undressed. Then, to her great surprise, he led her up from the bed and into the bathroom.

There, in the modern shower that gave a lovely fountain-like feel, they stood and washed each other in the warm, lively water that warmed their excited bodies. They kissed each other intensively, yes, they almost ate each other up and both enjoyed the pleasure. Lizette was in heaven and it felt as if she had finally come home. Lawrence's masculine chest pressed against her plump breasts and she could feel him from every direction.

They made love in the shower until they were completely exhausted. Afterwards, they put on their bathrobes and Lizette wrapped her close- cropped frizzy hair in a turban. Lizette couldn't help but look at Lawrence spellbound. So, this was what the poets wrote about with their long poems!

Genuine, lovely lovemaking was even more fantastic than people had claimed. It had taken many years for Lizette to discover it. She had thought that everyone had over exaggerated but to make love with Lawrence was so well worth waiting for thought Lizette. Lawrence whispered in her ear: "A penny for your thoughts!"

He took her hand yet again and brought her back to the inviting bed. There, he tucked Lizette in and said lovingly: "I'll be back in a moment, my love!" He then disappeared out of Lizette's suite.

Lizette abruptly fell asleep with a smile on her lips and had never slept so well or been so satisfied.

Lizette was awoken by a knock on her door. The sunlight that flooded into her room made her squint. The thoughts returned to her consciousness and she realized where she was and felt happy. Her whole body felt like a newly uncurled flower. There was a knock at the door again. "Yes! I'm coming!" answered Lizette. A servant came in with a wagon, which was full of delicatessens, which smelt of freshly brewed coffee, croissants and fruit. The servant lifted a silver lid to reveal bacon and scrambled eggs. Lawrence entered the room, carrying two champagne glasses and a bottle of Piper champagne this time. He thanked his butler Clifford and asked him to leave them alone. Lawrence smiled warmly from ear to ear and lightly hummed: "Good morning Lizette, my fantastic beauty from New York!"

Lizette wondered if he had not heard her Swedish accent. Lawrence, who was very sharp, must have had an idea that she wasn't American from birth (but who really was?)

Lizette's heart skipped a beat while she recognized the desire that was growing by being next to this charismatic, beautiful man. Lawrence held up a cup of coffee to his love and gave her a croissant with strawberry marmalade.

Lizette devoured the croissant while she enjoyed both the coffee and being kissed on the forehead, causing her to shiver with pleasure. "Have you slept well, my princess?"

"Yes Lawrence, it was the most beautiful night of my life!" Lawrence answered: "And even though I wasn't in your bed, my lady!" Lizette laughed and expressed her surprise that someone was quicker with a remark than she was. "I firmly believe that you have bewitched me, my lord, to a point where I can no longer talk!"

"We don't need to talk more today", said Lawrence slowly and took off his bathrobe and crept under the covers to a more than willing Lizette.

They made love slowly with passion until they both had to recover. Lizette had never felt so free. She thought that this experience with Lawrence was the most wonderful and natural thing that had ever happened to her. He got her to love her own body and not be ashamed of anything.

Lawrence opened the bottle of champagne after they had made love several times. They lay side-by-side, satisfied and exhausted and started to feel slightly intoxicated by the sweet drops that the Piper house had produced in France.

Life was just wonderful thought Lizette happily. They talked for several hours while they ate scrambled eggs, bacon and croissants now and again. The champagne ran out between the kissing and cuddling and was replaced by the strong coffee.

Lawrence told her that he had invited several friends and acquaintances over for a welcome party in her honor at the weekend but before this, he had planned to go out riding through the beautiful nature and explore Lawrence's estate if Lizette didn't object. Lizette answered: "Not at all, it sounds great!"

During the following three days, Lawrence and Lizette rode around the large estate owned by the Stewart family. Lizette loved the smell of the horses, which were Lawrence's and Lizette's closest friends during these intensive days. They galloped over the meadows and trotted around the lake; the fantastic colors of the autumn leaves made everything look like a painting.

Despite all the rain in England that Lizette had heard so much about, it wasn't all that bad. Sometimes it drizzled a little and sometimes it was sunny as if spring was in the air. It was much milder at this time of year in England than what Lizette remembered of the cold Swedish autumns.

Of course, it felt extra nice now that Lizette was so in love that she was about to crack; she had never experienced this incredible, magical feeling before. The girl called Louise from Sweden who was now the lady Lizette was being carried forward by the wonderful feelings in her whole body. It was really like a true fairytale.

Apart from the pleasant life with the Sinclair family that they had given her, she had never felt as good as she did now; together with her own count whom she loved more than anything else. There must be an angel who is watching over me, thought Lizette gratefully.

Lawrence shouted from his horse: "The last one to the stable will be surprised by something special after dinner!" Lizette whipped her horse; she sat well in the saddle and liked being on horseback. They galloped so that the earth splashed and their hearts beat faster. Lizette spurred her stately chestnut once again. Lawrence was now behind her and drew closer to the stable with Lizette in the lead.

Lizette won and was received by the stable hand Paddy, who took care of the beautiful and sweaty horse. Lizette jumped off the saddle on the mare and adjusted her jacket. Sure, she full of aches the day after all the riding but also after all the lovemaking thought Lizette and smiled coyly to herself.

She took several chunks of carrot out of her jacket pocket and gave them to the mare. At the same moment, Lawrence rode into the courtyard and exclaimed happily: "You are a real horse girl! If I had had any idea of your prowess in the saddle, I never would have started riding with you!" Lawrence winked at Lizette and blew her a kiss.

After the two lovers had had these fantastic autumn days on horseback together around the estate, it was now time for all the preparations for the welcome party in Lizette's honor. She observed, amazed, everyone who worked with everything from small to big things, from the preparations of the big rooms to the planning of the menu in the kitchen, everything that a lady of the manor would need to learn to control.

Lizette didn't yet see herself as the lady of the manor but the thought struck her that everything seemed to be unbelievably lavish, not a penny seemed to have been spared for her party. Workers from the whole neighborhood worked so that this party in her honor would be a fantastic and appreciated success. Lizette felt slightly nervous. What did she want from life? To be in New York and hold court for the upper class or spend time with her lover, Lawrence in England, on royal European soil?

As she sat in the vast surroundings of her beautiful bedroom in the castle, there was a knock at the door and Lizette was jolted out of her daydream.

It was Lawrence's butler who apologized and said in a deep tone: "Lord Lawrence asked me to fetch you, Miss Lizette, and take you to the pavilion on the south side." Lizette nodded and went into the bathroom when she heard the butler close the door. In the bathroom, she checked her appearance as it felt important to do so.

She became transfixed by her reflection and studied the woman she had become and wondered at the same time what Lawrence now wanted out in the pavilion. Lizette shuddered and put on an extra top. She left her room and went down the large staircase towards the front door. The butler stood prepared with Lizette's coat and gloves. Lizette dressed herself in her outdoor clothes and went out through the large entrance doors but with the butler following behind her.

Lizette knew that they didn't want her to become lost on the estate or be kidnapped, which made her smile. Her employers in Småland hadn't cared about the possibility of her being taken by bandits – when Louise worked as a maid. Now she was valuable and rich which Lizette had difficulty realizing. Lizette had always thought about how the rich man's world worked and had always believed that she suited that world right from the start despite her modest background. The mere thought of it made her smile as she made her way to pavilion.

The pavilion was lit with amazing kerosene lamps and outside, Lawrence had arranged an avenue of flaming torches on tall ornate iron poles. Lizette's chin almost dropped when she stood by the entrance on the way to the largest pavilion she had ever seen, because there were hearts on all the windowpanes. In addition, there were rose petals on the path between the torches and when she was almost there, the front door swung open as if to receive a queen.

Lizette stepped into the festively decorated pavilion. There was everything you could wish for; dainty salmon sandwiches, black caviar, roe, English biscuits and tasty sauces in beautiful bowls. Even lobster and oysters because Lawrence knew all too well that they were Lizette's favorite dishes.

When she came in, Lawrence took her hand and pulled her into the house and kissed her slowly. After the kiss, they were almost out of breath. A violinist played for them while Lawrence and Lizette were given a champagne glass filled with Dom Pérignon by Lawrence's butler who waited in the vicinity. When the lovers started to drown in each other's eyes, the butler and the violinist slipped out to leave the two turtle doves alone. Lawrence suddenly got down on one knee and took Lizette's small beautiful hand in his. Lizette felt so many mixed feelings overwhelm her. She had some idea that this magical moment might someday come but she was completely confused and didn't know how to handle it. Lizette knew that it would change her whole life yet again.

Lawrence said, from his kneeling position: "Dearest Lizette, if you will become my wife, I will be forever the happiest man in the world!" Lizette squatted down in front of the amazed Lawrence, surely no other wife-to-be had done that before. Lizette hugged Lawrence hard and whispered in his ear: "My dearest darling, I do BUT you must listen to what I want too!"

Lawrence took Lizette's left hand in his, put a ring with a large glittering diamond on her ring finger, lifted her up and said emphatically: "Your wish, my dearest, is my command!" Lizette nodded happily and said that in that case everything was how it should be. Lawrence opened the front door and the cool autumn evening streamed in.

Outside, the staff of count Lawrence Stewart applauded. After a few words of thanks to the staff, Lawrence shut the door and poured more champagne. They took their plates and enjoyed the delicatessens that had been laid out but what they really wanted was to land up in the same bed. They left the beautiful pavilion filled with lust and desire and hurried to the manor house. Once inside, they threw off their jackets and hurried up the stairs. The servants smiled and were excited because they had realized there would eventually be a wedding and possibly small children gracing the manor with their presence.

CHAPTER 11

The Engagement

Lizette's clothes dropped down on the floor thanks to Lawrence's skilled warm hands that undressed her with great intensity. He longed for the first mission as newly engaged; to give his bride-to-be wonderful caresses and he felt privileged to have met this beautiful creature. Lizette had everything he wanted in a woman and he didn't care one bit about her simple background. Her lovely presence was everything to the enchanted Lawrence.

Finally, Lizette lay completely naked in bed with only her new diamond ring on her finger and this time she was in Lawrence's bedroom and not the guest suite.

Everything had gone so fast that her doubting thoughts could not be heard because everything felt right. There was no return; it was her fate to marry Lawrence. They had the same sort of humor, the same view of life and even physically matched each other. He was the best thing that had happened to her. Everything was just as wonderful as she could have ever hoped for or wished for. Lizette trusted Lawrence and he trusted her. What more could you ask for?

He was also noble and rich which was also too good to be true. Even if it was now a fact that Lizette was not a pauper, she actually had wealth thanks to the Sinclair family.

Lawrence made love slowly, sensually and pleasured his beloved, soon-to-be- wife. Lizette gasped loudly as she came like never before. Before Lizette had met her soul mate, Lawrence, she had not known what orgasms were but she learnt to enjoy sex more and more each time they made love. Afterwards, they slept tightly as if nothing could separate them from each other.

The following morning, Lizette awoke to an empty bed. She loved to sleep in but most other people she knew were more early birds than she was. In the past, she had started work early and it had always felt like she had sand in her eyes in the mornings.

Lizette inspected Lawrence's elegant bedroom, which was in a class of its own. She stretched her entire body out on the lovely silk sheets and felt a genuine delight inside and outside and in every cell of her body. Both little Louise and Lizette felt completely at home.

This was what every girl and woman had dreamed about and Lizette was no exception; she had longed for this and now she was happily engaged! Lizette stared at the fantastic diamond on the ring she got the night before. It was unbelievable and fit to be worn by a royal. Lizette couldn't tell the fantastic news to her mother as she had passed on but she had a strong urge to talk to her pretend mother, Charlotte Sinclair. Lizette could barely let the thought sink in before the bedroom door opened. She quickly drew the sheets over herself.

Lawrence came briskly in and showered her with kisses and then said seriously: "Our lives will be totally changed now, my love!" Lawrence kissed her tenderly but at the same time so sensually that Lizette's heart began, once again, to boom.

Lawrence continued: "We shall have a welcome party for you in the morning, my darling, here on the estate. It will be both a welcome and engagement party, which is precisely what I had hoped for. You are the right one for me, Lizette".

When they had made love yet again, they showered together. Lizette almost fainted from standing next to the world's most beautiful man and from all the wonderful things that were happening. Lizette would be Countess Lizette Af Sinclair Stewart. It felt unbelievable and sounded really refined. If this was a dream, she never wanted to wake up again.

The most special weekend in Lizette's life was when it was time for Lizette to be publicly presented as Lawrence Stewart's fiancée. The party had already started on Saturday afternoon on the Stewart's estate in October, when an old English tradition called Halloween was celebrated in Great Britain.

As with Easter and May Day, magical powers were said to be in the air during the last days of October. In the past, some have said that learned men and women, druids and whole village populations extinguished their household fires on the 31st October. Some have said that the druids, in turn, lit a large bonfire where everyone later could fetch fire for their household needs.

Many years later, towards the end of the 1800s and into the early 1900s, this magical, last weekend in October, Halloween has been said to bea weekend for young lovers. It was something that Lawrence enthusiastically told Lizette in the last couple of days before the party. He told her that during the twenties, associations like Rotary, Lions and Scouts had started to take over the practice but also began to turn it into a general celebration and not just for lovers.

Lizette sighed lightly and said that they actually had Halloween traditions even in America. In the USA, she had learned that the weekend was celebrated to show reverence for deceased loved ones. A Halloween custom that came from Mexico involved relatives meeting up in cemeteries to offer and enjoy favorite dishes of the deceased. In other words, a party to the departed. "The Celtic tradition then, Miss Af Sinclair?" asked Lawrence jokingly and grabbed her silk ribbon that she wore around her waist and pulled her closer to her.

He then continued on with his lecture - while he kissed her now and then – about how Scotland and Ireland were Christianized in the 5th century and how, amongst other things, they had retained a Celtic festival that was called All Saints day which is celebrated in May which they then moved to the end of October. When he had finished, Lawrence carried Lizette to the bed and whispered sensually in her ear: "Regardless of who did what to whom and when, I love you, Lizette!" Lizette choked up with laughter.

It was eleven in the morning. The first guests would arrive in three hours and the bride-to-be and the groom-to-be seemed to have a promising future because they couldn't be torn apart from each other. When they had made love as never before, they heard a knock at the door and Lawrence's butler shouted: "My lord, a message!"

Lizette kissed her lover and jumped into the bathroom to get ready. She closed and locked the door behind her, stepped towards the mirror, looked carefully at herself and analyzed her reflection.

"Yes, Lizette, you have come a long way and have a promising husband that you have fabulous sex with!" Lizette smiled to herself and had never been so happy.

While Lizette prepped herself in the bathroom with everything from make- up to exquisite underwear that she had earlier prepared and laid out on a chair in the fantastic bathroom, Lawrence put on a smoking jacket and received the packet that had been delivered by his butler. He opened the box impatiently. A sealed envelope lay within and a beautiful horse halter in burgundy leather.

The letter read: "Dear Lawrence, I have heard that Lizette and you are getting engaged and we wish to be part of the announcement of your wedding tonight. Can you please give our Lizette this horse halter before the party and tell her to visit the stable. There is a surprise (we have arranged a little something with your staff)! Looking forward to seeing you soon and thanks for the invitation! We have arrived in London this morning and we'll soon be with you.

Congratulations from the Sinclair's and all the best to both of you. Love from William, Charlotte and Andrew Jr Sinclair."

Lizette came out refreshed wearing a perfume from the bathroom in her exclusive silk lingerie with perfect make-up. She asked her soon-to-be-husband with a longing in her eyes if it was Clifford who had delivered a packet. Lawrence answered slowly and replied that it had something to do with the stable. "You should go and see what it is."

"Me?" asked Lizette confused because she had never had to take responsibility for anything in the stable. Lawrence convinced her that before she put something amazing on, she should put on something more practical, which filled Lizette with curiosity.

"This is for you!" Lawrence gave Lizette the beautiful halter in soft, burgundy. She looked confused. Lawrence informed the bamboozled Lizette that someone was waiting for her in the stable and that she should hurry there and come back as soon as she could.

Lizette threw on a pair of riding trousers and a polo shirt. She had not arranged her hair yet and even though it was relatively short, she could tie it up in a ponytail. She kissed Lawrence and ran through the estate. The whole estate was decorated and there was a pleasant smell everywhere. The servants greeted Lizette with a smile when she rushed past the entrance where she put on a warm duffel coat in the hall. She rushed out in the direction of the stable with the burgundy halter in her hand. Patrick was there with one of the most beautiful brown horses Lizette had ever seen. It was love at first sight.

Around the horses neck was a burgundy silk ribbon with a card, waiting for her to read it. Lizette eagerly opened the beautiful envelope. There, in stylish handwriting read: "Dearest Lizette, we believe that you have come home. Here you have a friend that can watch over you and gallop away with you towards all your fantastic goals! We wish you and you soon-to-be-husband all the luck in the world! You have all our love already! Charlotte, William and Andrew Jr Sinclair."

Lizette let out a howl of joy that made the young horse leap to the side. Patrick held onto the mane while Lizette put on the new halter as she took away the large ribbon. Patrick then fastened a gold colored rope around the halter so that Lizette could walk her new friend.

The horse, which was a mare that was neither too big nor too little was perfect for Lizette's 165cm frame and inspired Lizette's hope for the future in England. Lizette said to Patrick that the horse should be called Hope. Patrick nodded, delighted by the happiness Lizette had together with Hope.

Patrick then told her that a stall had been prepared for Lizette's new horse if she wanted to see it. Lizette remembered that the guests were on their way and hurried away to Hope's new stall.

There, Lizette caught the sight of a new well-tailored saddle. What fantastic handcraft, thought Lizette filled with admiration. It was precisely the type of saddle that she always wanted. The snaffle looked shiny on its hook and Lizette grabbed the burgundy quilt and put it on the curious Hope. Then she asked one of the stable hands to give Hope food and pamper her. Patrick waited in the stable yard and saluted Lizette when she hurried past him on the way back to the castle. She laughed to herself at the dizzy headed Lizette and thought that Sir Duke Lawrence would never ever get bored.

Lizette was the perfect age; she would soon turn twenty-eight the following year and radiated feminine beauty. She was young but still mature and looked fantastic. The men were drawn to her like flies to a sugar cube but Lizette was a little old fashioned and there had been much more going on in her mind than just the thought of men since she had been very young. Everything had been about survival and having food on the plate.

Now that she had all of this luxury and all the necessities, she could finally enjoy love. It was maybe relatively late but the right time for Lizette. As she ran through the castle gate, she threw off her duffel coat to the housekeeper who happened to be standing there. Lizette shouted: "Sorry but the guests are coming soon and I am not ready!" Lizette double stepped up the large staircase to the second floor. She was red in the face by the time she reached Lawrence's bedroom where she found a note on the bed.

Lizette stared at the note that read: "My darling and soon-to-be-wife – I will be back soon!"

Lizette threw herself on the bed and breathed out. The clock read almost one and the guests would be there in about an hour. After she had taken a short break and took into the account the fact that she was now the owner of the fantastic Hope the horse, she felt even more at home.

The Sinclair family had left their mark at the home, which would be her castle with their wedding gift. Hope the horse gave hope and gave Lizette an almost goofy smile. Sometimes, she wondered how she had earned the praise and kindness of the Sinclair family in her life. Sure, she was kind and diligent but also a little wild. They had given her the base of security that she really needed and now she was not alone either. She had a man.

Lizette stared with big eyes at her beautiful engagement ring and got up to get dressed and meet Lawrence's curious neighbors, friends and relatives who would come to them that evening.

CHAPTER 12

The Italian Trip

The engagement party went on for three days. Lizette's original employer and benefactor, the Sinclair family, was there and Lizette's closest friends from New York, yes, even Selma, who Lizette had travelled to the USA with a long time ago. Selma had visited Lizette a couple of times in New York over the years but still lived in Chicago, a city she liked.

In between they had written letters telling each other about their different lives. Selma came with her husband, who she had met through Lizette in New York, and her son Karl from Sweden who was now a grown man. Lawrence's family, relatives and friends socialized with everyone but some of them turned up their nose at the fact that Lawrence had chosen a non- aristocrat as a fiancée.

It was real pomp and circumstance. In the evenings, despite the chilly time of year around Halloween, the younger guests threw themselves into the fountain into the wee hours, drunk and happy from all the champagne from breakfast to dinner. Love was in the air the whole time between Lawrence and his beloved Lizette and it rubbed off on everyone.

It felt like a precursor to wedding mania and the live orchestra played at full capacity. A well-accustomed, popular music group that entertained the guests varied the music skillfully. Besides this, there were other guests who played records in the pauses. Everything was mixed to create fantastic entertainment. The very popular songs were "My Man" by Fanny Brice, "The Song of Love" by Lucy Isabelle March, "April Showers" by Al Jolson, "I Love Her – She Loves Me" by Eddie Cantor and "Three O'clock in The Morning" by Paul Whiteman & his Orchestra.

It was the year before the Charleston started to seduce the festive upper class in the USA but it wouldn't be really hot until 1926-27. This party was on an estate outside London in the autumn of 1922 and was still enjoying waltzes and foxtrots. Lawrence and Lizette danced, absorbed in each other, and the guests clapped their hands around them. They couldn't take their eyes off each other.

When they were into their third day, even some of Lawrence's stiff relatives came to accept Lizette and act more positive towards her.

The following weeks until the wedding, which would take place on the 9th December, it was full speed ahead with all the preparations on Stewart's estate. Since their wedding had not been booked a year in advance, the wedding planners spent a lot of their time trying to book the most sought- after guests and get them to cancel their other engagements and activities and prioritize Lizette Af Sinclair's wedding with Earl Lawrence Stewart.

Many prominent people at the top of society were going to Stockholm for the Nobel Banquet, which was held every year on the 10th December. Lawrence felt that he didn't have any friends that were especially close to him in the science world, so he chose to ignore it. Lawrence's wedding would not necessarily be the event of the year but a wonderful gathering of good friends who would witness his happiness and joy when he married the sweet Lizette.

The news spread quickly through London's upper class that Count Lawrence Stewart would marry. Many women gasped and almost cried when they got to hear that they had failed to capture England's most sought-after bachelor.

When there were two weeks left to the wedding and the young couple was taking their daily riding tour, Lawrence stopped his horse and called for Lizette. She had learnt to know her beautiful horse called Hope and they were now inseparable. She galloped to Lawrence and stopped very close to his horse.

They breathed in the chilly air in the morning sun. There was a fog but the sun broke through slightly. Lawrence said: "Lizette, I would like to go on a short holiday with you before the wedding and the wedding party here at home on the estate. What do you say?"

Lizette became overjoyed. "Oh, it would be wonderful to get away and relax for a while, just you and me, my darling. Think about it! We could get away from all this planning hysteria!" answered Lizette in excitement. When they had come to an agreement, they rode back to the stable.

The following day, they drove down towards the south of England, driven by Lawrence's chauffeur in the shiny Rolls-Royce. They had two suitcases with them in the boot for the ten-day holiday in Italy. They drove through the English countryside for several hours until they eventually came to Brighton where they would take the boat to France. From France, they would continue the journey by train to Rome in Italy.

One day later, they sat in their first class cabin on the train on their way to Rome. They breathed out, hugged, kissed and were completely taken by each other. In the restaurant, they drowned in each other's eyes and could hardly do anything else other than look and hold each other.

After a while, Lizette said: "My darling, it feels as if we are on our honeymoon!" and gave out an enchanting laugh that captivated Lawrence. He never wanted to let her go. It felt as if they were the only human beings in the world because they didn't need anybody else.

Lawrence took Lizette's little hand in his large, powerful hand and whispered: "Darling, our whole relationship will be one long honeymoon." The gigantic diamond in Lizette's ring glittered in the restaurant car's dim lights, and they both radiated happiness. The two turtle doves sat there, drowning in each other's eyes again and again.

The waiter served the dinner silently; without disturbing them, whilst filling up their glasses, making sure they were never empty.

The weather was warmer when they reached Rome. They stepped, refreshed and newly awakened out of their cabin while a porter carried their two suitcases on a wagon. He led them to a taxi, which would take them to their hotel deep in the heart of Rome.

The hotel was The St. Regis Grand Hotel, an exclusive first class hotel built in 1894. Lawrence told Lizette that the St. Regis Grand Hotel in Rome, The Ritz in London (which opened in 1906) and The Ritz in Paris (which opened in 1898) had the same architect, namely Charles Mewés who lived between 1860 and 1914. Lizette laughed a wonderful laugh and said: "Darling, you are like a living encyclopedia!" and kissed him passionately in the back seat. Once at the hotel, a bellboy quickly stepped towards the taxi and welcomed Lizette and Lawrence in Italian. He placed the sturdy suitcases on a trolley. Lawrence paid the taxi and put his arm around Lizette while they entered the beautiful hotel.

While they checked in, the staff started to swarm around them. Lizette understood why when she heard Lawrence say that they would live in the Royal Suite; that was why they all bowed. Lizette felt like a queen! Goodness gracious me, thought Lizette, see what money can do!

The bellboy showed them the way to the elevator and took another elevator with their luggage. Lawrence had the key in his hand. Lizette kissed him in the elevator and said: "Lawrence, you make me, time after time, the happiest woman in the world. You have so many strings on your bow!" When they slowly approached a fantastic ornate door with the most incredible gilded details, Lawrence unlocked the door slowly and opened it.

Lizette almost fainted when she saw the magnificent suite where they would live. It had several rooms and even a dining room. They walked around and looked at the royal suite. Lizette asked her fiancée: "Who shall we entertain in this enormous dining room, darling?" Lawrence answered with a sensual look: "I had hoped that you would lie naked on the table for a couple of hours a day and eat grapes while I tried to paint you!"

Lizette started to chase Lawrence around the table for a while until he changed directions and chased her into the bedroom instead.

The bellboy knocked at the door and announced that their suitcases had arrived. Lizette giggled and after the bellboy had closed the door, they tore off each other's clothes and made love passionately in the gigantic bed.

Italy offered romance, warm weather and fantastic food. The week they were there and the days spent traveling were some of the best times in Lizette's life. She couldn't believe that you could be so happy. If she had known during the difficult times growing up in Sweden how her life would be when she grew up, she would have laughed every day. There in the dark forests of Småland outside Värnamo, she had not had it easy. She had no idea that life could be as fantastic as this when she was a girl. She thanked her guardian angel and made a Catholic sign of the cross as she saw the Italians do every day, to give thanks for everything in life.

Lawrence rested his head on his beloved Lizette's knee in the suite's lounge. He was stunned by love and infinitely grateful to have this woman in his life; she was the only one he had ever wanted to be his wife. He looked deeply into Lizette's eyes and took her small hands in his.

"Darling, tomorrow is our last day in Italy and I think we should go out to the shops and shop big! I have several ideas that I can tell you over dinner. For once, we shall dine in the restaurant here tonight and dress up; we have lived within the beautiful walls of the hotel suite too long". They both giggled as Lizette rang for room service.

She asked the maid to run a bath while she walked around the royal suite in an adorable silk bathrobe and enjoyed just being alive. Soon, she would take a well-deserved bath and get dressed for dinner.

The following morning, they traveled by taxi to the largest fashion house where Lizette got a "carte blanche". They were forced into buying a new suitcase for all of Lizette's new clothes, shoes and hats.

For lunch, they were near the Spanish Steps which were built between 1723- 25, and were called "Scalinata della Santissima Trinità dei Monti" in Italian. They breathed out and Lizette looked glassy eyed at her dream prince who was actually a count! She said slowly: "Lawrence, I have never loved somebody as much as I love you!" You, my love, are absolutely the best thing that has happened to me!" Lawrence leant over the table and kissed her intensively and everyone in the restaurant started to whistle and applaud.

As a last stop, they went to look at a car. Lawrence told Lizette enthusiastically on the way: "The car maker Alfa Romeo was founded in 1910 as A.L.F.A. – "Anonima Lombarda Fabbrica Automobili". In 1915, Nicola Romeo bought Alfa and changed the name to Alfa Romeo. The factory started making military equipment in Italy to prepare for the First World War but in 1919, Alfa Romeo went back to civil engineering and expanded during the twenties. Alfa Romeo had a broad production which also included, amongst other things, locomotives, motors for airplanes and boats but now, we will buy one of their finest sports cars!"

Lawrence laughed and added: "We will just order it. I'm not driving it the whole way home back to England!"

CHAPTER 13

The Wedding

The train journey home to England was as wonderful as the journey to Italy. They made love, talked and looked deeply into each other's eyes. They sat in the restaurant car and enjoyed the delicious dishes with good wine now and then but they mostly spent their time in their cabin. A conductor, who they had given huge tips, fetched everything they wanted and brought it to their cabin; everything from coffee and good bread to fine cheeses and wines.

In the end, they suffered from fatigue and slept all the way from Calais in France. When they eventually got off the train and off the boat at Brighton, they were collected by Earl Lawrence's chauffeur.

They still felt very tired from the long journey and slept like small children in the back seat. Lawrence's chauffeur had packed all of the suitcases in the large car's spacious boot. The journey made its last stop on the estate's grounds outside London that the Stewart family had had for generations.

There was snow on the ground of the estate that made it shine in the mood of winter. Lizette kissed Lawrence on the cheek and said: "Now I must rush to the stable and say hello to Hope. See you inside in a minute!" Lizette ran to the stable where the stable hand greeted her. She hurried to Hope's stall where the graceful mare Hope looked at Lizette with her big beautiful eyes and nudged her pockets with her nose. Lizette stood and talked with her for a long time and held her beloved horse. Lizette fetched some sweets for Hope who seemed very pleased to see her and not just because Lizette fed her carrots and sugar cubes. Lizette whispered softly in Hope's ear: "See you tomorrow sweetie!" Lizette left the stables and walked quickly towards the manor.

The snowflakes fell heavily over the estate and the wind had started to blow. Lizette held one hand onto her hat so that it wouldn't blow off her head. Once inside the castle, the whole staff welcomed her. She was told that her suitcases had been carried up to her room. While one of the servants took her coat, the butler said:

"Miss Lizette, Lord Lawrence is waiting for his bride-to-be in the library!" She smiled and thanked Clifford. Lizette went straight into the beautiful library where a large, flaming fire sparked and gave the room life and warmth. Lawrence sat in one of the leather armchairs in front of the fire with a cognac in one hand. Lizette kissed him and sat beside him in the wing chair. The butler came in and asked Lizette what she would like to drink before dinner. Lizette answered:

"A glass of whisky, thanks! Preferably with a little water." She turned to her darling and said that she had felt cold outside in the stables when she had told Hope the horse about their Italian trip. Lawrence warmed Lizette's hand and smiled. He said thoughtfully and seriously: "Lizette, don't be upset but do you want bear my fruit and for us to have children?" Lizette was startled by the fact that it seemed that Lawrence could read her like a book. How could he tell that she was distressed by the possibility of motherhood?

A servant came in with Lizette's whisky, which she took directly from the tray. She took a real swig and looked anxiously at Lawrence and replied with a weak voice: "Honestly speaking Lawrence, I don't know if the mother role is something for me even though I love children!" Lawrence kissed her and could taste the whisky drops on his mouth and whispered back:"Why are you worried? Children love you and you would easily make a fantastic mother"!

Lizette squirmed and expressed after a long silence:

"Darling, I am so afraid that something tragic will happen. Have you noticed that I almost never menstruate? This part of feminine nature is a must for a child to be born and..." Lizette bowed her head and started to cry. Lawrence took both her hands in his and sat on the rug in front of her.

"My darling, tell me what is troubling you!" Lizette sighed and told him about the strong feelings she had; she understood that Lawrence wanted an heir but that she was terrified because both her grandmother and aunty had died when they gave birth to their first child. Lizette's mother grew up without her own mother and it was the same for Lizette's cousins. Lawrence picked up a handkerchief and dried Lizette's tears. "My dearest, we'll just see what happens! You never need to feel the compulsion to give me children. You're everything that I wish for!"

Lizette kissed Lawrence passionately; they got up and hugged each other hard.

Inside, Lizette cried over the abortion and the horrible rape when she was seventeen. She didn't want to tell Lawrence. Patrick came in and announced that the pheasant dinner was served in the dining room. They sat down at the dining room table where the antique silver candelabra stood, burning a welcoming light. Lizette and Lawrence sat for a couple of hours and enjoyed the dinner and liked being so cared for. After the meal, they retired back to Lawrence's large bedroom and fell asleep, content in each other's arms.

The interest in Lawrence Stewart's wedding and his beautiful bride-to-be was the topic of conversation in much of England's high society. A lot of them were invited and all the pieces of the puzzle of the winter wedding on Stewart's estate started to fall into place.

Saturday the 23rd December was the big day. The wedding would be held on Stewart's estate north of London. Two hundred guests were invited which meant that everybody who wanted to attend were not invited. Lawrence had made the decision to set the limit at two hundred guests.

From the start, they had thought that a small wedding would suffice but the pressure from family and friends forced them to invite the whole family and friends to this winter wedding.

Lawrence was enormously popular and had a large amount of relatives, which meant that many who weren't invited were disappointed. Lizette didn't have so many that she wanted to invite but important guests were the Sinclair family as well as her Swedish friend Selma and a few other friends. She didn't invite any of her relatives from Sweden as she had lost contact with them.

It was now less than a week left to the wedding and today, after riding, Lizette would meet the tailor in London together with Charlotte Sinclair who was still in London together with her husband William and their son Andrew. They had stayed in England to be at Lizette's wedding.

Lizette could hardly believe her own eyes when she met Andrew Jr at the engagement party; how he had grown. He was a young man, wise to the world and more of an adult than a child.

Andrew Jr was in England for the first time. He discovered London together with his father William Sinclair when he did notany business to take care of. Thus, it was Charlotte and Lizette who visited the tailor, which was the best thing that could have happened. Lizette was so sincerely happy to meet her fantastic ex-employers and benefactors, Mr. and Mrs. Sinclair and their son and have them so close.

Lizette had the great honor of having Charlotte Sinclair with her during the fitting of the bridal dress and Charlotte even helped with everything that had to be done since the engagement at the end of October. Lizette was so happy to have Charlotte as her "extra mother".

In the USA, long silk ribbons mixed with flowers adorned the bridal bouquet but this wasn't the case in Europe or England. However, what was fashionable on both sides of the Atlantic was to lower the waistline to the hips according to the twenties style with a calf-length skirt and a beautiful tiara on top of a lace veil; it was all that Lizette would wear. Her bridal dress was in ivory white satin with pearl embroidery, which was the latest fashion. There was celebration and glamour, and a glittering magical shimmer in the air of the upper class. Lizette's era had just started and the year was 1922.

Charlotte whispered to Lizette during the fitting at one of London's best tailors: "Lizette, you look fantastic!" You are really the daughter I have always wanted!" Lizette tried to kiss Charlotte on the cheek but the tailor shrieked: "My dear Madame, we are trying to make a bridal dress fit!" Both Lizette and Charlotte started to laugh hysterically.

After two hours of fitting, the tailor had completed the impressive ensemble of the bridal dress with accessories and everything was to be sent to the Stewart estate. Lawrence had promised Lizette that the tiara would be finished by the wedding day. As they were about to leave the tailor, Charlotte asked Lizette if she wanted to follow her to the fashionable department store Harrods that everyone was talking about. The tailor who had heard every word said: "My ladies are you aware that the new Harrods was built between 1894 and 1905 because the old Harrods was destroyed in a fire?"

The tailor, a well-educated man, added: "The architect's name is Charles William Stephens – just so that you know. Thanks for today, your highnesses!"

Charlotte and Lizette started to laugh again (because they both knew that they weren't really highnesses) and thanked the tailor and his assistants and let him know that they were looking forward to seeing the finished bridal dress.

The following day was the wedding day and a servant girl, who knocked on her bedroom door, woke Lizette. She carried a tray into the room with a delicious breakfast balanced on top. There was even a champagne pink rose in a silver vase on the tray alongside a heavenly packet inlayed in gold lamé.

On the packet, there was a plaque fastened to a ribbon which had the engraved words:

"To my bride-to-be and life companion Lizette! I don't want to live without You and I love You more than You know, Your Lawrence."

Lizette had slept in the guest room on the last night before the wedding. It was a tradition that spouses should not have sex before the wedding but Lizette smiled to herself and though that she had never, in her life, experienced such wonderful love making as she had during the months with her beloved Lawrence. The servant girl poured a strong coffee for Lizette just the way she wanted and asked if Lizette wished for anything further. Lizette thanked the girl and excused her; everything was to her liking. The servant girl curtsied and closed the door behind her. Lizette sliced a piece of toast and spread some marmalade on it, chewed and carefully drank her hot coffee. She put the cup down on the bedside table and looked at the most exclusive packet she had seen; the gold lamé felt wonderful.

After she had kissed the plaque with the most wonderful message from Lawrence and removed the gold lamé, she opened the hard package carefully.

The most fantastic, glittering tiara that she had ever seen sparkled from the inside of the box. It lay on a bed of dark blue velvet. The diamonds were of three different sizes and it even had superb rubies that were like drops of red blood. It was a tiara that was called duga and it symbolized everything: celebration, joy, kinship and class.

During these few seconds, Lizette felt like the little poor Louise and suspected that she was dreaming. But she quickly realized that she had lived the upper class life for at least eleven years and that it was a considerable amount of time as she was twenty-eight years old!

It was Saturday the 23rd December and there was magic in the air. Lizette sipped the good coffee and realized that she had never been so happy. She lifted up the small vase with the beautiful rose in it and breathed in the scent from the fantastic rose. There was a knock at the door again. Lizette shouted: "Come in!" It was the servant girl again who explained that Lord Lawrence wanted Lizette to meet him at the stables in an hour. She didn't need to get dressed in the bridal gown for four hours so she could get ready in peace and quiet. Lizette thanked the young servant girl who seemed a little sullen and wondered if the girl was sick, or worse, jealous.

Lizette did not intend to tell Lawrence about the girl's attitude as she knew it would get her fired. Lizette knew what it was like to stand on the first rung of the social ladder but she had never actually been jealous of the upper class people around her. On the contrary, it had inspired Lizette as a child to seek a new life in the future.

Lizette walked into the bathroom and took a hot shower. She washed her hair and scrubbed her body in the same way she had seen the fine beauty salons in New York do. The removal of dead skin made the skin smooth and refreshed. She began singing "My Man" by Fanny Brice to herself. Imagine that she would be married in a few hours – life was really wonderful!

The guests had arrived at the estate that Stewart's had owned for generations. A winter wedding would take place there and the most sought- after bachelor in England would marry. His wife-to-be was said to have come from Long Island in the USA and bore the surname "Af Sinclair" but it had been rumored that she was really a simple maid from Sweden. It wasn't anything that anyone believed. The rumors were said to have come from jealous women who worshipped Lawrence and wanted to ridicule Lizette.

Anybody who was somebody had also seen Lizette in a life story report from her enormous flat on 5th Avenue and there was hardly a maid in the world that had made that kind of class trip.

It was finally time! Lizette had got some help putting on the perfect bridal gown that had been delivered from London together with a seamstress, in case there were any last minute adjustments. Charlotte was in Lizette's room and admired her own creation, which was actually what Louise was to some extent, when she stepped into upper class life and became Lizette in New York's high society.

Everything was thanks to Charlotte Sinclair. Charlotte's son Andrew Jr was with his father on the bottom floor. Selma was in Lizette's room. She would be Lizette's bridesmaid and there was also a maid who served coffee and champagne so that the day would feel a little more balanced for Lizette. There was a knock at the door and Lizette joked that it was maybe Lawrence who wanted to approve the bridal gown. Charlotte and Selma laughed and said that it would mean bad luck if Lawrence saw it.

The maid asked who it was before she opened the door because everything was secret. Lizette's choice of dress would probably influence the fashion in the whole of England and maybe, even in Europe. With her marriage to a man from one of England's oldest and noble families and one of the most sought-after men, Lizette's relatively anonymous existence would cease to be.

The maid learnt from the butler Clifford that all the guests were present and that the reception room had been fantastically decorated. Everything was prepared and ready. Even the priest was in place. The maid looked happy and conveyed what the butler had spoken about to the expectant bride.

Charlotte hugged Lizette and whispered to her: "As your extra mother, I want you to know, sweetie, that now is your time to shine and that we all love you!" Selma had tears in her eyes and could hardly comprehend the amazing dream that had become a reality for Lizette and she was unbelievably happy for Lizette's sake. They had both come to the USA as poor immigrants ten years earlier and their lives had completely changed.

Lizette walked out of the guest room for the last time as a guest; she had a companion who waited for her outside the door. Two small girls and two small boys were dressed as angels and carried baskets filled with rose petals. They walked down the stairs slowly while spreading the rose petals in front of the radiant bride. Lizette glittered while Charlotte Sinclair and Selma walked behind her. Since the wedding was private and in a home environment, the guests applauded when Lizette came into the reception room in her fantastic dress. It was, in other words, not as strict as a church wedding and the roaring twenties had, in principle, just started.

Lawrence stood before everyone together with the rosy cheeked, slightly chubby priest. Lawrence was very stylish with a fantastic tailor made suit and looked at his bride with pride and loving glances. Charlotte's husband, William, led Lizette to her husband-to-be in front of two hundred guests.

When the ceremony was almost over and Lizette's new magnificent diamond ring sat on her ring finger, Lawrence lifted Lizette's veil and kissed her like a real prince. They were married for real. The priest, almost embarrassed, slammed his fine small bible when Lawrence started to almost eat Lizette up in front of everybody.

The guests were served champagne and everybody toasted. Later, photographs were taken. There was a journalist who was a royal reporter at the party and he had been promised that he could take a series of photos of Lawrence and his bride, Lady Lizette.

The party continued long after midnight but after a while, the bride and the bridegroom wanted to retire to their bedroom as man and wife. Since the engagement party had lasted three days, they felt that one day and one night was just right for their wedding party.

Charlotte and William Sinclair said goodbye together with Lizette's much loved favorite "child", Andrew Jr. Selma promised to come back soon to explore Harrods in London with her family before returning to the USA.

The wedding gifts almost covered the whole room and there was a fantastic atmosphere in the air. Lizette and Lawrence stood happily in the hall and waved at the last guests who were leaving. After this, Lawrence chased Lizette up the stairs to their new-shared bedroom where they fell asleep, happy and at ease in each other's arms.

CHAPTER 14

The Catastrophe

Lizette awoke the following morning as Lady Lizette Stewart. Lawrence kissed her as she lay there, still dressed in her magnificent bridal gown from the wedding day. Lizette started to giggle and asked for Lawrence's help in taking off the enormous creation. "I guess that we were really tired after the wedding", said Lizette happily and satisfied.

Lawrence answered quickly: "I hear you, my love; you are now Lady Lizette Stewart and you are most certainly allowed to sleep in your wedding dress!"

Lawrence slowly undressed his beloved wife where upon they took a bath together in the suite's bathroom. Lawrence ordered up champagne and coffee.

They sat in the bathtub with foam up above their ears. They toasted, laughed and threw bath foam at each other like naughty kids. After an hour's bath, they got dressed in their riding clothes and walked towards the stables feeling slightly tipsy.

The Alfa Romeo stood in the courtyard having been delivered from Italy. Lawrence had patience and could wait before taking his new Italian beauty out for a test spin. Lizette went to Hope and asked the stable hands to saddle her and prepare her for a ride. When Lawrence's horse and Lizette's much loved Hope were saddled and ready, they sat upon their horses and rode out around the estate as husband and wife.

Lawrence and Lizette trotted beside each other and talked about everything that only they could talk about; they were made for each other.

Back at the stables, one of the stable hands took care of the horses whilst Lawrence and Lizette walked towards the castle to eat brunch. Lawrence said, impulsively to Lizette that he wanted to take the Alfa Romeo for a spin and would be back by the time Lizette had showered and was ready.

Lizette smiled: "I am surprised that you have been able to restrain yourself this long without taking her for a test drive!" Lawrence thanked his beautiful wife for being understanding and walked quickly towards the stall where he had placed the keys to the Alfa Romeo. "The Alfa" symbolized his and his wife's "pre-honeymoon" in Italy and Lawrence was really eager to take it for a test drive. The red Alfa shone in the winter sun on this Sunday.

Lawrence hopped into the sports car and sat comfortably – still dressed in his riding clothes. The Alfa Romeo's leather upholstery smelt good, making Lawrence smile to himself. There was something fascinating about new cars thought Lawrence. He started the engine that made a wonderful purring sound before he pressed the accelerator and took off.

He looked at his gold ring on his left hand that held the wheel. He really had everything that he had dreamt of apart from an heir. Lizette seemed to be embarrassed by the topic; becoming a mother and having a baby was a taboo subject but Lawrence was convinced that she would get used to the idea. When Lawrence had left the estate, he increased his speed to almost one hundred miles an hour.

It was slippery out on the roads and Lawrence failed to spot a horse carriage that was about to cross the road in front of him. Lawrence panicked and did everything to avoid the horse. Unfortunately, he had no way out; there were walls on both sides of the small gravel road. Lawrence drove into the stone wall on the right side of the road. The Alfa Romeo's front was crushed on impact and Lawrence was thrown towards the dashboard where his head became stuck and shattered glass rained over him.

The farmer with the horse, who had witnessed everything, was in shock and hesitated several minutes before he walked towards the sports car with smoke coming out of it. He shouted and hoped that Lawrence would move. When the farmer couldn't get an answer, he went back to his horse and drove it under cracks of the whip to the nearest house. They drove to the first one in the vicinity that he knew had a telephone. Within an hour, an ambulance was at the scene with Lawrence and his expensive crushed Alfa Romeo.

On the Stewart's estate, Lizette had showered after the ride with her new husband. She wondered what it was like to drive the new sports car and wished she had joined him. Just as Lizette was on her way down the big, curved stairs, Clifford, the butler called for her. He asked her to go to the library where he handed her a large glass of whisky and asked her to sit down.

Lizette wondered what had happened and became very worried when she saw how the butler looked at her. "Clifford, what has happened?" shouted Lizette, consumed with concern.

The butler swallowed and had tears in his eyes. He apologized and said solemnly that there had been a car accident and that it was feared that Lord Lawrence had died. Lizette fell to the floor and made a desperate, heartbreaking sound. The butler helped her up onto a chair and got her to swallow a large swig of the whisky. Afterwards, the butler left to make a telephone call to Selma, who was still in London. She promised to come back to the Stewart estate as fast as she could. Patrick and one of the maids helped Lizette, who was barely conscious, up the stairs to the bedroom.

Lizette was beside herself with grief and didn't want to live without her beloved husband. She was now a widow after just one day of being happily married! Selma had arrived and was by her side, talking to her in a comforting voice and in Swedish. She was really was her best friend. Selma said sternly to Lizette: "You will get past this!"

The newspapers had only just printed the exclusive news that the Count Lawrence Stewart was now happily married with pictures from the spectacular wedding on his estate with the American Lizette Af Sinclair. Lizette's dress was adorable and her tiara sparkled on all of the photos. The ink barely had time to dry until the next horrific message reached the public:

"LORD LAWRENCE STEWART DEAD IN CAR ACCIDENT!"

Lawrence had been so happy with the woman in his life and, suddenly, everything was gone and the young, grieving widow was beside herself with sorrow.

Charlotte Sinclair had been on an excursion to the countryside with her family during the Sunday and when they came back to their hotel, they saw the headlines in the papers. Charlotte started to faint and her husband managed to catch her before she fell. For the first time in her life, she was stunned and mute. Deeply shocked, her husband and son followed her to their hotel room. It was unbelievable.

Charlotte couldn't reach Lizette on the telephone, even though she knew that the young widow, who was like a daughter to her, would want her there.

The following morning, she reached the butler, Clifford, who told her that Selma was with Lizette because they couldn't get into contact with Charlotte.

Charlotte gave instructions on how to treat Lizette until she got there. "Let her stay in bed and give her food in the bedroom and see to it that Selma is there to take care of her the whole time. I will be there as soon as I can." Her idea was to take Lizette back with her to New York after the funeral. She then asked for the phone numbers to Lawrence's nearest family to help with the funeral and all other necessary arrangements.

Charlotte's husband and son took the boat home to New York without Charlotte because Andrew Jr had to go to school and her husband, William, had businesses he had to take care of at home in the States. After the conversation, Charlotte lit a cigarette, which was something she normally wouldn't have done.

It hurt in her soul and heart that Lizette's new and unbelievable romance was over. Charlotte, who felt like a grieving mother to Lizette, was filled with empathy and sorrow.

When Lizette had lived in her bed for several days, the butler told her that Charlotte Sinclair had arrived. Lizette had a swollen face after all the crying and anxiety attacks but it was thanks to Selma that she was still alive. When Charlotte came into the bedroom, Selma was dabbing Lizette's eyes. It was dark in the room, except for a few lamps, as Lizette had chosen to have the heavy velvet curtains drawn as protection against the outside world. She had not wanted to see the daylight over the last few days.

Lizette sobbed and said in a shaky voice: "How shall I ever live again without Lawrence?" Charlotte said to Lizette with a heavy voice: "Lizette, you have done precisely the right thing in grieving and it's all you can do". Charlotte took Lizette's hand and Selma was on the verge of crying. Life was really not fair. Lizette was, yet again, alone and she had not even turned thirty years old.

The funeral took place a couple of days later at the family grave, a short distance away from the estate. Noble men and their wives of yesteryear were buried in the churchyard and now even the young and dynamic Lawrence would get his resting place here too before his time.

Lizette was dressed in a black ankle long dress with a black veil and hat. She cried quietly behind the veil and walked next to Charlotte and behind them walked Lawrence's closest family and relatives.

The priest gave an emotional speech at the funeral and there were probably as many guests at the funeral as there had been at the wedding less than two weeks earlier. Lizette was beautiful but she didn't care about that on this tragic day when her beloved was being buried in a raw and chilly England. The beautiful coffin was made of mahogany, adorned with white lilies and white roses. When everyone had gone inside the church, somebody tapped Lizette's arm. It was one of Lawrence's cousins who Lizette recognized from the wedding. Her name was Bridget and she was a beautiful red haired girl in her teens.

Bridget whispered in Lizette's ear: "You meant so much to my cousin Lawrence; he had never loved anyone as much as he loved you and I know because I have followed him at a distance my whole life because he was my favorite cousin!" It was the finest moment at the funeral thought Lizette. The sweet, red haired Bridget made Lizette smile for the first time since Lawrence drove away with his Alfa Romeo. The journey ended with his death and with his beloved wife, Lizette, in a hell of terrible sorrow and loss.

Lizette dreaded the after funeral mingle and saying goodbye to everyone. It felt as if she had partly died herself and now everyone would look at the broken object she had become. Lizette sensed that everyone was staring at her and noticed that they were amazed by her strength during this difficult time.

Once back at the estate with all the guests, Lizette wanted to escape. She was twenty-eight years old and not old enough to handle this day of sorrow. She crept away from everyone and went, deep in grief, up to her and Lawrence's newly decorated bedroom and feel asleep on the bed. Her heart and soul were crushed in several pieces. After a moment, she collected herself and went down to join the guests again.

Lizette thanked the guests quietly and somberly when they came with their condolences regarding the misfortune that had affected her. Charlotte took over the role of hostess to help Lizette and collaborated with Lawrence's relatives.

Charlotte had represented her family for decades and was used to handling people in different situations. She was a colossal support for Lizette who found herself in her own "bubble" during the whole funeral day and could hardly be reached. Lizette fell soundly asleep and woke up when Charlotte came into the bedroom: "My little darling, everyone has gone now Lizette!" She tucked Lizette in and said thoughtfully: "Sleep now, my darling. Tomorrow is a new day. You'll bounce back stronger and restored again!"

Lizette felt some of the weight lift from her shoulders and was grateful that Charlotte was there with her. Lizette said in a weak voice: "Without you Charlotte, I would have died!" Lizette then slept for almost a whole day, still dressed in her black mourning dress.

When she finally awoke, she felt completely empty inside. She staggered into the beautiful bathroom and ran a bath. She cleaned the smudged mascara from her face that had run after hours of tears had trickled down her cheeks. She called after the maid and ordered a croissant, scrambled eggs and coffee and asked: "Is Charlotte here?" The maid replied and said that Charlotte had travelled to London and would come back tomorrow.

Lizette didn't know what day it was and forgot to ask. She took off her black funeral dress while her tears ran down her cheeks and felt a pain inside that she had never felt before. It felt horrifically painful to lose the one you loved more than life itself. Lizette went into the bathroom and poured bath foam into the bathtub, which swirled up in the rippling water.

Lizette put on her bathrobe when she heard a knock at the door. It was the maid who came in with her meal on a tray. Lizette neither knew what time it was or what was on the tray even though she had ordered it herself. She sat the tray on a stool in the bathroom, lay down in the bathtub and chewed on a croissant that seemed to grow in her mouth until she swallowed it in one big lump. She sipped some of the hot coffee and the scrambled eggs were really the only thing she could eat which tasted better than before. The warm water gave a sense of security and Lizette dreamt that she was in Italy; the journey with Lawrence which had been the best holiday in her life.

Suddenly she began to shake from the horror and fear of death due to her great loss. Why had Lawrence died? Why had he bought that stupid Alfa Romeo? Lizette believed in God to some extent and wondered why he had robbed her of the man that was so important to her. She didn't get an answer. Lizette felt completely empty and her old, inner self, Louise, shivered from loneliness.

There was a knock at the door but Lizette remained mute and speechless in the bathtub where the water had started to become cold. In the end, the door was opened to the bedroom and Charlotte stormed in and shouted Lizette's name. When she caught the sight of Lizette in the bathtub with empty eyes and a completely apathetic look, she rushed into the bathroom. She helped Lizette out of the water and dried her with warm towels and dressed her in a bathrobe.

Charlotte held Lizette and said in a convincing voice that she would be okay and that she loved her and that she would always be her daughter. Charlotte continued: "I had planned to stay the night in London but was terrified that something would happen to you, so now I am back with you!"

When they sat down in the stunning master bedroom, Charlotte told her that she had something important to tell her but she had to follow her down to the dining room where a surprise awaited. Lizette lay back on the bed and could hardly react. Charlotte had never seen anyone grieve so much as Lizette grieved after her beloved Lawrence.

"Dear Lizette, I can help you find something warm and simple in the closet.

Then we can go downstairs and drink a cup of tea in the dining room."

Lizette didn't have the energy to protest and let Charlotte choose something appropriate from the huge closet. They left the bedroom where Lizette had slept since her new husband had lost his life in the terrible car accident.

Charlotte took Lizette under her arm and they walked slowly together down the grand staircase. An English "afternoon tea" awaited them in the dining room with several varieties of biscuits and cakes to choose from. Lizette felt, for the first time for a while, that she was hungry. She chose a couple of freshly baked scones with marmalade and a slice of chocolate cake. Charlotte smiled to herself when she saw that some of the old Lizette was starting to return.

When they had sipped the tea and drunk a glass of liqueur, Charlotte said that it was time to look at her present for Lizette. Lizette took Charlotte's hand and said in confidence: "You are just like my mother!" Charlotte smiled and replied: "And you know that you are the daughter I have always dreamed of having!"

The butler came in when Charlotte gave him a sign. He carried a large basket full of tropical fruit that Lizette had only seen in films. The fruit basket also contained a large gilded envelope, which Charlotte asked Lizette to open. In the envelope, there was a fantastic brochure that featured information about a hotel called the Royal Poinciana on Palm Beach in Florida.

The hotel had opened in 1894 and was a magnet to the American upper class elite. It placed Palm Beach as one of the premiere locations for holidays in the USA. At the start of the 20th century, the hotel had been expanded and could now receive circa two thousand guests who were looked after by seven hundred staff.

Charlotte gave Lizette a warm and intensive look and said: "You have gone through a terrible tragedy and I think you need a change of environment, at least right now." She continued: "Henry Flagler is a friend of our family and he was one of the founding members of the Palm Beach elite in Florida and now owns several hotels there. Now he has helped me book one of their suites for you and me at the Royal Poinciana, a week after New Year and up to the end of March; approximately three months. There you can rest and enjoy the ocean, the serenity and the beach. I will be there by your side and we can have a wonderful time together – and you can mourn there too – nobody will make demands of you."

CHAPTER 15

Florida

Lizette finally agreed to go to Florida and stay there as long as Charlotte was there by her side. Charlotte organized everything on the estate. Lawrence's staff was told that they all needed a holiday after what had happened. Thereafter, only three people were needed on the estate until it could be ascertained what the new situation would be. Charlotte had spoken to Lawrence's lawyer and his family who stood behind her strategy.

Twelve people were handed their references, their final salary and extra holiday bonus but the butler, Clifford and the servant, Patrick, stayed until further notice. The stable hand would look after the stable together with people from the village. The maid would, also with help from the village, clean the house and serve food to the workers. Besides these staff members, there was security staff who kept a watchful eye on the Stewart estate until further notice.

Before Lizette's and Charlotte's trip to Florida, they would try to celebrate New Year's Eve. The New Year waited around the corner and Charlotte made Lizette stay at Riche in London, together with herself, during the festivities. It was so that Lizette wouldn't sink back down into deep depression, alone at the manor without her beloved Lawrence, when the clock struck twelve.

Lizette chose to stay in the hotel room after New Year's supper but she ate, at least, a delicious supper at the nice hotel in the presence of others. Many whispered and looked at Lizette because, in some way, they knew she was the Count Lawrence Stewart's widow. The news was still fresh and people saw that the young widow really grieved.

Many had spread nasty gossip about Lizette being after Lawrence for a title and money but others knew that Lizette Af Sinclair had her own money. Yes, gossiping about other people's misfortune was part of people's nature.

Lizette didn't care about them. She had survived the first two horrible weeks thanks to Selma and Charlotte but despite this, she still felt bruised by grief and felt there was little hope in surviving the next day.

The following days, their suitcases were packed with only the most essential accessories. Charlotte intended to take Lizette out for some shopping where they could find the latest summer creations once they had arrived in Florida. First, they would travel with the ship Berengaria to New York and then take the train to Palm Beach in Florida. The new steam driven trains had, naturally, first class carriages and were a popular way to travel to the tropical state of Florida. The upper class in New York had created palace-like houses in Palm Beach. It was the latest craze for the rich and famous.

The packing at the Stewart estate had been taken care of so Lizette and Charlotte had one final breakfast in the dining room. Charlotte had checked out of her hotel in London and had taken all of her luggage to the estate. The gentlemen Sinclairs had learned of the plans that Charlotte and Lizette would spend three months in Palm Beach and both William and Andrew Jr would come to see them there in March. Yet, Charlotte had no idea what Lizette would decide to do after the visit to Florida. It would have to wait. First, Lizette would strengthen her soul in Palm Beach and Charlotte would do everything to save her crushed "daughter" from apathy and anxiety.

The car was ready and Charlotte and Lizette waited while their luggage was loaded in a truck that would follow them. Lizette thanked the servants, who would remain behind, as they stood in the great hall. She had also been to see her horse, Hope, early in the morning. She was still too weak to ride but talked to her darling Hope for a whole hour in the stall and got a lot of love back. Hope smelt so good and comforted Lizette like no other, in a way that only beautiful and loving animals could.

Lizette gave a sob, hugged her horse and thought, at the same time, about Lawrence. She asked God why he had taken the love of her life away from her but she couldn't get a logical answer. She gave Hope some apples and carrots and promised her that one day she would come back but in the meantime, the stable hand would take care of her and the other horses. They had decided to sell most of the twenty racehorses but to keep Hope and three other horses.

Lizette suddenly felt like a stranger on the estate that had been her home for half a year. Now, when Lawrence wasn't there any longer, it didn't feel right to live in England.

Lizette ran into the house and sat in front of the fire in the library. Everything was packed and ready and breakfast would be served in the dining room. Charlotte and Lizette sat there and picked at the food while their luggage was loaded into a truck. They didn't say much to each other but Charlotte knew there was a faint hope that Lizette would recover but knew it would take time and wasn't sure if she would recover. When they were dressed and said goodbye to the staff, they went out to the car and stepped in.

The chauffeur closed the doors after Charlotte had made sure that the truck was loaded with everything they would need for Florida. It was early on a winter morning when the car left the Stewart estate. Lizette panicked just from sitting in a car. It was the first time she had done it since her beloved Lawrence had died in the terrible car accident in their "love car" – the Alfa Romeo that they had bought in Italy.

Charlotte had brought a small hipflask just in case Lizette would react with grief when they passed the place where Lawrence had died. Charlotte's perception was correct as Lizette's body started to shake and she began to cry when they passed by a cross, making the spot of the accident. Charlotte gave Lizette a small glass of whisky and held her hard. After crying intensively for one hour, Lizette finally fell asleep due to exhaustion.

They drove to London, a journey that took a couple of hours. The boat would leave late in the afternoon. Cunard Link had started the route London – Southampton – New York the year before and it suited Charlotte and Lizette perfectly.

Once they had arrived in London, they had several hours to spend before the ship left. Charlotte loved to be in good time and she wanted to settle into the cabin in peace and quiet. Lizette was almost apathetic since they passed the place where Lawrence had crashed and hardly had the will to live. Charlotte was like a mother and did her upmost to help the grieving Lizette.

It was foggy and cold in London. The only thing Lizette could think of was why there was always so much fog in London. It was question she didn't have the energy to answer.

The dock was full of people of all kinds. The chauffeur had driven up to the first class pier where the people of nobility were boarding, on their way to their first class cabins. The Berengaria looked magnificent. There were people everywhere who worked to prepare for the long cruise over the Atlantic and, besides this; there were many well-dressed and wealthy people who clung to the railings on their way onboard to an upper class world.

A carefree world of complete luxury awaited those who experienced the same world onshore. The poor hardly knew if they would get food for the day. Life wasn't fair but Lizette had always felt that anything was possible. Despite her wealth, she had lost the one she loved the most.

Charlotte and Lizette had a fantastic suite but Lizette hardly cared this time. The first class section had a big lounge and luxury suites with their own bathrooms. Lizette sat down heavily on the bed and didn't have the energy to cry anymore. There was a knock on the cabin door and Charlotte ordered a bottle of chilled champagne, a little fruit and something light to eat from the bellboy.

Lizette lay on her bed and breathed out. Charlotte could almost sense her pain in the air. It had been a terrible stressful situation since the sudden death. The wedding celebrations had barely finished before the fairytale had finished.

Charlotte had to be a rock for Lizette's sake and, naturally, didn't want to be anything else. When they were well onboard with all their luggage and on their way to the lovely climate of Florida, Charlotte finally relaxed. She was travelling with Lizette and it felt fantastic. Charlotte could never have imagined leaving her alone in the condition she was in.

Charlotte wanted Lizette to be happy and would try to make her happy again but it was a plan that was too early for Lizette; first the young girl had to recover. They had three months to spend in Florida and it would, hopefully, be sufficient healing time.

CHAPTER 16

Palm Beach

Nine days later, The Berengaria hooted when she neared the harbor of New York. Lizette had stayed in her cabin for almost the whole journey and Charlotte left her alone in peace. She knew that if you had recently lost the biggest love of your life in such a brutal way, it was unbelievably important to grieve in peace. This way, one could heal the wounds and start to live again. It was the knowledge Charlotte had got in her teens from her good mother.

Charlotte had had a fantastic upbringing in Boston and already belonged to the society there. Her parents were wise but also modern in their parenting methods. Charlotte and her three siblings had got everything that they wished for but the most important element had always been a stable and loving home.

Charlotte's father and mother had known all the important politicians in Boston and their wives and children. These prominent couples were often seen at dinner with her family and Charlotte snapped up everything political and she learnt a lot through listening to all the adults' conversations. Her father, Clarence Abbey, was a popular, outspoken man with his heart in the right place. His wife, Betty August, Charlotte's mother, was from a family of British origin and was very quiet and withdrawn.

Betty had come to the USA as a small girl with her family. Her father was an art dealer and died when little Betty was ten years old. Betty's mother, Elizabeth, became a widow early and she quickly learnt that it was important to grieve family members when they passed away. Elizabeth reminded her daughter Betty all the time that those who had passed would still be present after their death, watching over the living as angels.

Charlotte's grandmother, Elizabeth, was a wealthy lady who became even richer when her successful husband passed. Betty was their only child and she received a lot of attention and love and had the possibility to study what she wanted to.

This meant that Betty was far ahead of her time and studied at Radcliffe College, which was for women; at "the boy's university" Harvard, which was close by, she met her husband, Clarence. It was love at first sight and they were both very interested in politics and art.

Consequently, they had very much to discuss and with their similar interests as a base, they travelled to Boston to view artworks in the fine galleries. They drank warm chocolate at the cafés during the chilly season and chased each other through the leaves in the parks in the autumns. It ended with kisses and they swore that they would never meet anybody else. They possessed an unusually strong bond of love that would last a lifetime.

During the summers, they spent fantastic months at Martha's Vineyard where Clarence's family owned a summer house. Clarence and Betty married when they had both graduated "summa cum laude". They settled down in one of Boston's finest quarters in an enormous, red brick house where their four children were born; Charlotte was the third child.

They even had a swimming pool in the garden and Charlotte's and her siblings' childhood was fantastic. However, they suffered a big tragedy when they became a little older – Charlotte's oldest brother, George, died in a car accident. The whole family became devastated and it was Charlotte's wise mother, Betty, who taught them to handle the sorrow in the best way, as Elizabeth had taught her when her father passed away tragically.

This fine quality of helping and supporting others had, in other words, become a legacy and now, Charlotte had taken up the challenge to be a mother for Lizette seriously. It meant giving her the warmth and empathy to guide her through the roller coasterof life with everything that it entailed, happiness as well as sadness. Charlotte woke up out of her daydream and during the whole trip, she sat with Lizette as if she was her daughter. Charlotte didn't turn an inch away from her constant care of her favorite girl; it was her calling to create a balance in Lizette's life.

Eventually they arrived in New York. When the first class passengers left the Berengaria, they were met by the icy January wind in the big metropolis. Lizette and Charlotte shivered when the chill pinched their cheeks after the warmth they had had onboard in their cabins. They were both dressed in furs but the chill was persistently raw, especially by the water in the harbor. Charlotte had telegraphed her chauffeur to come from Long Island and fetch them and drive them to Grand Central Station in New York.

Charlotte's husband, William, and their son, Andrew Jr, did not have the possibility to meet them but Charlotte didn't let that disturb her. She had been married to her husband since her teens and they completely trusted each other, exactly like her mother and father had done. Charlotte honestly thought that it was nice to be alone now and then, so long as she knew that they had each other. It was now her mission to help Lizette through the difficult loss of Lawrence Stewart.

The chauffeur was happy to see Charlotte and Lizette and had brought an extra car with a young chauffeur for the luggage. Charlotte praised her chauffeur for not letting them wait and having saved them from the worst chill. Lizette sat completely quietly and Charlotte wondered how she would ever get the old Lizette back again.

The cortège took off towards the railway station. Once there, the youth helped to carry their luggage to the first class carriage, which would take them to Palm Beach, Florida.

Lizette and Charlotte took off their furs while their luggage was lifted onto the luggage car. They settled into their private coupé where the only luggage they had were their handbags as well as some smaller bags with the things they needed during the trip. Charlotte saw some information on Henry Morrison Flagler in the New York Times.

Charlotte told Lizette, who had now started to have the energy for some information, that Henry Flagler was the one who had founded Standard Oil and he had got the upper class to come to Palm Beach. It was the same man who had made it possible to take the train there with his own company Florida East Coast Railway. Charlotte reminded a very tired Lizette that they would stay at one of Henry Flagler's luxury hotels called the Royal Poinciana Hotel. Charlotte would let Lizette heal her soul there in the warmth.

After a fairly long but very comfortable journey, the train rolled into the station in Palm Beach in the tropical state of Florida. They found themselves really in the right place; a summer state which, in recent years, had blossomed in the form of a frontier spirit that attracted the fine people from the cold eastern states to have wonderful adventures in the heat. The wintery England and the ice-cold New York were distant memories.

When Lizette and Charlotte finally climbed out of the carriage, they were met with a damp, tropical warmth that surrounded them. Charlotte knew instantly that she had chosen the right place for her "daughter's" rehabilitation. It was precisely what Lizette needed but even what Charlotte needed too.

Their porters fetched their luggage while Lizette and Charlotte followed and soaked in the pleasing warmth and environment. They were ecstatic to be there even if Lizette still bore a horrific sorrow but you could sense a glimmer of hope in her face.

Lizette and Charlotte were shown to their waiting car where the chauffeur greeted them with a welcome to Palm Beach and showed them to the comfortable car. It was the Superior model of Chevrolet with a modern chassis that had just come out that year in 1923. The chauffeur told them enthusiastically about the car and much more on the way to the hotel. Lizette looked out of the window hypnotized and felt attracted to the turquoise blue color of the sea. Charlotte enjoyed the views around them too; it was wonderful to come to the warmth and something new and positive.

The luxury hotel, the Royal Poinciana, appeared like a mirage in the tropical idyll. Charlotte took Lizette's hand and said delightedly, when they were both examined the hotel from the car: "Here is where we will really have a good time, Lizette!" The chauffeur parked the car, opened the doors and whistled to get the attention of a bellboy who collected the luggage. It was time for the adventure at the Royal Poinciana to start. Even if Lizette was weak because of the loss of her beloved Lawrence, Charlotte felt that this was the perfect place for both of them right now.

Very attentive personnel met them. When they had checked in, they were treated as if they were royalty. They were taken to the exclusive suite that would be their home for the next three months; they even had a private butler at their disposal that would always be in the servants' quarter, close to their suite.

Both the women took a deep breath when they walked into the huge suite that was made up of six rooms. This was the most fantastic hotel that they had every stayed at. For the first time since her Lawrence had died, Lizette felt a little joy. She walked out onto the balcony and had a perfect view over the ocean as the suite was on the 5th floor. The sun was shining but the balcony was in the shade thanks to an enormous parasol. She sat down in a comfortable wicker chair with silk cushions. Charlotte came out on to the balcony, which was more like a terrace and kept Lizette company. Within a short matter of minutes, their butler appeared out on the balcony. He bowed and wondered what the ladies would care to drink. Charlotte ordered a freshly pressed orange juice and a fruit tray as well as other small snacks.

Lizette leaned back in her chair while their butler hurried away. For the first time, with a little energy in her voice, Lizette said: "Thanks my dearest Charlotte! You always know want I need! This suite in a tropical climate is solace for my soul!"

Charlotte took Lizette's hand and said for the first time during all of their years together: "What are mothers for?"

It was as if something magical exploded within Lizette. For the first time in her life, she had got to hear that someone was her beloved mother.

Charlotte had already given her so much and Lizette shook in her deckchair and looked with tearful eyes at Charlotte. Charlotte turned towards her, lifted her sunglasses and answered: "Dearest Lizette, are you with me for real now?"

Suddenly there on the terrace in the secure company of Charlotte, Lizette started to feel like she was alive again and her beloved Lawrence, in some way, would always be with her – deep within her soul. Even if he had left her alone on the Earth, Lizette would maybe be able to survive all the pain and sorrow anyway, if only she kept him inside her heart as a guardian.

Lizette leant back in her deckchair once again, took Charlotte's hand and sank into a deep sleep. Charlotte realized that it was a good sign that Lizette had shown some form of happiness and that she could relax.

Lizette had been so emaciated and pale since Lawrence died and she hadn't reacted to anything but just now, it seemed she had come back to life and had again become the way she usually was; filled with joy and an appetite for life. Charlotte felt some hope and sipped on the fresh juice. Then she made sure Lizette was sitting in the shade and was wearing her new hat in order to avoid getting sunstroke.

Charlotte got up and walked into their suite, which was absolutely wonderful. She strode around like the lady she was. She breathed out and it felt nice not to be traveling. The long days on the ship from England and the train later had been exhausting but had taken them to a slice of paradise. The beautiful and elegant Charlotte changed into her fine silk bathrobe. Their maid had been unpacking the suitcases while Lizette and Charlotte had sat on the balcony.

Charlotte went around the room and enjoyed the magnificent view through the large windows. The sea was attractive and the palm leaves rattled in the tropical wind. Charlotte stepped into the shower, let her bathrobe fall to the floor and washed her blonde, page styled cropped hair.

When she was ready, she sat, dressed in her bathrobe, once again, and wrapped her freshly washed hair up in a turban. Then, she walked with firm steps out to the mighty balcony.

Lizette still sat in the shade and was still in a deep sleep. Mrs. Sinclair gave an order to the butler to keep an eye on Lizette and to give her a lot of juice and water when she awoke. There was a high heat and the humidity was the same, as the weather in Florida usually was. Charlotte ordered a manicurist who could also do pedicures; she ordered a new red nail polish at the same time.

Two hours later, Lizette awoke. At first, she didn't know where she really was in relation to her dreams and reality. Lawrence had kissed her as if it was for real but it was a dream and it cut her heart with sorrow. Lizette shivered and peered out over the beautiful beach that she could see at a distance from the balcony. As a consolation, she was, despite everything, in tropical Florida. Lawrence's death had put pressure on her night and day. He would always be there in her soul. The change of environment had returned Lizette to her normal self and the warmth made it all feel a little easier.

Lizette stretched and looked around; as soon as she moved, their butler came in with a glass of cold water. She had to admit that she felt like royalty and if the truth could be told, she appreciated this kind of service in her life.

Charlotte had put on some music in their suite so Lizette got up from her chair on the balcony, slightly dazed, and walked into the suite. Charlotte was standing, singing to herself. When she saw Lizette come in, she rushed forwards and gave Lizette a warm hug.

She said happily: "Dear Lizette, you look much better and happier now, my dearest! We need a good and hearty dinner and I have booked a table in the large dining room here at the hotel!" She suggested that Lizette should take a shower and choose an appropriate dress for the dinner.

CHAPTER 17

The Rehabilitation

The fabulous fine weather in Florida helped to heal Lizette's soul and she felt better every day that passed. Charlotte and Lizette walked out early every morning to take long walks along the beach or swim. The ocean's presence meant so much to Lizette and she enjoyed walking along the long white sandy beach with sprays of seawater.

They were dressed in their new swimsuits, which hid most of their flesh, but even so, it was an enormous change compared to how the fashion had been a few years earlier when women couldn't show any skin at all.

Overall, it was a more colorful fashion than earlier and, best of all, thought Charlotte, was the silk stockings that had come onto the market as a positive surprise. The corset had now almost completely vanished; it had been a constraint for most modern women. It was a development that pleased Lizette. However, the brassiere was still a must considered Lizette and Charlotte. The fashion dictated that dresses should show some leg and shoes were in matching colors in everything from peach to gold instead of only black and brown.

The two beautiful, slender women walked at a very brisk pace despite the sand's resistance. They had comfortable shoes, their elegant swimsuits, large hats and sunglasses; in addition, they had lightweight beach bags with thin summer dresses and cash. After a one and half hour walk from the hotel, they stopped by an elegant beach restaurant. It was not really safe to walk any further than this. There, they drank ice tea with lemon and sugar to recover from the hefty walk they did every other morning. The other days, they swam in the mornings, in the hotel pool, followed by a gymnastic workout on the beach where you could stretch, throw a ball and use a skipping rope.

Charlotte seemed to know everything you should do to feel good in body and soul. When they sat at the beach restaurant and they sipped on their ice teas, Lizette said to her: "Charlotte, you should be a professor in how you heal a broken heart and a damaged soul!" Charlotte smiled assured. Lizette continued: "There is no-one in the world who has been as divine and sweet to me as you, except Lawrence!" Charlotte took Lizette's hand and held it tightly.

Lizette and Charlotte kept this vigorous training scheme during the first two months and Lizette became stronger every day but on one particular afternoon, she felt the need to walk alone on the beach and think to herself. Charlotte said she would be in the hotel library and read while she drank a cup of hot tea with honey. She had learnt to make this tea in England and would wait for Lizette's return to the hotel as she sipped it.

Lizette wrapped a thin shawl around her straight dress that went to her calves. It was a relatively short dress in the latest fashion. On the way to the beach, she met people who nodded in happy recognition and said hello. Lizette nodded back but most of all, she wanted to be alone with the sea and her own thoughts.

Lizette skipped along the long beach in her modern shoes and looked out over the fantastic horizon. The waves flowed and caressed the beach where she was. She walked slowly and talked silently to the God she somehow believed existed and conveyed her despair over why Lawrence had been taken away from her so brutally. She sighed to herself but, in some way, felt for the first time that she had accepted Lawrence was now in heaven and that his time on Earth was over. Lizette stopped, took off her shoes and stockings and waded out into the water and washed her hands. She left the shoes on the beach. Lizette stood in the water for a while and enjoyed the clear salt water; it was really like heaven to be in Palm Beach.

After being cooled by the sea, she went back to the hotel barefoot and carried her shoes. In the luxurious suite, Lizette found a note from Charlotte, which read that she was in the hotel's beauty salon, and would be back soon. Lizette looked at the clock. Charlotte also wrote that she should get ready because, later, they would take a trip down Worth Avenue, the shopping street in Palm Beach. Lizette became really happy at the thought. She continued in to her private bathroom.

A moment later, Lizette was about to try on some clothes when she heard Charlotte call out for her. She replied back: "I am here in my room Charlotte!" She came in to Lizette's room and said delightedly that Lizette looked radiant. Charlotte continued by giving Lizette clothing tips whilst she told her about the plans for the day. First, they would go to shopping, then they would eat lunch in Palm Beach and during lunch, she said that she had something important to talk to Lizette about.

The young women travelled in to Palm Beach with their chauffeur, dressed in elegant twenties dresses, silk stockings and hats. They went around and reveled in the clothes and everything else in the shops. Lizette was satisfied with just looking as she was not yet ready to purchase clothes but it was nice to look around.

The lunch was the high point. They sat in the shade of the restaurant and they ordered an ice tea each. Charlotte wondered how Lizette wanted to live her life when she came home from Florida. The answer was that she had not really thought about it and so far, only lived for now. She had no desire to return to the British life without Lawrence. It would only be sorrowful and hurt badly.

Charlotte pointed out that Lizette was an extremely rich, young woman and that she must take on responsibilities and think about her position as Lawrence's widow now that he was gone. She also suggested that Lizette should go back to her apartment on 5th Avenue during April and May and later, travel back to England to finish finalizing the inheritance. The Sinclair family's financial advisor and lawyer would assist Lizette. If there were things on the estate that Lizette wanted to have with her in New York, transport would be arranged through him. Charlotte also suggested that Lizette should keep her small amount of staff at the manor for a couple of years and wait to see if she really wanted to sell it.

The food consisting of lobster and good accessories was served. Charlotte said: "Since you do have not drunk anything alcoholic for more than five weeks, I thought it might be time that we sipped this excellent champagne." She had ordered a well-chilled Piper, which brought back memories from Long Island at the time when Lizette was still called Louise and worked for the Sinclair family. She got her first taste of champagne through them. Charlotte's intention was to take Lizette's constant thoughts of Lawrence away.

They sat and talked for several hours. Lizette was so infinitely grateful towards Charlotte; she was really was a lifesaver! It felt unusual to drink champagne thought Lizette after several weeks of not drinking a drop of wine. Charlotte answered smiling: "Everything has its time!" They giggled together like old times.

It was the first time Lizette laughed since the fateful winter weekend in England, when her beloved Lawrence died. Thanks to the light champagne in sunny Florida and after strengthening both body and soul during the long time spent by the ocean, Lizette could stand the hurt. The pain had been numbed so that she felt almost like her old self again.

CHAPTER 18

The Tragedy in Palm Beach

The weeks rolled by at a comfortable pace in a wonderful environment and it was time for Andrew Jr and his father, William, to visit Charlotte and Lizette in Palm Beach. They arrived there in March and Lizette was surprised at how happy she was to reunite with the former little boy, whom she had helped grow from a child to a man.

Andrew Jr Sinclair was now a young man who studied at a private school, Junior High, to prepare for the three years he would spend at High School in Boston.

Andrew's schooling had long since been mapped and included both the right college and university. He was a quick learner and didn't have any problems studying school literature. Had this not been the case, William and Charlotte had planned that Andrew would find his own way within other areas. The way things looked, he would be trained to take over his father's business but there were a number of years left before that would happen.

Lizette and Andrew Jr could, for the first time, socialize as almost equal adults this spring. They walked together down the long beach as soon as Andrew Jr and William Sinclair had arrived. Charlotte was thoroughly overjoyed to meet her husband and they spent a lot of time together just as Andrew Jr and Lizette did. "The youths" lived by the pool and the beach. One day, on the beach, Andrew Jr grabbed Lizette's arm like a real gentleman when a wave was about to soak them; Andrew lifted Lizette off the beach so that she wouldn't be completely soaked. Lizette thanked him and smiled.

On the beach, elegant couples sat in their deckchairs and there were changing rooms behind them painted in blue and white stripes, a popular pattern at the time. Children played catch with a ball and it was a wonderful feeling to walk on the white sandy beach in Palm Beach, a popular pastime. It was the elite of New York's society who came down to Florida to enjoy the wonderful climate at the right time of year.

Andrew Jr enjoyed Palm Beach just like a fish in water as Lizette did. He told Lizette confidentially: "I like it in school and everything is going well". Lizette nodded in approval. Andrew Jr continued: "But there is this girl that I like more than any other, apart from you of course!" Lizette laughed and patted Andrew Jr on the cheek. It was a cheek that wasn't like a baby's bottom any longer but one that needed shaving every day. Andrew Jr looked Lizette deeply into her eyes: "Promise not to tell my parents yet!" Lizette was drawn to the young man's enthusiasm and was so happy for his sake and nodded. They passed well-dressed people on the beach that looked curiously at "the youths" as they passed by.

Maybe many thought that they were a real couple despite their age difference, which made Lizette smile and almost become slightly embarrassed. She had been an extra mother for this stylish youngster who was now becoming a man.

Andrew Jr spoke about the popular car racing competitions at Daytona Beach, not far from Palm Beach. He forgot, in his eagerness, that Lizette had just lost her husband through a car accident. Lizette bit her lip when Andrew Jr wondered if they could go there while he was in Florida. Without thinking, he continued to happily describe the car racing competitions in Daytona Beach.

He informed Lizette about how compact the sand was and that it was a perfect base for competition racing at high speed.

Andrew Jr also told Lizette passionately about his idol John D Rockefeller who had built his winter home Casements on the outskirts of Daytona, during 1912-18, he believed. Lizette collected herself and told him about Henry Flagler who had bought St. John and Halifax River Railway in Daytona to incorporate them into the East Coast Railway in 1889.

Andrew Jr was impressed that Lizette always knew so much about so much and had, actually, extraordinary knowledge for a woman, as his mother had too. Andrew Jr really enjoyed talking to Lizette and she was more like a big sister to him than his ex-nanny. They walked back to the hotel.

In the middle of the idyllic situation, a woman ran towards them with a knife in her hand yelling that she would kill her husband who had betrayed her. Lizette pulled Andrew Jr out of the crazy woman's path.

When the hysterical woman had run past them in the direction of the pool, Andrew Jr said; "Has she failed to understand that most people of high society have affairs with each other?" Lizette agreed with him and could hardly keep herself from laughing. It was black humor, sure, but that was how you survived thought Lizette. Such things could conjure up demons in certain people, but Lizette was more mature. She assumed that the hysterical woman probably had married into a rich family where she didn't understand the rules of the game.

Lizette had, herself, been astonished at all the time the upper class people spent "playing games" She had been lucky to find Lawrence who had been faithful to her. Lizette sobbed and Andrew Jr put his arm around her shoulders and said, in a precocious way, that Lizette had been very fortunate with her husband and that he was deeply sorry at his passing. They sat at a distance from the pool and saw the woman again, floating in the pool with blood everywhere. She had apparently committed suicide. Elegant and aloof women, who walked past the pool in their big hats, said to each other: "What luck that we weren't in that pool!"

The hotel staff waited for the police who were soon at the scene and informed the guests that they were all invited to dinner in the large dining room and told people to keep away from the pool area. For the moment, all of the guests were invited to the terrace on the beach side, where the hotel would offer champagne and snacks.

Lizette said to Andrew Jr: "We should probably go up to the suite instead "sweetheart" and see if Charlotte and William are back". Lizette was strangely not so upset or affected by the "knife woman" and her tragic fate. The shock would maybe come afterwards because it was a horrible situation with a suicide at their hotel. In fact, it was completely incomprehensible.

Lizette and Andrew Jr came up to the suite and found Charlotte and William there who welcomed them. They all talked about what had happened by the pool and William claimed that some people had said that it wasn't a suicide. When the woman had run after her unfaithful husband in the direction of the pool, she had stopped by the edge of the pool where her husband had quickly gotten a hold of her. Nobody really knew what had happened after that. Lizette said shocked: "So you mean, William, that she could have been murdered by her husband?"

William nodded and sucked in a breath. The incident had put a dampener on the holiday paradise of Palm Beach and he suggested that Charlotte and Lizette should return to Long Island as soon as possible with the train departing the following morning, while Andrew Jr and he would travel to Daytona Beach to experience the car racing competition. They would stay at a hotel there instead. This was so that Andrew Jr could enjoy what was left of his spring break.

Lizette and Charlotte sat on the sofa and talked while William and Andrew Jr went off to pack. Their maid served coffee and the ladies were both shaken by the events at the pool. Charlotte asked

Lizette if she wanted to return to Long Island and figure out what she wanted to do in the future.

Did Lizette want to live in New York in her big new apartment and eventually sell or rent out the estate in England? Lizette sighed and wrinkled her forehead and felt that she didn't have any idea. She answered calmly and objectively that she at least didn't want to live on the estate in England right now. Lizette admitted that it would be too painful with the memories of Lawrence and all the wonderful memories of him would haunt her in the almost empty manor.

After hours of joint packing with the aim of taking the first morning train, they all chose to stay in the suite. William and Andrew Jr said a warm and loving farewell after several hours together with the women in the family. They went to Daytona even though it was free to eat in the dining room this macabre evening. Even if it was not yet clear whether it was murder or not, guests talked about the "pool murder" throughout the hotel. However, the dead woman's unfaithful husband had been put behind bars pending further investigation. If anyone wanted to get him out before trial, they would have to pay the sky-high bail.

The luxury hotel, Royal Poinciana, had had its reputation damaged slightly. Upper class society was shaken by the "pool murder" in Palm Beach, a place where nothing should threaten frivolity and luxury.

The following morning, Lizette and Charlotte sat in a first class compartment onboard the train, which would transport them home to New York. They did, however, leave behind an amazing time at the Royal Poinciana with its tropical surroundings. They were both happy and thankful to Florida as it had turned out to really be a consolation for all the pain. Lizette felt more whole as a person and had had time and the possibility to grieve Lawrence's passing properly. The only discomfort was the end of their stay in paradise, but as always in people's lives, it would be forgotten over time.

CHAPTER 19

Stopover on Long Island

Spring welcomed Charlotte and Lizette at their arrival in New York. The Sinclair family's chauffeur was, as usual, on time and in the right place because he had been called days in advance, in case there were any changes to the schedule. Charlotte didn't plan on telling her chauffeur about the "pool murder". Instead, he was told there had been a change of plans. They had come home from Florida two weeks earlier than planned. Moreover, it was not the chauffeur's job to keep track of everything - just cars.

Charlotte and William were popular employers and nobody employed by them had ever been dissatisfied. The chauffeur stowed the entire luggage in the new Ford station wagon. The ladies stepped into the car and it carried them to their much-loved Long Island.

Lizette had mixed feelings about England but had decided to keep Lawrence's estate outside London and rent it out for now. She came to the decision on the train journey. She realized that it was probably wise to have a property in Europe even if Charlotte had taught her to think commercially and to be more strategic than emotional. Lizette had learnt a lot from Charlotte.

Once on Long Island, calmness swept over Lizette, allowing her to breathe out easily. The journey to Florida with Charlotte by her side had made Lizette feel extremely good and it had been a fantastic time in the tropical warmth for both body and soul.

They drove in through the enormous gate to the Sinclair's residence where the whole personnel waited on the stairs, dressed in their uniforms. They curtsied and bowed to their boss Charlotte and greeted both of them welcome.

The personnel knew that Lizette had started as a nanny at their level once a long time ago but the rumor was that Lizette was an upper class girl from the start and only pretended to be a nanny from Sweden. When Lizette heard about the rumor from one of the maids, she burst out laughing.

It was one of the first times she had laughed so hard since Lawrence's passing. A sweet kitchen maid told Lizette, after she had spent a few days in the fantastic house on Long Island, that people believed that she was Sinclair's real daughter.

Lizette was happy about the fantastic rumors; now maybe she could, for once, close the books about her upbringing, which had been both poor and miserable far away in her home country of Sweden.

The time in Sweden was a past memory and Lizette, who had a brilliant memory, despite everything, didn't want to completely suppress the past. She wanted to be able to relate to the poor period of her life to constantly remind herself how lucky she was now. Lizette affirmed her roots, in other words, and didn't have an inferiority complex. She was far too intelligent to question her own success that felt wonderful, yet natural too.

Lizette flinched when Charlotte called for her attention. Charlotte smiled and apologized that she had interrupted Lizette's daydreaming. She suggested that they drink coffee and eat sandwiches on the veranda. It was spring after all, even if it wasn't as warm as Florida, she pointed out happily. Sinclair's majestic house was so wonderful to come home to again; it was a long time since Lizette had been there and the memories from her earlier life there occasionally washed over her like comforting waves. She had come the whole way from old Sweden as a seventeen-year-old and had had the honor to be Andrew Jr's nanny in the wonderful America.

The ladies were served newly baked bread and steaming fresh coffee. Charlotte asked Lizette, if she had got over the horrible murder in Palm Beach. Lizette admitted that she had hardly thought about it but said that it been an abrupt and horrible end to her wonderful rehabilitation.

They sat in the spring sun and enjoyed the veranda and discussed Lizette's decision to rent out the estate in England. Charlotte agreed with her decision, as it sounded wise. She said enthusiastically: "Lizette, you are still not fully recovered and it would not be a wise idea for you to live alone in your large apartment on 5th Avenue. I have really thought about what would be best for you. Have you heard of Grosse Pointe in Michigan?" Lizette enjoyed yet another swig of coffee and answered: "Is it the place where they make cars?"

Charlotte nodded but explained that that was more in the main city of Detroit, a small distance from Grosse Pointe. Michigan had been booming because of the success of the automobile industry and many of society's elite moved to Grosse Pointe. The car industry was at a high and everyone who was "something" wanted a home in the beautiful Grosse Pointe by the great lakes. Charlotte continued, saying that they had several friends there and a couple had let it be known that they were welcome to stay in their house by the water while the family was away in Europe for a couple of months.

Lizette didn't really know how to react. Charlotte told Lizette not to worry because Grosse Pointe was exclusive, nice and good. Charlotte continued to tell Lizette a little about its history.

The wealthiest Americans had started to live there around the 1850s. They had created a golf course, a country club, a shopping street in The Village known as Kercheval with fine boutiques. Lizette and Charlotte were welcome to live by the lake St. Clair on Lake Shore Road in a big, but not huge, exclusive villa. Well, it was actually eight hundred square meters to be precise, said Charlotte enthusiastically.

They stayed on Long Island for a week, packed and travelled to Grosse Pointe. They would, once again, take the train, which both Lizette and Charlotte had learnt to really like and feel good about.

They sat in the first class carriage and this time they were heading in a northwest direction. Lizette was feeling more like herself and more comfortable. They had finished everything that needed to be done with the estate in England and had had contact with the right people over there. The estate would be rented out and there was already a list of interested people. Lizette would draw a small fortune from the rental of both the estate and the horses. Her beloved Hope had a good place there and Lisette's stable boy would stay there and she was thankful for that.

Charlotte and Lizette used the rest of the time reading books and took a pause to eat a good meal or drink coffee but most of the time, they sat in their compartment and read so the journey seemed to take no time at all from New York.

They eventually arrived at the giant and spectacular train station in Detroit. A chauffeur waited to take them to Grosse Pointe. The chauffeur smiled at the beautiful ladies who had instructed him to take them to The Country Club in Grosse Pointe. There they would meet a woman who had the keys to the house where they would live for a couple of months by Lake Shore.

When they arrived at the impressive clubhouse, Charlotte asked the chauffeur to wait until they came back.

The ladies went into the clubhouse where they were watched by curious regulars. Charlotte went up to a porter and said that they were going to see a woman who was a member and would wait for them in the restaurant. Her name was Dorothy Swanson. Charlotte and Lizette were shown to the veranda where Mrs. Swanson waited. Amongst the round tables with a view over the golf course, the porter showed them to a corner table where a big busted woman of a mature age waited. Charlotte had met her once before in Grosse Pointe at a dinner party and had, thereafter, heard so much about her. Mrs. Swanson could predict the future. If Dorothy had lived several years earlier, she would have been burnt at the stake.

Eerily enough, her predications had turned out to be true for many of her clients. She wasn't a bluff but, even so, it was a little unconventional. Dorothy was colorful and had a charisma that attracted men of all ages but she hardly noticed herself. Dorothy had grown up in a rich family in Virginia where her father was the youngest son of a nobleman from England. He had made a decision to try his luck in local politics in Charlottesville just because he wanted something to do. Her father's relatives had owned sugar and tea plantations as well as coffee roasters. Dorothy's father had inherited everything at an early age. Her grandfather had kept slaves on his plantations and everything had turned into chaos when President Lincoln abolished slavery towards the end of the 1860s. Dorothy's grandfather, David, was a clever man who mopped up the mess by hiring young, strong people, white as well as black, who didn't demand especially high wages. This meant the family business flourished without problems, even though some of the slaves left the Swanson plantations after being freed.

Dorothy was psychic and had discovered her unusual gift at an early age. Before the car had been invented, she had revealed that a four-wheeled invention would revolutionize the world. Out of curiosity, she was drawn to Detroit when the car industry was the biggest news there and the most explosive subject in the world. It was there she met an eccentric genius within the motor industry, Paul Raffert, who also had a British background. They married when Dorothy was still young but not young enough to miss the fact that Paul was just after her money to finance his inventions within the car industry. But this didn't bother Dorothy. The only thing that bothered her was the fact that they didn't have any children.

Dorothy built up her own empire in their summer house in Grosse Pointe where she held secret séances for wealthy women when her husband, Paul, was in Detroit. Their love was not based on honesty and they drifted apart right from the start. Dorothy had always been drawn to women and used her position as Mrs. Raffert as a perfect cover. In addition, her own family, who bathed in money, could afford to support Paul's so-called inventions.

Dorothy had, at this time, put down her roots in Grosse Pointe and was conscious that her husband had another woman in their apartment in Detroit. What her husband didn't know was that Dorothy had a woman on the side too in Grosse Pointe, with whom she was passionately engrossed in.

Dorothy was a popular, social person and gave the most sought-after parties in the exclusive neighborhood. She knew everyone important and, because she was extremely curious, and because most women were a little afraid of her, she was always invited to every party. When the Jefferson family announced that they were about to travel to Europe and rent out their fantastic home to Charlotte Sinclair and her daughter, Dorothy was contacted for the keys to house. Dorothy Raffert was really the spider in the web in Grosse Pointe during this time and she loved it.

Charlotte walked towards Dorothy and gave a light kiss on the cheek and presented her much loved beautiful Lizette as her daughter. Dorothy smiled and called the butler who quickly came with a wine cooler that contained a bottle of champagne. Charlotte laughed and said to Dorothy: "I have heard how much of a popular host you are and now I understand why!" Dorothy smiled back and revealed that she always had admired the Sinclairs' fantastic home on Long Island. "You maybe don't know, Charlotte, but my father knew your husband's father and he has spoken well of your fantastic house".

She continued: "When I was a teenager, my father brought me to your house and at that time your husband was just a baby." Charlotte listened fascinated while the butler served them champagne. Lizette observed Dorothy Raffert and thought that she was an exciting lady but also a little dangerous too. She didn't wish to have her as an enemy.

Dorothy continued to tell stories about rich families like the Fords and Dodges who all lived in Grosse Pointe and were going to build houses there. All those who owned land in Grosse Pointe were very wealthy. It was the place to live during the 1910s and the happy 1920s and would remain so for a few more decades, predicted Dorothy.

Everyone who lived in Grosse Pointe had servants' quarters on their land; the rich had more servants than they did family members. There were gardeners, waiters, wash women, butlers, cooks and everything else that was needed. The women had private dressers and, sometimes even lady's companions. It was another world from the one Lizette came from. While Dorothy passed on everything she knew about everything and everyone in Grosse Pointe, they enjoyed the champagne, finally ending up giggling uncontrollably together.

After long sessions of gossip, drinking and laughing, they thanked Dorothy for the entertainment and got the keys to the house by Lake Shore Road which would be their home for the next two months.

The chauffeur, who was sitting nicely in the car, leapt to his feet when the women came outside and asked him to drive to their temporary home. When they arrived, Lizette was amazed at how excited she felt looking at the house for the first time.

It was so beautiful and was situated by the water of Lake Shore. Charlotte noted Lizette's positive reaction, held her and said: "Lizette, we will have a good time here for two months". She added that she knew a circle of interesting people who lived in the area who they should meet. So far, Lizette had met the most odd and eccentric of them all, namely Dorothy Raffert. Charlotte said that now she would be introduced to more or less normal and successful individuals. Lizette laughed and said: "What or who is normal?" Charlotte nodded and smiled.

The chauffeur carried their luggage into the fine villa where a maid, who took care of all the practical arrangements, met them. She presented herself as Betsy Winger and showed Lizette and Charlotte around the house. When they had seen most of it, the ladies retired to their rooms, and literally fell back onto their beds and fell asleep within minutes.

CHAPTER 20

Grosse Pointe, Michigan

The following morning, they heard the maid knock on the bedroom doors announcing that breakfast was served on the terrace by the sea. Charlotte wrinkled her nose at the brisk tone; they normally wouldn't get up this early. She would talk about it with Betsy during the day and explain that they didn't need to have a fixed schedule during the two months. It was only eight o'clock in the morning and they were there so that Lizette would feel better, change the environment and have a good time.

A quarter of an hour later, Lizette and Charlotte sat on the terrace and ate poached eggs and toast with orange marmalade as well as drinking large quantities of coffee. Lizette laughed at the whole situation of being forced out of bed even though they had rented the villa to have peace and quiet.

Charlotte rang for Betsy with the gilded table clock. Betsy walked leisurely out onto the terrace and asked in an irritated voice what she could get them. Charlotte replied with a wonderfully calm and collected voice: "What would you say, Betsy, if I gave you a three week vacation?" Betsy looked suspiciously at both Lizette and Charlotte. In a dry voice she said: "Didn't you like my breakfast?" Charlotte replied with a friendly but firm voice: "Please Betsy, we are here to have a peaceful time after a number of tragic incidents and we don't want our lives steered. You will get three weeks paid vacation from me and you can go and pack immediately!"

Betsy looked at them both with enthusiasm and with some skepticism. Charlotte guaranteed that she would be paid so long as she packed and was ready to go. Betsy nodded, curtsied and ran back to the house. Lizette and Charlotte started to laugh loudly.

After a while, Lizette said: "My beloved mother, now we will have to cook breakfast ourselves and I will assume this as my responsibility because I have always been good at it!" Charlotte answered: "OK, my dear, but I'm the one who will cook lunch and dinner!"

Lizette looked surprised but Charlotte laughed and said that there were also restaurants. Lizette served them more coffee from the silver pitcher that Betsy had put out. After twenty minutes, Betsy ran down to them, dressed and ready to go. Charlotte thanked Betsy for her understanding and wished her a wonderful vacation. Charlotte opened her handbag and took out a fifty- dollar bill. Betsy stirred with large eyes and looked as if she was about to faint. She did the deepest curtsy and promised to be back in three weeks.

Charlotte wondered how she would travel from the villa. Betsy told her that she had called her brother who would fetch her down the road. He would be there in thirty minutes which was roughly the amount of time it took to get to the gate, said Betsy, turning away to begin her walk. She hurried away as if she was scared that Charlotte would regret her decision. Lizette giggled and realized, yet again, how lucky she was having changed her position from downstairs to upstairs; but she had no plans to become a bully.

Charlotte interrupted Lizette's daydreaming by telling her about all the invitations that had been waiting for them on arrival. "What do you say, Lizette, accepting an invitation to celebrate the 4th July – our much loved national day – with the Ford family?" asked Charlotte enthusiastically. Lizette was in such a good mood that she only nodded and said that it sounded like a nice and exciting invitation.

Charlotte was amazed at how energized Lizette finally seemed. She had finished grieving by the sea in Florida, which had been therapeutic, and Charlotte was proud and happy that it had given the result she had hoped for.

Not just anybody could have gone through the large losses as Lizette had done. Charlotte thought about how passionate Lizette was with such an outstanding personality. She had noticed this the first time she met the little Swedish girl who had grown into the role of her own daughter.

Charlotte thanked her lucky stars and took one last swig of coffee when they had gone through all the invitations they would accept while they were in Grosse Pointe. After they had looked through a majority of them, one remained. It was an invitation from the mayor and his wife to a popular party on an island in an area of beauty in the closest city, Detroit. The large, beautiful island of Belle Isle was situated there where people used to go to enjoy the lovely rural surroundings by the water. There, amongst other things, was an exciting zoo, The Boat House Club, restaurants and leisure activities. The Boat House Club was frequented by guests from high society; it was a club for the wealthy who liked to watch rowing competitions, swim in the enormous pool or take a drink and relax.

Charlotte suggested a dozen events and parties during the two months they would be there. Finally, Charlotte thought that they could end their visit by participating in the rowing competition on Belle Isle, and the spectacular festivity that would take place at The Boat House in the presence of the mayor and his wife. Lizette thought that it sounded nice and agreed with Charlotte on all points.

At one o'clock, their chauffeur, Kurt, drove up with the Ford. Kurt lived in the gatehouse and had worked for the same family almost since the car had been invented, around 1908. He mentioned that he had heard that Betsy had been given a vacation but if Charlotte still needed a maid or washing girl, he had a daughter that could take care of things when it suited. Charlotte thanked Kurt and said that it was exactly what she needed, when it suited.

They drove along Lake Shore Road, which had an unbelievable view over the water to the left and, to the right; there was a view over the exclusive estates. Kurt told them all about the owners and gossiped a little about the latest rumors in the local society.

Lizette pointed to the yacht club and wondered if they could go there some day. Charlotte answered happily:"Yes, we can for sure – if we are successful in meeting new friends with memberships there who hopefully have a nice boat."

A moment later, they were sitting in a restaurant on the shopping street of Kercheval where Charlotte ordered a local fish dish. They drank fresh white wine with the fish. Lizette enjoyed being in Grosse Pointe as it felt so idyllic. She had hardly had the time to think about her husband's tragic passing since they had arrived.

Charlotte waved a serviette in front of Lizette and exclaimed: "A penny for your thoughts!" Lizette sighed, suppressed a sob and answered Charlotte that she had just thought about Lawrence for the first time since coming to Grosse Pointe. Charlotte felt sympathy for her beloved bonus daughter welling up inside her.

Suddenly, something caught the attention of both women with interest; a gentleman in a pin-striped suit came in through the door to the restaurant. He was very well-dressed and looked at Lizette with interest. He whispered something to the head waiter who led the man and his company to the table beside Lizette and Charlotte. The round tables in the restaurant were beautifully laid out with cream white tablecloths and beautiful lilies in high vases. The man introduced himself as Mark Rodge Jr; Charlotte nodded and Lizette smiled. They both knew that the Dodge family was one of America's richest families. The Dodge cars were as popular in the 1920s as Ford had been before.

After talking to the ladies during the meal, everyone headed in their own directions. Mark Jr wondered if they wanted to accompany him on the family's yacht "S/S Dolphine II" the following day and go on a sightseeing tour of the great lakes, which would take ten days.

Lizette asked directly if they were the only guests. Mark Rodge laughed and told them that there would be twelve guests onboard with approximately twenty-five servicemen. The "S/S Dolphine II" was 78, 5 meters long, 10, 8 meters wide and equipped with two steam engines that could reach 12 knots boasted Mark Jr. Lizette looked impressed. Charlotte smiled and wondered politely if not all of the guests had already been invited. Mark Jr answered with a charming smile that he was the owner of the yacht and had decided himself who he wanted to be there. He knew that he had not invited a couple this time, so Lizette and Charlotte were very welcome to be two of the guests tomorrow.

Charlotte laughed and Lizette giggled, even if both of them felt a little uncomfortable taking somebody else's place that quickly. Mark Jr said that they would not regret it as this luxury trip included everything you could wish for. It would include skeet shooting, games, Shuffleboard and, of course, festive meals where wine and champagne would flow. To add to this, there would be a gramophone onboard with a great selection of 78s including Irving Berlin, Jack Palmer, Spencer Williams as well as Gene Austin and Roy Bergere that would play the whole trip.

The following day, the chauffeur had driven Charlotte and Lizette to the Rodge family's estate in Grosse Pointe by the water. The property was enormous; it was like a large palace in heavy, masculine designed stone. Lizette pointed and Charlotte looked out at the glittering water. There on the glassy lake floated the "S/S Dolphine II" moored to the quay. It was early in the morning and several well-dressed couples were waiting there for Mark Jr Rodge. The ladies were dressed appropriately in long pants instead of dresses and jackets to feel at ease as they stepped onboard the boat. The women had evening dresses for the dinners in their luggage as well as other sets of clothes for different activities that might take place out on the great lakes. They would probably swim too, which is why both Lizette and Charlotte had packed the latest swimwear they had bought in Palm Beach.

The weather was fantastic and Lizette was surprised at how warm it was in the state of Michigan during the summer. It was clearly much warmer than in Sweden during the same time of year despite Michigan being close to the border of Canada and being one of USA's most northerly states.

Lizette asked if Charlotte missed her beloved husband William. Charlotte lied this time and said no as she didn't want to worry Lizette. She reminded Lizette that both William and Andrew Jr would be with them on the National Day celebrations with the Ford family. Lizette looked deeply into Charlotte's eyes and said: "But Charlotte, it is still June!" Charlotte answered by reminding her that time went fast and went even faster at her age. Lizette hugged Charlotte and whispered in her ear: "Thanks for always being here for me!"

Mark Rodge Jr had come down to the quay and stood on the pier in front of the guests and wished them all welcome. "Now, I hope that we will have a fantastic cruise with my family's much loved 'S/S Dolphine II' and most of all, I want to wish Lizette and Charlotte Sinclair an extra special welcome. They have come all the way from Long Island outside New York to be a part of this cruise". Everybody's glances turned towards Charlotte and Lizette. Some of the guests pursed their lips whilst others smiled and whispered about how powerful William Sinclair was and how popular Charlotte Sinclair's parties were on their estate on Long Island in The Hamptons.

They all stepped orderly down onto a smaller boat that took them out to the 'S/S Dolphine II' where the servicemen awaited.

The female service staff had prepared the cabins and fixed the small details onboard and the chef had prepared the food with the kitchen boys.

Every day, the guests would be given beautifully hand written menus; the advanced menu had been meticulously planned in good time. Everything from seafood to meat dishes and delicate desserts were now onboard. A sommelier from Europe had spent a long time finding the right wines to suit the chef's dishes. The coolers were filled with the most expensive and exclusive white wines from Alsace and other regions and there was plenty of champagne. The red wines were kept at room temperature. For classification within the wine branch in France in 1855, the wines from Médoc got the chief distinction "ler cru classé". There were such wines as Château Latour, Château Lafite Rothschild, Château Margaux and Château Haut-Brion. These prominent wines were all onboard for the journey on the "S/S Dolphine II". Dom Pérignon champagne, launched in 1921, was also kept onboard. The bottles had been imported from Europe via a tobacco billionaire in New York who had presented the champagne to Mark Rodge Jr. Only the best green grapes from the best crop were used to make this fantastic champagne and at the time of its release in 1921, it had been said to possess a "distinctive bouquet comprising of sandalwood, vanilla and praline".

Lizette was silent during the short tour out to the magnificent yacht. There were seven people in the small boat, half the guests as well as Mark Jr Rodge. The remaining guests would be collected and brought to the yacht afterwards. Charlotte talked and laughed with a woman around her own age, seeming as if they really liked each other's company. Lizette was glad for Charlotte's sake but she was petrified that she would end up alone for the ten days on the lake. She was so used to Charlotte taking care of her and that she was the focus of her attention every step she took after Lawrence's passing, that she almost felt like half a person without Charlotte's total attention. Lizette realized it was dangerous to be so dependent. If Charlotte was now socializing with others onboard, Lizette could hide under a hat and sit on deck while she sipped champagne and read a book she had with her: "The Beloved Woman" by Kathleen Thompson Norris.

Kathleen Norris wrote about the upper class in California and Lizette liked to read about it. She was still completely taken by the fact that she was now considered a part of the upper class and lived the life of luxury. Now and then, she thought about the fact that she had grown up poor and she had difficulty in believing it now. It was just a completely different life to what she was used to until she as a seventeen-year-old went to America. What if there really was reincarnation, thought Lizette, that you could live so many different lives and that the soul would come with each new "guise".

They had suddenly arrived and Lizette came back to reality after her daydream. They berthedat the luxury yacht "S/S Dolphine II" and the guests were helped up along an exclusive roped ladder made of wide mahogany steps so that it was more stable compared to other types of rope ladders.

When they had come onboard, Mark Jr suggested that they all check out their cabins and wait for their luggage there. It would take at least thirty minutes before the "S/S Dolphine II" would leave and there were refreshments in every cabin. The service crew would show them to their cabins. The two ladies had been given a double cabin in the bow. Lizette exclaimed: "I just love it, Charlotte!" They chose a bed and sat down in the armchairs in the lovely cabin. Charlotte asked Lizette if she wanted some coffee or a glass of champagne, which stood in a cooler on the table. Lizette answered that she could start with the champagne. It made them both giggle hysterically as if, suddenly, there wasn't any grief in the whole world. It was a burst of laughter that neither had experienced before during all the years they had been like mother and daughter.

Charlotte took Lizette's hand after wiping away the tears of joy. She looked happily at Lizette and expressed her feelings: "With this, dear Lizette, we have become more than friends heralding a new, fantastic era!" Lizette understood what Charlotte meant. Lizette was no longer a child but an adult friend who Charlotte liked as much as when she was a bonus child earlier on.

In the middle of the laughter, there was a knock at the door that made both Lizette and Charlotte jump. They started to laugh again while they let in the service staff that brought in their luggage. Charlotte took a five-dollar bill out and the man's face lit up, bowed and left the lady Sinclairs to continue enjoying their champagne.

Among the guests, there was a Patrick "Joe" Flemming. He was thirty-six years old and had a good education from Harvard University. Patrick had made a real fortune in real estate and in liquor smuggling during prohibition and there were a lot of rumors about that. The spirits flowed through Patrick amongst the upper class and he was their stealthy hero.

Patrick had brought a famous actress from the silent films with him; they kissed each other on deck from the first moment. She was Ivory Kelly and was known for her dazzling white complexion and long legs. Contemporary stars on the silver screen during this time included Charlie Chaplin, Buster Keaton, Mary Pickford, Lillian Gish and Douglas Fairbanks. Ivory got the men to yearn and languish and women wanted to be like her. Ivory had blonde hair that attracted many admirers. In reality she had mousy hair, but there you go, a hairdresser could change everything to make it better!

Another guest onboard was Rosie O'Connor who was a banker's wife, but she loved everything the film industry could offer. Since she came from a wealthy family like her husband banker, they could have screenings at home. She told Charlotte and Lizette everything she knew about the film world. The Sinclair ladies had come up on deck after they had got dressed and ready. They sat down in comfortable deckchairs next to Rosie, who waved her arms in the air to get Charlotte and Lizette's attention and told them about the sensational demands well-known actors made of film companies and not vice versa. Their star status could, in principal, give them just as much power as a politician had.

Acting was almost considered prostitution from the beginning; it had, however, the reverse effect on cinema audiences. They felt that going to the movies was a sensational experience and, secretly, most people who went to the movie theater were in love with their idols on the silver screen. Since America didn't have royalty, the film stars came to represent the role as fine people in the young nation of the USA.

Lizette observed the film star Ivory Kelly. Lizette was fascinated by how young she seemed in comparison to all her roles on the silver screen. She often played thirty-year-old "femme fatale" roles. Ivory's self-confidence shone like the sun that hit the mahogany deck.

The men looked curious when they understood that a known actress was onboard but when they got to know she was Joe Flemming's lady, they realized that they didn't have a chance. They absolutely didn't want to annoy Patrick Joe Flemming who basked in power and money. While Ivory was enjoying her own fame, wearing a tight dress that attracted all eyes, Patrick had sat down with Mark Rodge Jr to talk business in the finest cabin onboard – the ship owner's cabin.

Mark made it clear to Patrick that he was not interested in any spirits but he wondered if Patrick could make a number of actresses available for a car exhibition the following month.

"S/S Dolphine II" steamed slowly out onto the great lakes. The eleven guests socialized on deck. Some played Shuffleboard, some gossiped about the latest news in society whilst some lay in comfortable chairs under parasols, sipping their drinks.

Lizette nodded off and when she awoke a couple of hours later, it was cooler out on deck and she had been left alone with the exception of a crew member who was picking up cushions and cleaning up after the guests.

Lizette asked him where everybody was and he pointed to the lounge. Lizette fixed her hair and went into the lounge where most of the guests were socializing; the ladies smoked cigarettes using ivory cigarette holders while the men had a corner to themselves where they enjoyed cigars and engaged in "masculine conversations".

The ship sped mile after mile without anyone noticing the engines as the beautiful ship was driven by elegant and silent steam engines. The upper class during this time was extremely privileged and there weren't any paparazzi around to speak of. You could be left in peace and there were many chambermaids who were neither the gossiping nor complaining type who just kept to their own class. However, there were those among them who were energetic, who broke loose and could enjoy a so-called class journey. One of these was Lizette but even if she had talent and was smart, she had her dear Sinclair family to thank for her success.

CHAPTER 21

The Adventure at Sea

The dinner was served every evening in the beautiful dining room. The food was almost as divine as the French imported wines. One evening, there was knock on Lizette and Charlotte's cabin. It was Patrick Joe who wondered if Lizette and Charlotte wanted to come out to the lounge for a drink.

One evening in their cabin, Charlotte had spoken about the love games that often went on behind closed doors of the upper class. She also explained that she had never been interested. She told Lizette that almost everything was allowed and that it was up to everyone to choose to take part or not. She warned Lizette about the risk of disease if you weren't careful. Lizette blushed during the conversation. There was a tingling in her body for the first time since the last time she had made love to Lawrence.

It was like a rush just to be onboard and be served all the good drinks that it felt natural to be drawn to sex again. The men onboard were good-looking and Lizette was really attracted to Patrick Joe Flemming. She knew that his film star girlfriend was with him onboard but Lizette couldn't help feeling the way she did.

She was at the age when love and eroticism, in some magical way, seemed to lure her into sexual hopes but she didn't want to appear loose. Charlotte said that it was allowed to have a relationship amongst the fine people when you belonged to this category. Charlotte asked Lizette to go with Patrick if she thought it could be fun, while Charlotte chose to go back to sleep.

Lizette, who suddenly felt wide awake, put on a suitable glamorous smoking jacket with silk stockings and garters that could be perceived as being a risqué outfit. She then slipped out of the cabin and heard Charlotte say: "I love you" when she closed the door.

Lizette came out of the hallway, saw the party in the lounge and walked there carefully in her low satin shoes. She proceeded like a queen over the teak floor and the fine rugs and felt everyone stare at her. Patrick Joe was sitting on a leather couch and welcomed her. Mark Rodge Jr and another woman, who sat close to him, both nodded to Lizette. Mark's woman was Katherine Day from Boston. The film star Ivory Kelly had disappeared without a trace thought Lizette. Patrick Joe gave Lizette a light kiss on the cheek. He smelled spicy, masculine, and of a little tobacco and was a little too inebriated but then again, all the guests were all the time on this journey. Patrick snapped his fingers and a waiter immediately showed up. Lizette said that she wanted a glass of ice tea without alcohol! Mark Jr and Katherine started to kiss each other intensively on the couch. It seemed as if the whole boat was asleep apart from the two couples. Lizette realized that she was suddenly one of them. Patrick told Mark Jr and Katherine to leave and he wished them a pleasurable night.

Lizette blushed like a child, which she felt embarrassed about. Patrick Joe got on his knees in front of Lizette and told her that she was the most beautiful woman he had ever seen. Lizette could not help it and exclaimed: "But what about Ivory?"

Patrick stood up and took Lizette's small hands and gave her a kiss, which was completely wonderful; Lizette trembled and the womanizer Patrick sensed that straight away. Lizette was shaken by Patrick's masculine and sensual presence – he even had good taste in clothes and shoes and he knew how to put himself out there. In addition, his dark locks were very attractive in combination with his intensive blue eyes. Lizette awoke from her temporary coma-like trance, after having drunk the whole glass of her refreshing ice tea. They walked out onto 'S/S Dolphine II's' beautiful deck. Lizette let Patrick Joe understand that she wanted to go back to her cabin alone but she when she turned around to leave, Patrick pulled her closer and whispered wonderful things in her ears. Once again, Lizette felt how she trembled. What was it that Patrick had? He seemed to own the ground he walked on and would soon own her on this night. They kissed each other deeply and intensively and he fondled her in places that were forbidden.

Lizette knew that she would go along with most things and Patrick Joe was well aware of it. He knew the owner of the boat, Mark Rodge Jr, so well that he knew that there was a reserve cabin for unexpected situations, and on this occasion, it was Flemming's turn to make use of it.

The handsome Patrick held Lizette hard and led her to the secluded cabin but what Lizette didn't know was that he had arranged everything. He knew that Lizette Af Sinclair would be in Grosse Pointe with her so-called godmother Charlotte Sinclair and he had asked Mark Rodge Jr to invite the ladies after having followed them from a distance. Patrick knew everything about Lizette and he was completely obsessed with her.

To hide it, he had brought the film star, Ivory Kelly, as his companion. She was now sound asleep as Patrick had slipped several sleeping tablets into her wine. Now, here he was, alone with a woman he wanted more than any other.

Imagine what money could arrange, thought Patrick when he started seducing the young and beautiful Swedish Lizette onboard one of the world's most beautiful yachts. Lizette gave herself to Patrick that night in the exclusive cabin. It had been so long since she had lost Lawrence and she really needed to have some intimacy with a man.

She understood that Patrick was taking advantage of the situation but he seemed to be very fond of her. She just enjoyed it and thought that they probably wouldn't see each other again. Right now, all she needed was to touch a man's beautiful chest, wonderful hands and seductive penis, which, together with the tip of his tongue gave her three incredible orgasms.

They held each other hard for several hours, sweating with passion until the early dawn. Eventually, Patrick stood up and pushed open a champagne cork from a well-chilled champagne bottle, which had been prepared for them. Lizette did not yet realize that everything had been well planned.

Patrick served the beautiful woman with one glass of champagne after another as she lay in bed with her cream-white naked body entwined with the silk sheet between her legs. He desired her tremendously and would make love to her for a week without a pause. He had imagined all of this when he had seen a picture of her in a gossip magazine in New York in last December when she married the British nobleman Lawrence Stewart.

Patrick knew all about this Swedish woman who had come to America without anything, but that was his own little secret.

Lizette, on this rare occasion, took a cigarette out from a cigarette case that lay on the bedside table. Somehow she sensed that he was after something. She lit the cigarette and stopped herself from coughing, managing to look unconcerned as she blew out some smoke rings.

She grabbed the sheet and pulled it closer to her bust to cover them. She then said astutely, looking at Patrick who stood naked: "Patrick Joe Flemming, who are you really?"

Patrick smiled sensually and said: "I am a rich man who has just made love and has fallen head over heels for a new star". Lizette could not help but laugh even if she could hear the alarm bells ringing. It felt as if he knew her inside and out although they had never met before.

Patrick Joe was unbelievably charismatic and had a way about him that made women fall head over heels. He was well aware of this but not all women appealed to him. Lizette had something that attracted him and he realized that he was taken with her.

Lizette extinguished the cigarette in the ashtray that was readily available by the bedside; Patrick started to stroke her back with his magical hands. Once again, Lizette trembled with pleasure. She was ashamed that she felt the way she did, as it was in some way a forbidden fruit. It tasted better than she dared to admit.

CHAPTER 22

Patrick Joe Flemming

'S/S Dolphine II" was on the way home to Grosse Pointe after ten days out on the great lakes. Charlotte was aware of the passion that had arisen between Lizette and Patrick Joe Flemming and she knew that Lizette needed love from a man and Flemming was not just any man. Yet, Charlotte was also very aware that he was a womanizer but had let Lizette play onboard anyway. Lizette had crept to Flemming's cabin every night after the first night they had spent together.

Patrick had got his actress, Ivory Kelly, to fall for Mark Rodge Jr instead.

He had more or less forced Mark Jr to take over the film star even if he already had a woman. Mark Jr, in turn, was not one to turn down an offer. He loved film stars as most Americans in the upper class society did. They didn't marry any of them and saw them as passionate playthings that were more like trophies. Mark Jr didn't take love seriously and had convinced himself that he wanted to remain a bachelor for many years more.

All the guests were on deck for the last morning after ten days on the lakes and waited for the boat to anchor. They were dressed up, their bags were packed and everyone was very satisfied with what they had experienced on one of the world's most beautiful yachts on this journey with Mr. Rodge Jr. It was a journey which was full of passion, fantastic food, drink and fascinating interaction. Many had had flings in the cabins with one or several partners but now it was time to respectfully leave the fantastic journey and go back to reality. At least as much reality as the wealthy upper class engaged in for seven days a week the year round.

They all had important tasks though. They were often heirs of hardworking creative pioneers and geniuses, and some of the families had even invented the car.

Others were large oil magnates and had become enormously rich when the car conquered America and the rest of the world. Others were large ship owners, real estate moguls and artists who had had their best times during prohibition. The ironic thing was that the alcohol had not flowed more than it had then but everything was hidden behind the scenes.

The most enterprising people from Europe had settled in America to find a new and better life. Many of these fantastic people created large fortunes in different branches in the big western nation. Apart from the oil, the USA had other natural resources: metals like gold, iron and copper.

Paradoxically, the rich business owners' spoiled sons and daughters devoted themselves to partying and living the luxury life in their upper class environment. In most cases, it was the third generation that often lost the fortunes that their forefathers had founded. During "the roaring twenties", nobody reflected over hard times, which would maybe come. Many of the family businesses that were founded by the forefathers would continue to be strong for a number of coming decades.

Lizette and Charlotte were helped onboard the smaller boat. The service staff had even brought over their luggage. Lizette felt that her whole body was sore but the pain was of a pleasant kind. She could hardly believe what she had been through. Charlotte knew that Lizette needed the intensive sexual adventure with Patrick Joe Flemming to get a little distance from Lawrence's tragic passing; sex was sometimes the only cure, she thought.

Lizette sat on the boat and looked as fresh as a daisy even though she was suddenly unbelievably tired. She just wanted to go back to the house in Grosse Pointe that they had rented and lay in her large bed – without company this time – to digest everything that had happened and to allow herself to sleep for several days.

That is what happened. Lizette slept off her love and champagne intoxication in the villa by the water. She was so smitten that she didn't want to eat anything. She only wanted to dream of her latest love and doze off. Charlotte forced Lizette out of bed after two days. While Lizette had slept, Charlotte had got a new maid at short notice that wasn't as difficult as Betsy, who could stay on vacation as far as they were concerned. This maid was called Mrs. Davies. She was in her fifties and was easy to work with. Mrs. Davies set the table in the dining that faced the water.

Lizette came down in her silk bathrobe and was happy that the table was made and had all the tasty dishes you could wish for. She was really hungry just from seeing all the delicious breakfast food that smelled great. There was freshly pressed orange juice, scrambled eggs, crispy fried bacon, fresh bread that Mrs. Davies had baked the same day and strawberry marmalade. The first thing Lizette longed for was coffee which Mrs. Davies could read in both Charlotte's and Lizette's faces. The ladies were waited on by the pleasant housemaid, who knew what etiquette was and how to carry herself. They enjoyed their breakfast at eleven o'clock. Charlotte asked Lizette discretely if she had fallen for Patrick Joe. Lizette sighed and said heavily: "Yes, dear Charlotte, I really have and it is the dumbest thing I have ever done!"

Charlotte answered her bonus daughter and friend mildly: "Liz, I believe this is exactly what you needed. With time, your body and soul will be restored with or without him and you will probably be ready for what you want to do. That could be one romance or several. Physical passion is nothing you should ever take for granted but it can actually provide unimaginable power as we humans need sex. Enjoy the adventure you had with Flemming onboard but don't think too much about it, darling!"

Lizette took Charlotte's hand and said with tears in her eyes: "Charlotte, you have been the most important person in my life ever since I came to America as a seventeen-year-old girl and for that, I am eternally grateful!" Both women smiled at each other and knew that they meant so much to each other.

They would spend the last days in Grosse Pointe with Henry Ford at the popular boat club on Belle Isle outside Detroit. Before they would celebrate America's national day, the 4th of July, they had almost become regulars at the boat club on Belle Isle. There was an Olympic size swimming pool and besides being able to swim and row in different boat teams, the bar, the music and the company were distinguished. It was, in other words, reserved for "The Jet-Set".

At this point in time and onwards, the multi-gold Olympic champion and "inventor" of the surfing sport, Duke Kahanamoku from Honolulu lived on Belle Isle. There, he put on outstanding swimming performances at the boat club in the large pool.

Lizette was enthusiastic when she heard that "The Duke" had even won a gold medal in swimming at the 1912 Olympic Games in Stockholm. For Lizette, it was the magical year that she had come to America.

Now they all stood there, the cream of society, by the pool on Belle Isle, admiring the nimble and skillful Duke Kahanamoku from Hawaii. He had not only put on swimming performances but also advertised the surf sport on a board. He said that the sport was best tried on Hawaii where the water was warm. Lizette turned to Charlotte and asked if she had been to Hawaii. She answered no but added that she would like to travel there, to the tropical paradise in the near future. They continued to enjoy the performance by "The Big Kahuna". Afterwards, they sat down in comfortable seats and conversed with friends and acquaintances for several hours while they were waited on. The days went so quickly in Michigan. They lived the good life and Lizette was surrounded by admirers like bees around a honeycomb.

CHAPTER 23

Return to New York

Charlotte and Lizette had celebrated the National Day with the Ford family in Grosse Pointe. Their only son was very good-looking and would take over the Ford empire but in Lizette's head there was only Patrick Joe Flemming. He had woken up Lizette's sensuality onboard the 'S/S Dolphine II'. It was a feeling so strong; it was like strong glue that wouldn't let go. Even if Lizette didn't want to admit it, she was obsessed with Flemming. She didn't dare tell Charlotte how strong the feeling was; it was terribly difficult thing to both tell and admit to.

The day came when they would leave the house by the beach and both ladies would travel home to New York. Lizette had succeeded in getting over most of the loss of her husband, Earl Lawrence Stewart, during the fantastic journeys to Florida and Michigan with her extra mother and friend Charlotte Sinclair. One part of her had died with Lawrence and made her a little ruffled and almost half bohemian but in an upper class way, where there wasn't a fixed daily schedule.

Lizette didn't miss the English estate at all. Lawrence not being there was all too macabre but the exception to this was her horse, Hope. Lizette thought about how suddenly life could be thrown in a different direction and how things could change in a simple second. Lizette sighed deeply.

Charlotte meant so very much to Lizette, for which she was extremely grateful for. Unfortunately she had had a sexual adventure on the trip to Michigan, which had made Lizette crazy with desire. She had become crazy about Patrick Joe Flemming during the luxury cruise. It was maybe good in some ways, thought Lizette trying to convince herself. It would, after all, be pretty tragic to be an 'old maid' at the age of twenty-eight. Thankfully, she still had her sense of humor and was no longer an insecure seventeen-year- old, which meant she could laugh at her mistakes.

The loss of Lawrence was so devastating for Lizette that she thought about being 'tipsy' on a daily basis to dampen the pain. Even if the young girl Louise had had thick skin, the adult Lizette was light years away from the girl who left Sweden for America.

Charlotte smiled and wondered what bothered Lizette when they were on the way home in their first class compartment. Lizette, who was talkative by nature, could be quiet about her feelings sometimes because they ran deep and she did not want to talk about them.

Lizette collected herself and told Charlotte a white lie: "Yes, I thought that Ford's place in Grosse Pointe was smaller than your estate on Long Island and they have started the ENTIRE car industry!" Charlotte smiled and said: "Different times, different privileges. My dad was rich and we have inherited money. It's why William and I could get the best together." Charlotte paused a little and continued: "There have been difficult times; we have rebuilt our empire a few times but old investments have been our savior on a number of occasions."

She looked deeply into Lizette's eyes, opposite her in the compartment, and added: "Sometimes, William and I have been poor and I mean without money. We have had our fine estates but, sometimes, not had the funds to heat them up; that's how life can be." Charlotte continued: "Ford's property was considered noble in the day but everything changes".

Lizette nodded and thought that she would have never guessed that the upper class had had to fight for their lives, but the struggle had been different and surely harder for the working class than families like the Sinclairs and Fords.

Lizette respected the working class but now tried to keep a distance from them. She admitted to herself that her higher status in society had got her to, sometimes, have different opinions than before. Yet, she also admitted that there were many unsavory and tasteless types of people in the upper class; class could definitely not be bought for money. Either you had it or not. Lizette's companion, Alice (who Lizette studied etiquette with), had been right when she told Lizette about upper class behavior; about spectacular parties and about the wild sex life that went on within the upper class society. Lizette was now one of them and a part of her was ashamed of it but, at the same time, her morals had also disappeared. Lizette had believed that Alice's imagination had run away with her and had been so naive and not understood how everyone got theirs behind closed doors amongst the wealthy, spoiled upper class people. The difference between the poor and the rich was that you had expensive bedding, caviar and champagne in the upper class bedchambers and fine, subtle mannerisms outside the bedroom.

But when it came to sex and passion, it worked more or less the same in all classes, philosophized Lizette while she struggled not to drown in the memory of Patrick Joe Flemming's lips against hers, while his powerful hands explored her naked body.

Charlotte could, regardless of what Lizette thought, read her like an open book. She cleared her throat and patted Lizette on the cheek. "You must understand that you have taken part in pleasant sex games and it was an escapade, my darling, and I went along with it so that you would get a little more perspective on the loss of Lawrence!" Charlotte grabbed Lizette's shoulders and shook her lightly. "Dear Lizette, you should be aware that Flemming is a notorious womanizer. Take care and do not fall for him! Look at him as your lover and nothing more because if you take Flemming more seriously, you will be skating on thin ice!" Then, something broke inside Lizette but she bit her lips and nodded, admitting that she had been an easy victim.

A few hours later, they rolled into Grand Central Station in New York. Lizette was completely exhausted. Charlotte had surprised her yet again, how well she knew her and what she needed.

She put her arm around Lizette's shoulders and they went into the sea of people on the platform towards their car with Sinclair's own chauffeur. Charlotte said: "Lizette, I believe you need to be on your own at the moment. We have been together intensively over the last few months and I know that you are strong enough to get by now and onwards!" There was lump in Lizette's throat but she felt that there was a need to be alone; Charlotte was really the best mother in the world. They stepped into the Rolls-Royce and the chauffeur lifted their luggage into the boot with help from the bellboy.

Charlotte told Lizette that everything in her apartment on 5th Avenue had been prepared for her homecoming. Even the maid, Sarah, was there and all other personnel too said Charlotte on the way from the station. Lizette took Charlotte's hand and said quietly that she loved her extra mother. When they reached Lizette's own apartment, Charlotte said subdued: "I will call you in a few days and see how you are. In the meantime, I think that you should read, sleep, go to a spa, contact your friends and just enjoy living!"

Lizette stepped out of the car and the doorman whistled for a porter to take care of Lizette's luggage. She waved at Charlotte who had once given her the key to one of Manhattan's most fantastic homes. She wondered how she had been so lucky; it was a life-long question.

CHAPTER 24

Home Again

Once back in her apartment, Lizette was welcomed by large deep red roses across the hall and living room. Sarah came up to her and greeted her. She asked Sarah who had sent of all the red roses. Sarah fetched an envelope and gave it to her dear mistress, Lizette Af Sinclair Stewart, with a smile. In the coziest corner of the parlor, she took off her hat and sat down in an armchair. Lizette asked Sarah for a big cup of tea with honey. Lizette felt that she wanted to be healthier after all the alcohol she had drunk recently. Lizette opened the envelope carefully and tried to dampen her eagerness. It was from him, Patrick Joe Flemming! He had found her address and had showered her with an ocean of flowers for her homecoming. Patrick had formulated their romance onboard in a poetic way and Lizette's heart beat quickly and she felt sexually aroused after everything that had happened on the 'S/S Dolphine II". Her face turned red and she felt hot.

This was the forbidden fruit and she was not at all in love with Patrick, which, at the same time, worried her because it was only physical stimulation to be with this "playboy".

Sarah came in with a cup of tea and smiled: "Dear Miss Lizette, it's so wonderful to have you at home in New York again!" Lizette stood up, hugged Sarah and whispered that she had been on a very long journey with indescribable happiness and sorrow. Lizette thanked her maid for coming back to her position, which Charlotte had organized. Sarah curtsied and commented that everything had been freshened up in the apartment, that the bed had been freshly made and cleaned and that the fridge was full of delicious food. Lizette thanked her and said that it was wonderful to be home again to her dream apartment, but after many deep breaths, Lizette laughed hard and wondered what they ought to do with all the roses.

Sarah smiled and said: "They will brighten up the rooms for a bit longer. You just have to take care of them and I'll make sure to do that in the right way". Lizette asked Sarah to run a bath for her to wash away the dust from travelling.

Lizette walked around the apartment while the bath was being attended to by Sarah. Lizette held a rose in her right hand and smelt the scent from the beautiful flower, while she walked from room to room. In her left hand, she carried the letter from Patrick Joe Flemming. There must be several hundred roses in the apartment, thought Lizette. She read Patrick's letter over and over again. He wanted to see her again and wanted them to be lovers. He wrote that he desired Lizette more than he wanted to admit and that he had difficulty sleeping as he only saw her cream white skin in front of him. He fantasized about Lizette's long sexy legs that excited him and the frizzy- cropped hair that made him happy when it tickled his face. He described her voluptuous breasts and wonderful kisses. Lizette giggled to herself. What a wonderful life she led, she had to constantly remind herself. She didn't know if she wanted to laugh or cry.

Once she had laid down in the bath, which was full of foam, with a cup of tea instead of 'bubbly' on the bathtub's edge, Lizette enjoyed the wonderful water and dunked her whole head. Maybe she had been a mermaid in an earlier life. Lizette loved the water, the sea and spa treatments more than anything. She opened her eyes, sat up in the tub and took a swig of honey tea.

Sometimes, she had more serious thoughts. Lawrence was no longer around and who would be her family in the future? Would she ever have her own children? She knew that there had been problems with childbirth in her family. In addition, she had a tragic abortion. It was like playing with death to challenge the body to give birth in her family. There were big risks, she knew it, but at the same time, Lizette knew that her biological clock was ticking – that it was now time to become a mother. Lizette felt sick as if she was hung-over. That she could be pregnant did not cross her mind. It had been seven months since Lawrence had passed away in the tragic car accident and Lizette had menstruated to schedule every month as usual. She really would have wanted to give birth to his son but it had not been fate. Maybe she was feeling sick because she was exhausted after her orgastic life. It was normal to have a child at her age; she was twenty-eight years old and it was a relatively old age to be a mother at the time. The dreams of children would gnaw away at her over the course of the year.

After the loss of Lawrence, she wanted, in some way, to create a new life.

Lizette dunked her head in the deep bathtub again and washed her whole body using a sponge with sweet-scented oil. She stepped out of the bathtub and washed her hair in the modern shower with many showerheads where the water sprayed from all angles. She finished with a cold shower and swung the newly washed bathrobe around her. She wrapped her hair up in a turban with a towel.

She went out to Sarah in the kitchen and asked her to ring Patrick Joe Flemming's servant and thank him for the flowers.

Lizette strolled into her large bedroom and went through the closet to find something appropriate for summer. She didn't find anything that was suitable and she felt tired after the warm bath and all the traveling. Instead, she crept down in to her wide bed and lay naked between the cool, sweet- smelling sheets and fell into a heavy sleep.

The Third Part

CHAPTER 25

Four Years Later, 1927

It was the end of May 1927, early in the morning and Lizette had just stepped out of bed to be served breakfast. The newspaper was on the table, which described Charles Lindbergh's flight over the Atlantic.

He had made the first solo flight over the Atlantic in his airplane 'Spirit of St. Louis', a flight that had taken thirty-three and a half hours. Lizette admired Lindbergh who had undertaken this dangerous journey and, to add, he was a Swedish descendant. Lizette sat up in her bathrobe while Sarah filled up her cup with coffee. Lizette was terribly hung-over and tired!

During the last four years, the parties had never ended. They had been the most unbelievable years of the roaring twenties and Lizette had been one of the most popular hostesses in New York, "she had been the toast of Manhattan".

The music she danced to had been the Charleston which had been a dance that had come from Charleston in South Carolina. It was the twenties famous dance and the whole decade has been called 'The Charleston Era'.

The first recording of the melody was made by an orchestra in 1923, but it wasn't until it was seen and heard in the Broadway revue"Runnin' Wild", that it became a world success. Lizette thought about this while she sat in the breakfast room at home, at the end of May.

She had been to Broadway when the whole ensemble bathed in popularity thanks to this performance; after that the party was started amongst the "upper class with no tomorrow".

It was an exciting time and during the four years, Lizette had, on several occasions, bathed in a fountain filled with champagne out on Long Island at the famous Cassey mansion, when she herself did not hold the popular 5th Avenue parties in her own apartment.

Lizette's relationship with Patrick Joe Flemming had been doomed to fail from the first moment, but this was obvious, as Flemming was known for keeping several mistresses at the same time. It had been a dangerous game, which had ended in tears and hatred.

Lizette had become pregnant against all the odds but miscarried and it had probably been a good thing, thought Lizette bitterly. She didn't want to have a child who would grow up and hear that he or she was a bastard. Lizette had started to look older at thirty-two years old with platinum blonde hair and several laughter lines round her mouth and eyes. Despite this, she was still a beauty.

The memories of her simple roots from a poor childhood in Sweden had almost disappeared. After all the luxuries Lizette had experienced during the roaring twenties, she wondered, sometimes, if she had dreamed about her childhood. Unfortunately, she had become a chain smoker after her two stormy years with Flemming, who had behaved like a pig. He was a big name in politics now.

Patrick Joe Flemming had an enormous hunger for sex and political power. He had got everything he dreamed of and as a business on the side; he delivered spirits to the upper class. In other words, Flemming was "one really bad boy".

Charlotte Sinclair had desperately regretted that she didn't stop Lizette from having an affair with Flemming on the 'S/S Dolphine II' when they had been to Grosse Pointe on vacation in

1923. She suffered from seeing how Lizette had been damaged from this relationship. She had been a good mother for the young Swedish girl Louise, as she had been through the years when Lizette was the socialite queen, but knew that Lizette had to be responsible for her life in the end.

Charlotte had done all that she could for her beautiful "adopted daughter". Her son, however, was no party animal at all but went from strength to strength with his studies and did very well. Charlotte hoped that Andrew Jr would give her grandchildren, as Lizette was unable to have children. Andrew Jr was, after all, Charlotte's biological son, but she loved Lizette as if she was her own real daughter. She had done so since she had arrived as a seventeen- year-old from Sweden and had taken care of their son.

Lizette took out her ivory cigarette holder and lit a cigarette. Sarah came and cleared the table and served yet another cup of coffee. Lizette twisted uneasily in her chair and said lovingly: "Thanks Sarah, what would I do without you?" Sarah patted Lizette on the shoulder as an answer and disappeared out into the kitchen. Lizette went back to reading the paper and caught sight of an interesting article.

She read the article out loud to herself: "The Royal Hawaiian Hotel, that opened its doors in February with a style inspired by Rudolph Valentino, with 400 elegant suites, has become a success on the tropical island of Oahu." She continued enthusiastically and looked at the black and white photos of the hotel and the fantastic beach that you could picture in front of you, even if the photos in the paper were bad. The luxury hotel was called "The Pink Palace" because it was pink and adorned Waikiki beach in Honolulu. Lizette started to dream about a tropical vacation.

It was almost summer and this summer in New York would be awfully hot as usual on Manhattan, almost stuffy, and Lizette didn't want to be on Long Island or in Central Park this year. You could swim on Hawaii and it was a completely different thing. She called for Sarah and jumped out of her chair. Sarah came running in and wondered what was going on. Lizette looked at her maid with big eyes and looked almost like a film star with charisma and beauty. "Sarah, what would you say if I said that we should pack our bags and travel to the tropical paradise of the island 'Hawaii Oahu' for a while?"

Sarah had never been on such a vacation before in her whole life or traveled so far away. She understood that it wouldn't be a real vacation for her and that she would be looking after Lizette while they were there, but Lizette was the best employer that Sarah had had in her whole life and she felt very privileged.

Lizette never treated Sarah like a servant but more of a family member and Sarah was unbelievably happy that Lizette wanted her to go but asked: "Miss Lizette, are you sure that you want me to go with you on the journey?" Lizette stood up, grabbed Sarah and said firmly: "Sarah, you know that I am alone again and I don't want to have a new man in tow. From here on in, I am the one in charge over the men in my life and nobody will deceive me or treat me as badly as Patrick Joe Flemming has done!"

She added: "You will join me, Sarah, and you only need to use your organization skills and help me with the essentials over there. I won't be throwing so many parties, so you won't have too much to do, don't worry. But I will also ask Selma if she wants to come along as well. You know my old Swedish friend who lives in Chicago!"

Lizette took a final deep drag of her cigarette and rushed out into the parlor. She kept a telephone directory and an elegant telephone on the leather desk. She got hold of Selma right away. Lizette apologized for not being in touch for so long but could hardly wait to ask Selma about joining her for a trip to Hawaii. Selma fell completely silent and then told Lizette that the children were at private school and would be going to holiday camps during the summer.

Lizette suggested enthusiastically: "But if we leave next week…" Selma interrupted and said that it was too short notice for her but if Lizette could stay in Honolulu for a while, she would be able to join her a little later and keep her company. Selma was more than happy to do this, she said humbly. Lizette screamed with joy and ran into the bedroom after she had finished her conversation with Selma.

Lizette whistled while she started to pack and shouted for Sarah to open a magnum bottle of champagne – they would go to Hawaii! Sarah knew, just as Lizette did, that Lizette was drinking too much but neither of them said a word to each other about those bad habits.

As Lizette had had a miscarriage, she believed that everything was allowed. She could have all the bottles she needed for comfort. Lizette was, in some ways, "a poor rich girl" although she had, funnily enough, been a poor farm girl from Sweden. But since everybody who was somebody in New York longed to be invited to her parties in the magnificent apartment on 5th Avenue, many people pretended to be ignorant about it, even though they had heard about it. Some people who claimed to know whispered that it was all a malicious rumor.

Lizette carried herself like the queen of Manhattan and you could not see a trace of the poor farm girl she had been born as according to wicked gossip.

Lizette's new platinum blonde locks were perfectly styled like a beautiful cap. She had big beautiful hazel eyes and the smoky make-up was perfect for the time. She had a willowy figure with clothes that fit her like a glove. Her clothes always suited every occasion.

Lizette had, on top of everything, become a fashion icon. People already envied her. Many men fell hook, line and sinker for Lizette but her aversion to having a stable relationship always won. She flirted and teased men who did everything she said. Even though her intention was not to be mean, she sometimes treated men like toys. Unfortunately, in many ways, Lizette had become bitter when it came to men. She preferred the company of many friends, a handful of really close friends and, maybe, at most, stuck to flirting and temporary relationships. Returning to a stable relationship with someone was not on Lizette's mind. She had been asked recently if she wanted to be in a Hollywood film. Lizette had laughed at the proposition and given a direct no as an answer.

To be an actor or actress had advanced from being considered being loose to a professional vocation during "the roaring twenties". Movies with sound, known as "talkies", had just been launched in 1927 and the movie industry was hotter than ever. Even the famous and popular actors had started to appear in the movie's dramas. People loved these dramas because they showed people's real feelings. You could dream of another life by following your favourite actors on the silver screen. It all resulted in the moviestars becoming enormously famous.

The telephone lines had also spread over the whole country in the 1920s. This fascinating time was called "prosperity forever" and people convinced themselves that the rise in wealth would last forever; the state of the market with its crises and depressions belonged to history. But towards the end of the 1920s, investors started to realize that the market might be saturated and, all of a sudden, after everyone had invested in shares and bonds, the stock market bubble grew.

US Steel, GM and Ford were some of the companies who lured the public to buy shares in them. Previously, the stock market was only for the rich upper class. This changed with cutthroat advertising insisting that everyone could get rich on shares. The fact was that almost three million people invested in the stock market in the USA with help of brokers in 1927. The companies wanted not only men to invest but also women, as they wanted more buyers. In the USA, the order of the day was: "Live now and don't worry about the future!"

Consequently, Lizette and her friends lived each day as if it was their last but for some reason, Lizette refrained from these impulsive investments. It felt odd to buy a piece of "paper" for money she reasoned.

It was maybe her sound common sense that came to her rescue even if her advisors teased and even mocked her. They believed that she should be made to understand that she would not just buy a "piece of paper" but be part owner in something bigger, which gave a fine return. In addition, it would make her even richer.

Lizette always smiled at the stock market and considered, wisely, that if it all went to hell – she would support Ford and all the other big owners when they didn't have any money any longer. It was either this or throwing her money onto the fire to be part of something bigger. She didn't want to do it.

Everything that the Sinclair family had done for her, through being incredibly generous in giving her economic independence was something she didn't want to gamble with. Charlotte had told her several times about how physical investments had always saved them during their ups and downs. Lizette now had an estate in England with a large plot of land as well as her apartment on Manhattan.

Lizette had also bought several paintings by famous artists, both modern and "old" and had invested in precious metals. She had been given lots of jewelry from men she had courted and didn't feel any need to be bewitched by the stock market.

Lizette thought about what she had read in the New York Times recently: two men, Maitland and Hangenberger, had succeeded to fly non-stop from Oakland in California to Hawaii. The plane was an American army plane, a Fokker C-2-3 with three Wright 220 Tri-Motor engines. The airplane had got the nickname "The Bird of Paradise". She almost wished that she and Sarah could fly to Hawaii but the technology wasn't quite there yet. It would have taken a long time to fly the route but as she had crossed the Atlantic many times before, it would have been a quicker and more exciting way there. She wondered if she would get to experience it during her lifetime. "Sarah, where is the champagne?" Sarah came scurrying in and apologized but said that she had been in contact with deliverers and employees to let them know that Lizette's home would be vacated for a while.

Lizette grabbed the well-chilled champagne and pushed the cork out of the magnum bottle like a professional, as if she had never done anything else before; there was some truth to it even though her employees usually did it for her.

Lizette had the latest fridge in her luxury-equipped apartment and it was a really big project to keep it stocked. In any case, the fridge was a luxury that she was now used to and her craftsman took care of its maintenance.

Lizette asked Sarah to book the boat that would take them from California to Hawaii after she had booked the train the whole way to Los Angeles.

Sarah smiled at Lizette and thanked her again for being allowed to go on the trip with her. She had told a friend in confidence that it was a journey she could never have dreamed of. Lizette patted Sarah on the cheek and returned to the champagne, poured a glass and lit a cigarette. She took a deep drag and looked out over Central Park through the big window. Sarah rushed back into the room with a large ice bucket for the champagne. "Miss Lizette, now I will book our tickets in first class!" Lizette enjoyed her cigarette and nodded regardless of not listening to Sarah. Her thoughts wandered from all the parties during the last four years and felt that it would be healthy to get away and experience a climate change. She had been in Florida several times since the first time she was in Palm Beach with Charlotte.

Lizette had never been to Hawaii though, and now it had become so popular – thanks to the new luxury hotel "The Pink Palace", which had been opened to all actors who flocked there and spoke of Honolulu and Waikiki Beach. It was a place that Lizette wanted to visit herself and see if the things she had heard were a reality.

She had seen "The Duke" from Hawaii doing swimming performances on Belle Isle in Grosse Pointe several years earlier. "The Duke" had been an Olympic Games gold medalist several times and people's interest in Hawaii and surfing had risen thanks to his performances around the country.

CHAPTER 26

Hawaii

A couple of days later, Sarah and Lizette sat on the train from New York. Lizette felt satisfied as she sat in the first class restaurant's carriage. They had gone onboard early this Thursday afternoon at the start of the summer. Lizette took a deep drag on her cigarette and looked out at the scenery, which swept by outside the window. Sarah rested in her compartment. They had separate compartments next to each other. Lizette wanted to spoil Sarah because of everything that she done for her over the years. Lizette had never been able to reciprocate while they were at home in New York but now, Sarah would have a little time for herself and not only take care of her mistress.

Lizette wrote a list and ticked off everything that she had arranged before the journey. She had made sure that she had no pressing engagements. Everything was, in principle, already fixed and organized so that Lizette could stay on Hawaii as long as she wanted. Lizette didn't yet know how she would find this famous paradise; if she would like it. She recalled that Florida had always appealed to her and that she actually enjoyed the tropical climate immensely. The rumors about Hawaii were that it wasn't as damp as Florida, that it had a more temperate climate and was more comfortable.

Lizette thought about the story she had read about Captain Cook who came to Hawaii in July 1776 with the ship Resolution and Discovery. The natives had treated him as a god. His expedition continued north where they were stopped by ice. They returned to Hawaii over the winter. When they came back for the second time, he christened Hawaii "The Sandwich Islands". The natives noticed that he wasn't a god at all. Consequently, they killed him on the 14thFebruary and, some say, ate him. Lizette could not help laughing to herself when she thought about how macabre it all was.

A waiter came over and asked if Lizette wanted another cup of coffee. Lizette nodded and swallowed a mouthful of hot, black coffee. She didn't want to eat anything before lunch because she was concerned about her figure. Sarah cooked some scrambled eggs that they enjoyed before they were driven to Grand Central Station.

Lizette pondered over her list. Her hair was perfect and the blonde, short look suited her. A gentleman suddenly asked if he could sit down and presented himself as Oscar Wilding. Lizette, who had no interest in being social, sighed without being conscious of it. He apologized and said that he didn't want to disturb but asked if they could eat dinner together a few hours later.

Lizette looked suspiciously at the bearded gentleman. He said that he had heard of Lizette Af Sinclair's parties and had seen her picture in the paper and added that he had something important to tell her and asked for her attention for one dinner.

Lizette replied politely but warily: "What could be that important, Mr. Wilding?" Oscar Wilding answered quickly that if they could meet in the dining room at seven o'clock, he would explain everything. "Well, I will listen and, until we meet, I will wonder what you want of me", answered Lizette with sharpness in her voice. The man nodded and quickly left the restaurant carriage where all the gourmet food you could wish for was served at lunch and dinner. Lizette got up and went towards Sarah's compartment with a swaying, sexy walk that made all the men to turn around.

She knocked on the door to Sarah's compartment and was let in when Sarah heard who it was.

Lizette ran into Sarah's compartment and told her about the mystical man who wanted to eat dinner with her. Lizette suggested that Sarah should sit at the table behind them and listen to everything he said. She said that an early dinner would be good so they could book two tables next to each other. Sarah, who had slept for a while, was a little dazed but understood.

The evening sun shone in through the windows of the famous train, which chugged its way through state after state. The first class restaurant carriage was almost full. Lizette was waiting in a cubicle for the mystical Oscar Wilding. Lizette thought that Wilding should sit opposite her, because behind that seat, Sarah, who had her ear to the wind, was ready to hear what the strange man wanted to talk to Lizette about.

A quarter of an hour late, Oscar Wilding entered the restaurant carriage. The scenery outside the window had kept Lizette company for the half an hour she had sat there waiting for him. While waiting, she had drunk two cocktails. Lizette, who had come in good time, had let Sarah drink coffee so that she would be able to concentrate on what the man had to tell. As a reward, Sarah would get to share a fine wine with Lizette when the mystical man had left.

Wilding excused his late arrival and sat down facing Lizette. She observed this odd stranger and found that he didn't have the slightest shred of attractiveness or charisma.

Wilding cleared his throat and wondered what they should order. Lizette nodded to a waiter who quickly came over to the table. The waiter suggested the sole for the ladies and the tender steak for the gentleman.

Lizette, who had eaten the best food during the whole of the 1920s, replied to the waiter that it suited her fine. She looked at Oscar Wilding, who also agreed and made it clear to the waiter that he wanted his steak rare. Lizette said that she wanted a dry, full-bodied and strong white wine for the fish dish. The waiter asked if she wanted a whole bottle. Lizette nodded while Wilding only ordered a glass of red American wine for the steak but he wanted a cocktail as an appetizer. Lizette agreed and ordered another gin with ice.

Lizette shifted her gaze and looked to see if Sarah had ordered something to eat. It didn't seem as if she had yet, but first of all it was necessary to find out what Oscar Wilding wanted. Lizette would spoil Sarah rotten later.

When Lizette's and Wilding's gin had arrived at the table, the stranger started to talk and said emphatically: "Miss Lizette, I am a professor in economy and want to give you the following information that I hope you will take with all seriousness!" By this time, Lizette was falling apart at the seams – She asked herself - What could this man have to say?

Wilding started to preach about a big economic crisis that would affect the whole world within a couple of years, sooner rather than later. It would be best for Lizette to continue to live as she had been doing, namely to invest in physical things and not in paper.

Lizette interrupted and wondered if he meant shares and bonds. Wilding nodded and continued to describe the horrible scenario that awaited the upper class if you wagered your money on exactly those things. An hour's description of how the wonderful time that had been like a velvet blanket for the rich and privileged would end in horror frightened Lizette. There were many amongst the rich that had persuaded themselves that tomorrow only had positive surprises and, according to Wilding, it would all soon be gone.

When the food had been served and their wine glasses had been filled, Lizette took a bite of the superb fish and wished that Oscar Wilding was only a nightmare but when she looked up from her plate, he was there, in the land of the living.

Wilding continued to talk about how many would lose all of their fortunes and would probably commit suicide as a result of the losses. By now, Lizette was drinking the wine like water. She lit a cigarette, looked sharply at Wilding and said: "If you know everything about this tragedy, why don't you go to the press with this information?"

Wilding hesitated and said quietly: "Lady Stewart, I would become a target for murderers and everyone would hang me out in the press as a lunatic who tried to take the good life away from the rich." Lizette jerked in her chair and said trembling: "How did you know that I was married and was called Lady Stewart?"

Wilding scraped his beard and took Lizette's hand in his and whispered: "Look at me as your guardian angel that has been sent to you from Sir Lawrence Stewart's supporters."

When they had finished their dinner in silence, Oscar Wilding grabbed his napkin and dried his mouth, swallowed what little wine he had left and told Lizette that he had one more thing to talk about. Lizette had forgotten Sarah by now and was now almost hypnotized by the stranger.

Wilding coughed and said: "The best thing you can do now, Miss Lizette, is to live a long way away from New York for a few years until the stock market crash is over. Unfortunately, there will be a depression in the 1930s but with your assets you'll be able to make it through well and still have a lasting fortune."

With these last words of encouragement and after all the misery that professor Oscar Wilding had conveyed, he rose up quickly and said that he would be getting off at the next station; he kissed Lizette's hand and disappeared.

When he left Lizette by the table, she turned to Sarah wide-eyed. Lizette exclaimed: "Oh Sarah! Did you hear everything?" Sarah nodded and asked if she could sit opposite Lizette. Lizette answered: "Of course you can, my dear!"

Sara had not eaten so Lizette ordered in the fish dish and a bottle of white wine for her as well as a little cheese for herself and a little port wine. They sat there whispering and analyzing what Oscar Wilding had suggested and wondered who had sent him. Lizette smoked like never before and Sarah enjoyed being served, feeling as if she was a part of the upper class.

CHAPTER 27

Waiting for Selma

The train and boat trip that Sarah had been offered was a fascinating experience even though, through the years with Lizette, she had got to taste the good life when the parties had finished. The difference now was that she was herself a guest and was being served by staff and it tasted much better. Now they had arrived at Oahu after a peaceful boat trip over the Pacific.

Honolulu was on Oahu and it was by the ocean on Waikiki beach they would live in the so-called "Pink Palace" which had become a legendary hotel despite only being opened in February of the same year. It had, in fact, become the favorite hotel of movie stars as well as politicians and businessmen.

Lizette and Sarah were met in the lobby by service minded personnel and were shown to their suite on the fifth floor. The view from the suite was stunning; the azure blue waters outside the window were like sweet relief for the eyes. They went to rest in their respective bedrooms. Lizette slept for twelve hours and woke up in the most fascinating tropical climate she had experienced. Hawaii was infinitely better than Florida, she thought. She showered and got herself ready. Sarah stood at the ready with towels and told Lizette that she had been awake for three hours but didn't want to disturb. Lizette thanked her and asked: "Is Sarah ready for breakfast on the hotel terrace?" After a short moment, they were in the courtyard fully enjoying the exotic environment that they were surrounded by. One side of the courtyard was open to the beach.

Lizette said enthusiastically to Sarah: "What a lively pace of life and wonderful atmosphere, Sarah!" She nodded happily and thanked Lizette yet again for being asked to be there with her. A waiter came with the coffee, pineapple rings, marmalade and toast. Lizette laughed and said: "In New York, I have never had pineapple for breakfast!"

Sarah said with dismay: "I could have bought it if I had known!" Lizette answered that the point was to eat it in its origin, in Hawaii, and added:

"And you don't need to worry Sarah. You have served me everything I have loved to eat during the years!"

After breakfast, when they were on their way from the table, a butler crept in with a telegram for Lizette. He carried it in on a silver tray and delivered it carefully wearing white gloves. Lizette thanked him, gave him a tip and opened the envelope eagerly. The telegram was from Selma who messaged that she would be there in about ten days and would stay with Lizette on Hawaii for two weeks. Lizette cried out with happiness and told Sarah the good news.

Lizette, with Sarah in tow, went up to the suite to get ready to go to the beach. Once there, when they found their own little beach cabin where they could store their things, they found there was complete joy in the stunning paradise. Hawaii was really a taste of Nirvana. Lizette felt freed from the fiery rhythm and rush in New York. She loved "her home city" but Hawaii was precisely what she needed after years of being a hostess in a big city.

Sarah sat up in her deckchair and seemed to feel a little uncomfortable under the parasol that shaded both of them. She was not really used to being part of this privileged group.

Lizette laughed and said to Sarah: "You must get used to enjoying the luxuries in life if you want to be with me here Sarah. I have just got the idea to move here for a few years." Sarah, startled, answered skeptically: "Miss Lizette, is this true? Would you move to Hawaii?" Lizette smiled and answered Sarah smiling: "Yes, you heard what this mystical man on the train said. If it is true and there will be an economic world catastrophe which will start in New York, we'll be better off here." Lizette took a deep breath and said, thoughtfully, to Sarah that she had experienced love at first sight with Hawaii. The climate was perfect, the surroundings divine and there was tropical fruit to be eaten every day – there was nothing wrong with that.

Sarah was completely bowled over by all the new impressions and was confused with her mistress talking about moving to Hawaii. Sarah, who had never been outside of New York earlier, was in a light state of shock. Lizette asked Sarah to relax while a waiter approached. "What a perfect arrival, Sir!" divulged Lizette to the waiter. "You need a drink Sarah!" said Lizette and ordered two refreshing tropical drinks. Sarah almost fainted in her deckchair because of all the new information and experiences she was receiving.

Lizette asked the waiter to hurry and, just in case, bring an ice bucket containing a magnum of the finest champagne they had as well as the drinks.

While they waited for their drinks and champagne, Lizette suggested that they should bathe in the sea but Sarah said NO in a friendly, firm way.

"Okay. Suit yourself my dear Sarah!" said Lizette as she ran out into the warm and inviting crystal clear water. She threw herself into the first wave that came and enjoyed being in this paradise. The sandy beach stretched out as far as the eye could see and their hotel was the first and only one on Waikiki beach, but Lizette got a sense that it would all change. There couldn't be anybody who WOULDN'T want to be here.

When Lizette had bathed for a while, Sarah waved from her deckchair and Lizette assumed that their drinks had arrived. She walked out of the water and put on her shoes that were on the edge of the beach. The sand was far too hot to walk on barefoot.

Lizette soon sat beside Sarah in her deckchair and asked the waiter to open the champagne after she had sipped the other tangy drink for a while. Sarah declined the champagne; there was a limit to mixing with the upper class. The drink had done her good, though. While Lizette enjoyed the champagne under the parasol Sarah slumbered. So, they spent their time waiting for Selma to arrive from the mainland.

Sarah knew that Lizette had been especially generous towards her because she had no equal with her. Sarah had become something of a substitute in many ways but it didn't matter to her; she was very thankful to her fantastic employer.

CHAPTER 28

Finale

Some of the wagons full of furniture had arrived on Hawaii when Selma had gone back to Chicago. While she was there, Selma had been a fantastic help in finding the right house for Lizette in paradise. Moreover, Selma would come back to Hawaii to celebrate Christmas and New Year a few months later. They had had two wonderful weeks together and Sarah had taken care of them in the best way. Lizette had asked Sarah to keep what Oscar Wilding had told her to herself as she didn't want to worry Selma unnecessarily.

She had asked Selma to consider whether or not she wanted to join her and live on Hawaii now that her children were adults and her husband had passed away. Selma had promised to think about it until her next trip to Hawaii.

Lizette had started to move into a large colonial villa by Diamond Head, which was a place she loved. To be on the beach as often as she could, she had taken the decision to enjoy lunches and dinners at "The Pink Palace" and had, therefore, always had a suite booked at the hotel in her name, which would be available when necessary.

An American president called S.B. Dole had been installed on Hawaii in 1895 when the Americans had established a republic on the tropical paradise. Lizette thought about it and felt that it was a little tragic that the Americans had mutilated the kingdom of Hawaii, but on the other hand, she thought about Captain Cook, who some said had been eaten by the locals just over a hundred years ago. So for Lizette and other white people, they thought it was lucky that the Americans had taken command of Hawaii. She didn't want to get into any discussions about it because Hawaii was now her home and she wanted to feel secure in the fantastic paradise that Hawaii was – with an American touch.

Lizette's new house had belonged to an advisor to President Dole and had a long history. She had chosen the furniture from her New York apartment, which gave stability to her new house but chose to mix up the décor with domestic furniture from the islands.

Charlotte Sinclair, Lizette's beloved mother, had taken the responsibility for the move and had overseen everything in New York. Charlotte was so happy that Lizette had decided to move from all the partying in the big city and live on Hawaii instead. Charlotte thought that life on Hawaii would make Lizette go swimming and get other habits. In addition to that, she felt that it wasn't wrong to travel from the Hamptons on Long Island to Hawaii during the cold months and visit Lizette.

After two years on Hawaii, the thing she had heard from the mystical train passenger Oscar Wilding happened. There was chaos in New York at the end of October 1929. Shares and other bonds lost their value and company after company lay in ruins. Broken owners of large companies that had gone bust jumped out of their office windows in the middle of Manhattan and met a horrific death. It was an awful tragedy, which completely made the stock market lose its spirit and affected all the rich people who had suddenly lost everything. The only survivors were the ones who DIDN'T invest in shares and bonds. Charlotte Sinclair and her daughter Lizette Af Sinclair were some of those who survived this horrible event that would go down in history as a black chapter.

Since Lizette and Charlotte still had real estate and land, they still had stable and physical wealth.

Lizette was amazed to hear the radio news and sent a prayer, thanking Lawrence that she had his estate in England. She also thanked, at the same time, the messenger on the train, two years earlier. It was thanks to Oscar Wilding that Lizette had not been tempted to buy any shares at all or sell some of her assets. Of course, Lawrence's death was still worse than any stock market crash.

Lizette was thirty-four years old and sat on her terrace with a view over the ocean in paradise, slightly bruised by life. While Sarah was preparing lunch inside the house, Lizette sat with a glass of ice tea and thought back to her old life. Life wasn't always black and white. There were grey zones both for the poor and the rich and no overall happiness was to be found in either camps, according to the innocent Louise and the worldly wise Lizette who had been both rich and poor.

Life was full of phases of joy and sorrow. Lizette was now a hardened lady and realized, of course, that money could brighten up life and pay for a ticket to freedom, which was worth its weight in gold. Even if money was never everything, it was unfortunately a prerequisite for getting to live a life of freedom.

Lizette thought that it was so beautiful on Hawaii and took a sip of the refreshing tea. Lizette was forever grateful for all the fantastic luck in her life. Her colorful life story had started on the lowest level and now, many years later, she realized that she had got almost everything she could wish for.

The biggest tragedy was that her beloved husband, Lawrence, had died. Lizette could still see him on the estate in front of her. Lizette often dreamt of Lawrence and she loved him more than life itself. They fact that they never had any children saddened her. She would have liked to have kept a part of Lawrence which could carry on his wonderful personality, thought Lizette, filled with sorrow. Lizette accepted her lottery ticket in life, albeit with some bitterness. Her heart said that if she could have had her choice, she would have chosen a life of love with Lawrence above every party and sex with strangers.

Besides the miracle of love which was the finest thing that existed in every way, you must survive being satisfied with what you have got, no matter what, and always keep on fighting. Everyone would be affected sooner or later by something positive or horrific. It was simply a question of being strong through it all. Life's ups and downs had given her exactly that – strength! "Strength over time!"

To be able to enjoy the time you have on Earth it was important not to become bitter, thought Lizette, at the same time she admitted to herself that she had nearly become bitter during the last year she lived in New York.

When it came down to assets, she was almost cold and terrified to become poor again. Her soul, though, belonged to Lawrence. Everything was about love and money and, naturally, she would keep the beautiful apartment on Manhattan and her estate in England regardless of what happened. Her only desire, at this point in time, was to enjoy Hawaii and keep those she loved in her heart. Hawaii was a place that was tender to her heart and soul, a tropical Eden; it was like a consolation and gave Lizette both vitality and love.

Crickets played here all year round, the ocean had an awesome presence as well as the lovely beaches and the scents of wild exotic flowers. It gave Lizette spiritual and mental satisfaction. Imagine that there was such a place on Earth, thought Lizette to herself as she sang "Aloha, Mahalo sweet Hawaii", before getting up to go into her beautiful home she had created in paradise to see how Sarah's lunch was coming along.